SILVER CRESCENT

BY

ELIZABETH JANE MORGAN

Cover Design by Vila Design
Interior Design by Ebook Launch
Published by Elizabeth Jane Morgan
Printed by IngramSpark

Paperback ISBN: 979-8-218-62185-8
Ebook ISBN: 979-8-218-62186-5

Silver Crescent, #2

First American Edition: May 2025

10 9 8 7 6 5 4 3 2 1

www.elizabethjanemorgan.com

TABLE OF CONTENTS

In loving memory of Dorothy, Milfred,
Betty, and Verne.

CHAPTER ONE

THE RHYTHM OF MEMORIES

Ba-bum! Ba-ba-bum! Ba-bum-ba!

I awoke to the sound of beating drums. The sound was loud, persistent, and unsettling, like listening to an irregular heartbeat. After a few moments, the noise faded away and I was left alone with the crickets chirping and my two sleeping companions.

Just a dream, I thought, closing my eyes, but sleep eluded me as my mind raced.

Bum-ba-ba! Ba-bum!

I sat up straight. There it was again. I glanced sideways at my friends, Mag and Artie. They didn't even stir.

Sighing, I turned my gaze to the room. It had once been beautiful, with a large, soft chair, a comfortable bed, and a small bookshelf mounted on the wall. It had been abandoned for eight years. Time had not been kind. Huge chunks of the chair had been ripped away, the bed had been smashed, and books lay scattered on the floor. When we first arrived, Artie and I had gathered the books and stacked them in a corner, while Mag had cleared the broken bits of furniture from the center of the room.

"We didn't have to come back, Pen," Artie had said. "We could've stayed somewhere else. Surely, there are other places besides Tealeaf."

I had shaken my head. "No. This was my home, long ago. I needed to come back. Besides, we have nowhere else to go. Tealeaf was the only place we could stop, between here and Cherry Grove."

"Yes, we can't keep Maude and Cissy waiting," Mag had said, yawning. "Relax, Penelope. We'll get there tomorrow."

A flash by the window caught my eye, startling me back to my surroundings and the present. My heart racing, I got up and crept across the room to check. My eyes were adjusting quickly to the dark, but I still almost tripped over a loose floorboard. Stifling my cry of surprise, I felt my way cautiously, until I made it to the window and looked out.

Whatever I had seen had disappeared. I was staring out at the dilapidated, old town square of Tealeaf. The village had been destroyed eight years ago by a dark wizard. He had transformed into a powerful golden dragon, all in an attempt to find and kill me. My mother, Alice, was a witch. She fought and drove back the fearsome dragon, buying us time, but not enough. She managed to escape with me, my brother Malcolm, and my sister Lydia in tow, but our father died in the attack.

I had never learned the dark wizard's true identity. I only knew him as the golden dragon.

As the terrified villagers fled for their lives, Tealeaf was razed almost to the ground. A few buildings survived, like my old house, but even then, it was crumbling.

"Penelope, what are you doing up?" Mag asked me drowsily.

"It's nothing, Mag. I thought I heard something. Go back to sleep."

She nodded, dropped her head to the floor, and instantly began to snore. I was ready to do the same.

Bum-ba! Ba-ba-bum!

I turned. Outside, a lone figure, gray and ominous, stared at me through the window.

My breath quickened. I shrank into a shadowed corner, fearful of meeting the intruder's gaze. I fingered the silver rose, my most powerful magical object, wondering if I should use it to scare the figure away. Still, I hesitated.

The silver rose was capable of incredible feats of magic, but it wasn't limitless. If I used it too often, the magic of the rose would be lost forever. I slipped the silver rose back into my pocket. Unless the situation became dire, I wouldn't need it.

I shuffled closer, squinting at the figure, unable to make out any distinguishing features. Tealeaf was supposed to be abandoned. Maybe whoever it was had stayed and survived all these years. I felt a tingle of excitement.

That turned to disappointment as the figure stepped forward into the moonlight and I saw a wolf with black tips on his ears.

I don't know exactly how long I stared at the wolf and he stared back, but there was something familiar about him. I couldn't quite put my finger on it. The wolf walked right up to the window. He was gazing wistfully at me with bright, green eyes. He looked so sad that I wanted to give him a hug.

As the clouds rolled in, covering the moon, the wolf scratched something, a word, into the dirt, turned, and trotted away.

"Wait," I said. Now that I knew that the wolf wasn't a threat, he couldn't just leave. I had to meet him, talk to him, though I couldn't say why. He was like a friend I had long forgotten.

I hurried to the door, almost tripping on the same loose floorboard as before. After checking to make sure I hadn't woken up either Mag or Artie, I dashed out of the house and onto the street.

The night was cold for late July. I could see my breath as I skidded to a stop next to the word the wolf had scratched into the dirt.

I held out my hand and said, *"Funner."* Instantly, a small ball of fire appeared in my outstretched palm. Like my mother before me, I was a witch. I could use magic, even without the silver rose. I looked at the wolf's word.

Lupine.

"Lou-pine." I didn't have the faintest idea what that meant and a quick scan of the area told me that the wolf had gone. There weren't even any paw prints to show me which way he went. My shoulders slumped and the fire went out. Since I had no leads to go on, I started to walk back inside, when a voice called, "Penelope."

The wolf had returned. He was standing, waiting for me in the shadows of the next house.

"Lupine?" I asked. "That's your name, isn't it?"

He nodded.

"I feel like I should know you. Who are you? Why are you here?" With each question, I took a step closer.

Lupine didn't answer, but he didn't run either.

"I have magic. I can understand you," I said. "Please, talk to me."

Lupine turned and started to walk away. "Come," he said. His voice was deep and familiar, but I still couldn't place him.

"What about Mag and Artie?" I asked anxiously. "I can't just leave them here."

"They'll be fine. Trust me, Penelope. No harm will befall them this night."

This night. I didn't like the sound of that.

Pushing aside my apprehension, I nodded. Whatever this wolf wanted, I would handle it quickly and make it back before Mag and Artie woke up. And if not, well, my friends could take care of themselves until I returned.

"I'm coming."

"Thank you." Lupine headed further into Tealeaf. After one last look at my old house, I followed.

The streets were even eerier now that I was outside. The wind blew fretfully, shaking the branches on the trees, some of which rattled ominously against the windows. I shivered. I hadn't stopped to grab my cloak.

Ba-bum! Ba-ba-bum!

I glanced around the silent and deserted village, searching for the drums and their source. Someone had to be playing them.

Instead, I was confronted, not by a monster or a swordsman or even a dragon, but with memories. As I passed by the next house, I could picture myself as a small child, before Tealeaf was destroyed.

* * *

I was eight years old and lived with my parents, Alice and Edric, my older brother Malcolm, and younger sister Lydia. I ran outside and spotted Malcolm.

"Mal!"

He didn't seem to hear me. Rolling my eyes, I hurried along in his wake, darting in front of him, forcing him to stop. I glared, hands on my hips, giving him my best pout.

"No, Penny," he sighed, before I could even say a word. "You can't come with me."

"Why not?" I whined.

"You know why," Malcolm said gently. "Dad and I are off to track down wolves in the woods. That's no place for someone as young as you. Those wolves are vicious."

"You're ten! You're not much older than me!"

"But I am older than you and Dad asked me to go with him."

We stared at each other, neither of us even blinking, until I blurted, "You can't go, Malcolm!"

"Penny…"

"Those wolves aren't dangerous!"

Malcolm gave me a sharp look. "How would you know?"

"Mal," I began, when a familiar voice called, "Are you ready to go, Malcolm?"

We both turned. Our dad had walked up and was smiling at us, a bow and arrows strapped to his back. Dad was a tall, brown-haired man, with bright, green eyes. Malcolm was a miniature version of him.

Malcolm shook his head disbelievingly at me, before he spun on his heel and walked away. Dad patted my shoulder and said, "Don't let your brother bother you. See you later, Penelope."

I stood there, watching them leave with a pang. I had to stop them.

* * *

In the present, I found myself standing in front of my next-door neighbor's house, where Malcolm and I had disagreed, eight years ago. It was now in ruins. The roof had collapsed and I could see claw marks on several splintered pieces of wood. A dragon's claw marks.

As I stood there, lost in thought, something soft and cold touched my hand. Startled, I looked down and found Lupine staring up at me with concern.

"I'm all right, Lupine," I sighed, turning away. "Just thinking about my brother. I miss him so much."

"Maybe I can be of assistance," Lupine said quietly. "Wait here." He trotted away toward the tree line and out of sight.

Before I could even start to wonder where he had gone, Lupine was back, carrying a bow in his mouth.

It was like the one my dad had been carrying that day, long ago. My eyes wide, I met Lupine's gaze. This had to be some sort of cruel joke, it had to be. Lupine's expression was calm, if a bit sad, as he offered me the remnants of my past.

Trembling, I took the bow. The moment it was out of his mouth, Lupine walked toward the center of town. Taking a deep breath, I adjusted my grip on the bow and followed.

As I hurried after the wolf, I was visited by another memory.

* * *

Malcolm and Dad were striding through town. Dad was carrying his bow loosely in his hand, with a full quiver of arrows on his back. They were going to stop a pack of wolves that had been terrorizing the villagers. I didn't believe it. I'd seen the wolves from my bedroom window. They hadn't done anything but play in the garden, but some people in Tealeaf thought the wolves were dangerous and went after sheep and chickens.

I watched as Dad and Malcolm joined the other men as they prepared for their hunt. I couldn't let them do this. I had to go with them. I had to save the wolves, if I could. Checking to make sure nobody was watching, I slipped behind my neighbor's house and headed for the town square through the back way. I was right on the edge of Tealeaf, with the houses on one side and the woods on the other. I wasn't scared, though. Nothing in the woods would harm me.

* * *

I caught up with Lupine in the town center. He was standing next to a cracked stone fountain that was shaped like a mermaid. It was odd that the stone mermaid was entirely intact, but the circular base was split neatly down the middle.

"Lupine," I said gently, kneeling down beside him, "what are we doing here? Does this have anything to do with those drums?"

"Drums?" Lupine said. "So, you heard them too?" He shook his head. "Of course you heard them. How could you not? I'm sorry this has fallen on you, Penelope, but I need your help."

I felt a wave of protectiveness toward the wolf, though I couldn't explain why. I took his paw. "I'll help if I can. Please, Lupine, tell me everything."

He gazed deeply into my eyes, as if he was trying to memorize my features. "Do you remember the day the men of Tealeaf went out hunting wolves?"

"Yes," I said, taken aback. "But I don't understand."

"Think back, Penny. What happened that day?"

"I tried to stop them from going into the woods. I didn't want any wolves to be hurt."

"Right, but what did you do after you went into the woods?" Lupine asked. He sounded patient, but I could see his ears twitching frantically. He was listening for the drums.

I stared off into the distance, thinking. What had happened that day in the woods?

* * *

It didn't take me long to find the wolves. All I had to do was walk to a nearby clearing where they made their home. They were all there. The four wolves glanced up anxiously when I appeared, but relaxed immediately when they saw it was me. There were three adults and one pup. I assumed two of them were the parents, especially when one of them stepped protectively in front of the baby. They tilted their heads and looked at me curiously.

"You need to leave now," I gasped.

Ba-ba-bum! Ba-bum!

Someone started beating a drum. My blood ran cold. "The villagers… they're coming!"

"Thank you, Penelope," the largest wolf said gruffly. She was clearly the alpha. "You really are your mother's daughter. Thank you." She then gave a short bark of command to the other three and they all took off into the woods. The pup was the last to leave. He gazed at me sadly with large green eyes, before he trotted after the others.

Breathing a sigh of relief, I turned to head back into the village, when I spotted a small purple lizard on a nearby tree, staring directly at me.

"Well, well, well. What have we here?"

I turned and cried out in surprise. A woman with frizzled white hair and watery blue eyes was smiling down at me.

* * *

Blinking, I found myself back in the present, kneeling next to Lupine. The sky was gray, making his green eyes seem even brighter. Dawn was fast approaching.

"Lupine," I said quietly. "I understand now. *You* were the wolf puppy I saved all those years ago. How did you ever escape from the villagers?"

Confusion flickered in his eyes, but I ignored it. Clearly, Lupine was embarrassed that I remembered him as a pup and didn't know how to respond.

"It's all right," I said, fondly. "You were cute then and you're even more handsome as an adult."

Lupine shuffled his feet awkwardly. He started to say something, seemed to think better of it, closed his mouth, and shook his head.

I decided to change the subject. "Well, it was a nice reunion, Lupine. I never thought I'd see you again, but I have to get going. My friends are waiting." I stood, preparing to leave, when Lupine darted in front of me.

"You can't leave yet, Penelope. I still need your help. Don't you want to know where the drums are coming from?"

"It was just the villagers, wasn't it?" I said, frowning. "That's why I was trying to rush you out of the clearing eight years ago."

"And tonight? There aren't any villagers living here anymore."

He was right. There were only four of us in Tealeaf at the moment: Mag, Artie, Lupine, and me. Mag and Artie were asleep. Lupine clearly couldn't play the drums with his paws. I definitely didn't do it. There was only one logical explanation.

Someone else was in the village with us.

"All right, Lupine. I'm listening. What do I have to do?"

Lupine wagged his tail. "Follow me," he said. "It's time to visit an old friend."

Chapter Two

The Search for the Spell

It was nearly dawn when we arrived at the outskirts of the village. A single house sat huddled against the trees. I froze when I saw it.

"This is your friend's house?" I said. "Absolutely not. I can't."

Lupine sighed. "Penelope, please. It's not that bad. She's your friend, too."

"She is," I said, gazing out at the rubble on one side of the house. "It's just that I owe so much to Maude. I saw her a couple of days ago."

"Maude?"

"You may know her better as M. I can't go in that house, Lupine. There's nothing left for me here. Only memories."

Mad Maude, or M as she was called in Tealeaf, was an old witch who had lived in the village as far back as I could remember. I'd gotten to know her before Tealeaf was abandoned. She was eccentric, but nowhere near as crazy as the adults had led me to believe. She taught me all I knew about plants and how to listen to them, to know if they were safe. Not only that, Maude and her pet lizard Cissy were my friends.

"Trust me, Penny. There's more to this house than just your memories."

I turned away from Lupine, wondering. Wondering where Maude and Cissy were now.

* * *

I was done for. I followed the woman to the outskirts of Tealeaf, the purple lizard riding on her shoulder. I was shaking. Why, oh why, did I let myself get caught? And by this old hermit, no less. Her name was M. All the children were terrified of her. They said she rarely left her house and when she did, she would mumble incoherently and cast wicked spells that ruined everyone's crops.

Maybe someone would save me, I thought, but everyone was gone, all searching for the wolves. I hoped the wolves had escaped.

There was no way I was escaping from M. She would probably turn me into a newt before I could even take two steps. I wondered if that's what happened to the lizard. Maybe she had been a child M had captured and was now forced to do the witch's bidding.

I shivered.

"We're here," M said, causing me to jump.

"Please, let me leave," I begged. "Please, M. I promise not to go into the woods by myself again. Just let me go home."

M cackled, which didn't fill me with confidence. "You promise to not go into the woods? Oh, really, Penelope, you disappoint me. Of course you're going into the forest again, but this time Cissy and I are going with you. Not tonight, though. Come over for tea tomorrow. Now, run on home. Your mom will be waiting."

* * *

I approached the house cautiously with Lupine at my side. It was a wreck. The top of the house was caved in, the door was smashed, and every window was shattered. Apart from that, though, the rest of the house was in good shape.

"Why are we here, Lupine?"

"We're looking for a piece of paper. We have to find it, before anyone else does."

"It's been eight years. If nobody's found it yet, what makes you think you can now?"

"Because I know where to look."

"That's nice for you, but why do you need me? Why are you searching for a piece of paper?"

"It has a spell on it," Lupine said. "You'll need it if you want to defeat the golden dragon. I would do it myself, but I can't get past the glass on the ground."

Squinting, I saw the broken glass glinting in the pre-light of dawn.

"If this is about walking on the glass, I'm sure I can use magic to help," I said, pulling out my magical amulet. My mother had given it to me as a fourteenth birthday present. The amulet had a brass setting and was shaped like a star, with a large, oval ruby mounted in the center. I had always seen it as a pretty piece of jewelry. I had never imagined it would be magical. I used it when I didn't want to risk the silver rose's power.

Lupine's eyes widened when he saw the amulet. He cleared his throat and looked away. A single tear slid down his cheek.

"What's wrong, Lupine? One spell should remove the glass and then you can come in."

"No, it's not that." Lupine gazed at me intently. "Save your magic, Penny. I know what happens when you overuse it."

How did Lupine know about my silver vision? I didn't even know about it until a week ago, when my magic resurfaced. When I was eight, my mother had blocked it as a means to protect me from the golden dragon.

It had made sense at the time. My magic had been unpredictable, prone to explode out of me at the most inopportune times. Once, while unconscious, I caused a tree to start sprouting yarn balls. My mother's actions had allowed us to escape, but it set my training back almost a decade. Whenever I used too much magic, everything around me turned silver. It was extremely disorienting to have the world all suddenly become one color.

Luckily, it returned to normal relatively quickly, especially when I had Artie there to help me. He was asleep back in my old house, though.

"All right, Lupine," I said slowly. "I'll do it your way. What am I looking for?"

"It's an old, faded paper. It looks like it will crumble to pieces if you touch it. Handle it very carefully and bring it back out here. It's somewhere on the far side of the room. In the wrong hands, the results could be disastrous. We have to find it, Penelope."

Taking a deep breath, I nodded. I could do this. "Be back soon."

I walked into the house.

* * *

I returned to M's house the next morning. It didn't look as creepy in the daylight. My mom had reassured me that M meant me no harm, but still, I hesitated. As I stood there, mustering the courage to enter, I heard a chittering at my feet. I looked down and found Cissy the lizard gazing up at me.

She motioned for me to follow and skittered toward the house.

Taking a deep breath, I started after her. M and Cissy couldn't be that bad, right? Otherwise, they wouldn't have let me go.

I stepped through the door. The inside of the house smelled like lavender. I had expected it to be dark and musty. Instead, everything was bright and cheerful, if a bit cluttered. Shelves upon shelves of books filled every space of the wall. There was a small table set with two cups, ready for tea.

M appeared with Cissy on her shoulder. She smiled at me as she bustled to the table and began pouring water into the cups.

"Tea is served."

* * *

Back in the present, I blinked in my surroundings. The inside of Maude's old house was dark and musty. I was disappointed. I had expected it to still be bright, cheerful, and smell like lavender. It was cluttered, even eight years later, but that was more due to all the books and knick-knacks being knocked to the floor. I stepped carefully around a book titled, *The Witch's Brew: 101 Uses for Cat Hair, Wolfsbane, and Cheese.*

Smiling, I opened the book at random and read:

Wolfsbane is an effective remedy against werewolf bites, but nothing compares to the medicinal properties of cheese.

I snapped the book shut and set it carefully on a partially collapsed shelf, which wobbled slightly, but stayed upright. I continued through the room.

Slowly, I picked my way through the mess of papers strewn across my path toward the opposite wall. I stopped. There, beside the window, hung an old, faded drawing I had given to Maude. It was a picture of a dragon, but it looked more like a lopsided bird. Why had Maude kept it? It was just a child's drawing.

As I approached the picture to get a closer look, I heard something crunching under my feet. I glanced down and found myself standing on broken glass. Good thing Lupine had stayed outside.

Sidestepping the glass, I checked to make sure nobody was around. Lupine wouldn't mind if I used a bit of magic. I was inside, away from prying eyes. I could use my powers and no one would be the wiser. Lupine might even thank me for finding the paper so quickly. If I collapsed, I'd recover.

I placed my hand on my amulet, took a step forward, slipped, and fell. I lay on the floor, stunned, before I pushed myself up into a sitting position.

Even though there was nobody there to see me, I felt my cheeks burning with embarrassment. Clearing my throat, I tried again, *"Endoraken."*

Reveal.

* * *

M and Cissy were sitting at the table.

"Join us and have some tea," M said, pointing me to a chair. She rose and bustled out of the room.

Gingerly, I sat down and looked around. In front of M's chair was a blue cup with a sunflower painted on the side. Another cup directly across from me was green on the bottom, with a combination of red and orange on the top, making it look like a sunset.

As I reached for the sunset cup, M came back, carrying a green teacup with a yellow star on the side. "Don't touch that!" she cried. "That's Cissy's tea!"

I gasped in surprise, but M didn't seem to notice. She just sat down and placed the green star cup in front of me.

"Drink," she commanded. "Don't worry, it's perfectly safe."

I watched as both M and Cissy drank from their cups. Cissy had to put her front claws on the rim and lean forward. They gulped. Nothing happened. I took a tiny sip and found that I liked it. It tasted like lemon.

"Now, my dear," M said, softly. I winced, ready to be scolded. I shouldn't have been out in the woods. She continued, but not in the way I expected. "You were very brave saving those wolves."

"Thank you," I said. Before I could stop myself, I blurted, "Do you like wolves, too?"

M smiled. "They're some of my best friends. You can learn a lot from animals." She paused, considering me. "How would you like to learn magic?"

"I would love it! But what if I don't have magic? What if I'm a mundane?"

The old witch cackled. "Mundane? Anyone can learn magic, my pet. You know, I have an old ruby that would make a perfect amulet for you. I just need to find a setting for it first."

* * *

"Penny? What's going on in there?"

I blinked, trying to regain my bearings. My head was spinning. There was a light shining off to the side, which was not helping matters. A few moments passed, before my headache subsided and I realized Lupine was calling for me. I glanced out the window and saw him pacing.

He turned his head and saw me looking. "Do you need me to come in, Penny? I don't care about the glass."

I shook my head, trying to clear it. Last time I used magic to induce a memory. "No. I'm fine, Lupine, really. Don't hurt yourself on my account."

"All right, but hurry, Penelope." His ears perked up. "Somebody's coming! Go! I'll hold them off!"

Nodding, I turned back to the rest of the house. First things first, where was that light coming from?

I was not prepared for what I saw. My old drawing was glowing with a soft blue light.

Before I had time to register what this could mean, before I could even examine the paper, a sharp bark from Lupine warned me that our visitor was almost upon us.

"Easy, boy," a familiar voice said. "I'm not here to hurt you. I'm looking for my friend."

Eyes wide, I looked out the window. Lupine's fur was standing straight up as he advanced on a blonde boy in a green cloak.

"Artie!" I cried. I couldn't let Lupine hurt him. Without thinking, I snatched my drawing off the wall and ran outside. I barely noticed as the blue glow faded and warmth spread up my arm.

Chapter Three

Friends in Unlikely Places

I found Artie and Lupine twenty feet from the front door. Lupine growled and snarled at Artie, whose back was against a tree. Artie was holding Lupine back with his silver knife, but he seemed reluctant to attack.

"Artie!" I cried, sprinting to them.

"Penelope!" His eyes brightened and he gave me a relieved smile. "Where were you? Mag and I woke up and you weren't there. We were frantic. Mag went to look for you in the woods." He tried to take a step forward, but Lupine snapped at him again.

"Lupine, stop! Artie's my friend!"

The wolf slowly relaxed. "Are you sure?"

"Yes! Now, leave Artie alone!"

Lupine didn't move. I was starting to get nervous. What if he didn't back down? I fingered my amulet, ready to defend my friend.

Artie cleared his throat. "Lupine, is it? I'm not here to hurt Penelope. We've been traveling together. Mag and I were simply worried and went looking."

Slowly, Lupine nodded and backed away. "I'm sorry," he said. "I needed Penelope's help to retrieve an item. Now that she has it, I'll be on my way." He turned to leave. "I can see I'm not needed anymore."

"Wait, Lupine! All I found was a child's drawing. I still haven't found what you're looking for. You can't leave!"

He glanced toward the horizon. I looked as well. The sun was slowly rising.

Without warning, Lupine took off for the trees at the edge of the woods. He stopped in the shade of the first tree, before turning back.

"I've stayed too long," he said. "I have to go before they find me. Penelope, you need to keep the spell safe. You can't let it fall into the wrong hands."

"What are you talking about?" Artie said.

Lupine ignored him. "Come sundown, this village will not be safe anymore. Find your friend and get out as soon as you can." His fur started to ripple, even though there was no wind. "Good luck, Penny." And he vanished into the trees.

I stared at the place Lupine had been standing. I didn't have the right paper, did I? I glanced at my old drawing. If this paper really did contain a spell Lupine needed, I couldn't just let him leave, especially if Tealeaf wasn't safe. I had to know what I was up against.

"Pen," Artie said. "What is going on?"

Taking a deep breath, I said, "I have to find that wolf. Lupine sent me inside for this paper. I want to know why."

I stowed the drawing in my bag and started for the trees. I hadn't gone more than two steps, when I felt Artie take my hand. I stopped and looked back.

Artie's unruly blonde hair swept over his eyes. He pushed it back and gave me a determined look. "I'm coming with you, Penelope."

I didn't have time to argue. "Come on, then. Lupine can't have gone far."

Together, Artie and I hurried into the woods after Lupine. We were still holding hands.

* * *

Ten minutes later, I was sure I had gotten us lost. I may have explored these woods as a child, but the forest had changed. Trees weren't where I remembered them, a small river cut across a field that I knew had once been a meadow, and the ground seemed to be scorched in places.

Artie and I stopped next to the river as I tried to get my bearings.

"I think this is the meadow where I used to pick flowers with Lydia," I said fondly. "Good times."

Artie pulled his boots out of the mud. "Not much of a meadow now though, is it?" he said quietly.

"No. No, it isn't. What happened, Artie? What changed?"

"Eight years is a long time, Pen." He knelt and scooped up a handful of the scorched earth. "The golden dragon must have burned this part of the forest." He stood up. "But why here?"

"I don't know," I began, when a familiar female voice interrupted me.

"There you two are! I've been looking everywhere for you!"

A redheaded girl wearing a red cloak came strolling toward us. She was taller than both me and Artie and moved with the ease of a cat. She was currently in her human form, but in reality, she was a dragon. She had the power to transform between the two at will. Her amber eyes flashed with intelligence as she took in the scene.

"Hi, Mag," I said, smiling. "What took you so long?"

"Ha, ha," she said dryly. "Very witty, Penelope." She snorted, smoke curling from her nostrils. "Would you kindly explain why you ran off? You left me, your poor dragon guardian, wondering where you went. Artie was so worried about you that I had to go traipsing all over Tealeaf, searching for you."

"I'm sorry, Mag. An animal needed my help. Long story. We're trying to find him right now. You haven't seen a large, gray wolf anywhere, have you?"

"No," she said, growing serious. "Not directly, at any rate."

"What do you mean?"

"Tufts of fur snagged on low-hanging tree branches, the scent of canine in the air, and claw marks on fallen logs. He must have been in a hurry to leave such an obvious trail."

"Pen," Artie called. He was standing next to a nearby tree. "Mag's right. Paw prints."

I hurried over to him. "Wolf tracks?"

He nodded. "But that's not the weird part."

"Artie, there's a wolf somewhere in these woods, who asked me to search for a spell in the ruins of a witch's house. You and Mag have already picked up his trail as though it were nothing. How is none of this weird?"

In a quiet voice, he said, "Look up, Penelope."

At first, all I saw was a normal tree. But then, I spotted something bright and colorful in its branches.

"Birds?" I said, squinting.

"No," Artie said, shaking his head. "They aren't moving."

He was right. These things were swaying slightly in the breeze, but otherwise weren't moving. I couldn't get a clear look at them through the leaves.

"What do you think those are?"

Mag joined us at the base of the tree, but the moment she tried to step past me, she slowed and a blue pulse of energy seemed to push her away. She stumbled back a few paces, her eyes wide. "I don't believe this!" Her expression darkened and she stormed off toward the river, muttering to herself.

"Mag?"

She rounded on me. "Seriously, Penelope? Why would you cast *another* barrier to keep me out?"

"But I didn't," I said, frowning. The only spells I had used were to find Lupine's paper and create that ball of fire to read his name etched in the dirt.

"Oh, you cast it all right," Mag huffed. "I can sense your magical signature through our bond. This is just like Tealeaf all over again."

When the golden dragon attacked eights years ago, I had unknowingly shielded Tealeaf with a magical barrier. The damage had been done, however, and the village abandoned.

"How do you sense magical signatures?" Artie asked.

"The dragon guardian bond allows me to detect this sort of thing,"

Mag said, waving her hand impatiently. "But I can't get past, not until you remove the barrier, Penelope."

"I'll try my best," I said. "Give me a moment, Mag. I just want to check on something first."

She nodded as I approached the tree. The blue pulse flashed again, but besides a strange tingling sensation, nothing happened. Why did this particular tree seem so familiar? Maybe I played here as a child? It was certainly possible, given how close Tealeaf was. But why would I place a barrier around it?

I looked up and saw what was hidden in the branches. I couldn't believe what I was seeing. I started to climb, determined to get a closer look. I needed to satisfy my curiosity once and for all. If I was right, suddenly the barrier made a lot of sense.

I pulled myself onto a sturdy branch, when a voice said, "Here for the toys, Penelope?"

I was so surprised, that I almost fell out of the tree. When I regained my balance, I found a small black cat reclining on the branch above me, his legs hanging lazily over the side.

"Cadmus! What are you doing here?"

Cadmus was a magical lion. He could shrink to the size of a house cat and grow back to lion-size whenever he wanted. I'd met him on the same day I got my magic. He was one of my best friends, after Mag and Artie.

"I could ask you the same question," he said. "I believe I was here first."

"We're looking for a wolf," I explained. "You haven't seen him, have you? His paw prints are at the base of this tree."

"Large, gray, black tips to his ears?"

"Yes!"

"Never met him before in my life," Cadmus said, yawning. "Now, besides searching for a wolf, what brings you up here?"

"Pen, is that Cadmus up there with you?" Artie called.

"Let's talk on the ground," Cadmus said. "It'll be rude to leave Mag and Artie out of this, especially since your spell blocks Mag from the tree."

We started to climb down, when Artie exclaimed, "Penelope! Mag is gone!"

Startled, I looked at the ground, which was not a good idea. I leaned out a bit too far. My feet slipped from the branch. I threw my arms around the nearest tree limb, stopping my fall.

"Oof!"

I was left dangling, with only my arms to support me, my feet swinging wildly as I searched frantically for a foothold.

Cadmus leapt lightly onto the branch next to me. "Need some help?"

"I'm fine," I grunted, as I strained to pull myself up. I sighed in relief as I found a small knothole to jam my foot into. "Go find out what's going on, please. I seem to be stuck."

Cadmus nodded, grew into the size of a lion, and jumped to the ground, knocking a round, blue object to the ground as he went. *I can't believe it's the same tree,* I thought, not even flinching at his increased size.

Artie and Cadmus started talking beneath me. I didn't pay much attention, because just as I threw my leg over the branch, a loud *crack!* rent the air.

Again, I started to fall.

"Pen!" Artie cried. "Use *Ohen!*"

"*Oh—*" I began, when suddenly, I stopped falling. The "up" spell had worked, without me even uttering it.

Willing myself down, I slowly began to descend. As long as I concentrated, the spell would keep me in the air. I'd used this incantation before, but something felt different. My magic was still lowering me safely to the ground, but some other force seemed to be there. It wasn't invasive, it was more like a friend whispering encouragements in my ear.

I touched down gently beside Cadmus, took a step forward to regain my balance, and almost tripped on something. Kneeling, I scooped up the round, blue object that had fallen from the tree, shoved it in my bag, and straightened. I would deal with it later. I looked around. Cadmus was staring at my bag, his eyes narrowed. He looked ready to pounce. Understandable, really, given what it was. Artie, however, was leaning against the tree, looking exhausted.

"Artie?" I said, taking his hand.

He sprang upright like he had received an electric shock. "Who? What?" he said wildly.

"Are you all right?"

"Fine! Never better!" He cleared his throat and said in an overly cheerful voice, "Just felt a bit dizzy there for a moment. I'm fine, really, Penelope."

I frowned. An idea was forming in my mind. I shook my head. No, it couldn't be. I was simply confused. My magic had responded to my panic, that was all. *I* stopped my fall, right?

Pushing my ridiculous idea aside, I said, "What happened, Artie? Where's Mag?"

"I don't know. We were just standing here at the base of the tree, when Mag stiffened. She said something about checking Tealeaf and ran off. It must have been important."

"It was."

We all turned to see Mag jogging back toward us. Her hair was on fire. It tended to do that when she was agitated.

I rushed toward her. "Did something happen in Tealeaf?"

"Yes," she said, her eyes flashing. "You've got to see this. Tealeaf is about to get a lot more interesting."

Chapter Four

Voices in the Fog

With Mag guiding us, we returned to the Tealeaf town square. The place was deathly quiet. I shivered. Not even the birds were chirping.

"Mag," Artie said. "There's nothing here."

She rolled her eyes. "You humans never notice anything. Don't you sense— get down!" Mag ducked behind the nearest building, dragging Artie and me with her. Cadmus shrank back down to house cat size and squeezed into our hiding place.

"Mag?"

"Shh! Watch!"

Easier said than done. A mist was rolling in and I couldn't see more than three feet in any direction.

"Where did this fog come from?" Cadmus said, his nose twitching. "It wasn't here a few minutes ago."

He was right. A moment ago, the early morning sunlight had been shining brightly, but now, an eerie fog was slowly covering Tealeaf. It was unnatural.

Mag placed a finger to her lips and practically shouted, "SHH!"

I didn't bother to point out that Mag was making more noise than the rest of us combined. When you're standing next to an irate dragon, in human or dragon form, it's best not to enrage them. Mag's eyes flashed dangerously. She was one word away from burning someone to cinders.

Nobody spoke. The fog became denser. Everything was blanketed by a sea of white.

A movement caught my eye. At first, I thought it was just a trick of the light, but then the mist cleared enough to reveal a girl. She looked to be about my age, with gray eyes, long brown hair pulled back into a ponytail, and the prowling gait of a panther. She wore a dark blue blouse, black slacks, and a gleaming silver breastplate on top. The uniform of a guard. We watched as she stopped in the middle of the square, not far from where we hid. I held my breath, thankful for the fog.

"Oh, no," Artie sighed. He sounded resigned. "Not her. Anyone but her."

"Who is she?" I asked.

"Her name is Rowena," he said, not taking his eyes off her. "Let's just say, we've had a few run-ins."

He glanced at me, a hint of amusement dancing in his eyes. "It's not what you think, Pen. Rowena is not my friend. She's one of the most dangerous people I've ever met. She despises me because of who my father is, because I'm a thief. I'd appreciate it if she didn't discover my presence."

"She'll find us within minutes, if you two don't shut up," Mag snapped irritably. "Artie, what are our options? How do we get past Rowena?"

"The simplest way? We run. We run and we don't look back."

"How's that working out for you?" Cadmus asked.

"Not well," he admitted. "But there's fog. She can't see us."

"But she can hear us," I said. "Look."

Everyone turned. Rowena was heading straight for us.

"New plan," Mag said. "Penelope, Artie, I need you two to distract her while Cadmus and I work on a way to clear this fog. We're flying out of here."

"Why are we the distraction?" I asked quietly, as Rowena moved closer.

"Because unlike you and Artie, Cadmus can stay quiet for an extended period of time. That, and Artie should have some experience with Rowena, especially if they've met before. Now, get going. I need all the time you can give me. Make as much noise as you can. That should draw her away."

"Meet us at Maude's house in thirty minutes," Cadmus said. "We'll rendezvous there."

Artie looked less than pleased. He nodded stiffly, and together, we crept forward. As we watched, Rowena slowly turned and started walking in the opposite direction, muttering about how she must have been hearing things.

"Will she chase you, if she sees you?" I murmured. We were still close enough for her to hear us.

"Definitely," Artie said. "Rowena is nothing if not persistent."

This gave me an idea. "Artie, do you trust me?"

"With my life, Penelope."

"Nothing that dramatic, Artie. Mag said to create as much noise as possible, to draw Rowena away. What's the easiest way to do that?"

"To offer myself as bait." He stopped and stared at me, before shaking his head. "Clever, Pen. It just might work. But how do you know she'll follow me in this fog?"

"You said it yourself. Rowena will chase you, no matter what. Please, Artie. Mag's counting on us."

"All right," he said reluctantly. "You're sure she won't see us?"

"Yes. With a fog this thick, she'll be lucky to see anything. She just needs to recognize your voice."

"What about us? We need to see, too."

I held up my amulet. "I've got us covered. I know a spell that will help."

"Let's get this over with."

Rowena was at the opposite end of the square, still within hearing distance. Not wanting to take any chances, I whispered, *"Endoraken."*

I collapsed against Artie as my vision clouded with silver. Strangely though, it wasn't the bright silver I was accustomed to. Instead, it was dull and muted.

Artie lowered me gently to the ground, while I focused on taking deep breaths. After several moments, my vision cleared. It was a much faster recovery than usual. Maybe I was finally getting used to my magic. I could now see far enough through the fog to know where I was going. I glanced at Artie.

He gave me a thumbs-up. He could see, too.

It was time to put our plan into action. Artie helped me to my feet, turned toward Rowena, and called, "Rowena, so good to see you again!"

There was a falsely joyful ring to his voice.

Rowena jumped and spun around, but Artie and I were already on the move. The plan was to lead her on a merry little chase around Tealeaf, to give Mag time to clear the fog. We just hoped my spell hadn't cleared the area for Rowena, as well.

"Arthur Quick! Where are you?!"

"Looks like it worked," Artie whispered as we sped toward the fountain in the center of the square.

"I'll say," I muttered, as we paused to catch our breaths. The sound of racing footsteps over cobblestones reached my ears. We had to keep moving. "Artie, get ready to run. Head for Maude's."

"Arthur Quick!"

He winced at her voice, before yelling, "You're just as pleasant as the last time we met, Rowena!"

We sprinted off in the direction of Maude's house. The closer we got to the southern end of town, the slower we had to go. The cobblestones were cracked in places. Trees bordered the path. Artie and I held hands as we ran.

"I will find you, Quick! You can't get away from me forever!"

"What did you do to her?" I asked, as I dodged a low-hanging tree branch.

"Me? Nothing! I didn't steal anything from Rowena!"

"Well, she's angry about something," I said. "Can't you talk to her about it? Explain that you only steal from those who wrong others?"

"Ha! Talk to her? That's a good one!" Artie laughed humorlessly. Raising his voice slightly, he shouted, "Rowena hates me with a passion, don't you, Ro?"

"Call me that one more time, *Arthur*, and I will strangle you with your own cloak!"

Grinning, Artie said, "She's a bit violent."

"Clearly." I was taken aback by the vehemence in Rowena's voice. "Maybe we should go faster."

Artie glanced behind us, before turning back around. "Agreed."

We kept running, thinking only of staying ahead of Rowena, Artie taunting her all the while. As we rounded a corner, Maude's house in sight, I put on a burst of speed and stepped right into a hole. With a cry of surprise, I lost my balance and fell. My ankle was throbbing painfully.

"Ow," I whimpered, scrambling to my feet. Unfortunately, my right foot wouldn't support me and I crumpled.

"Pen! Are you all right?" Artie cried, bending down to help.

"I'm fine," I said, through gritted teeth. I couldn't stop. I had to keep going, otherwise, Rowena would catch up to us before we could even reach Maude's house. We had a good head start on her, but I could hear Rowena panting a little way behind us.

I tried to step forward, but pain shot up from my injured ankle. Artie put his arm around my shoulder and helped me to hobble a couple of paces. We would never get to the front lawn, let alone the door, at this rate.

While I appreciated Artie's support and was reluctant to part with him, I knew what had to be done. I pushed him away from me. "Run! Leave me here, Artie."

"What? No! Penelope, I can't leave you alone with Rowena!"

"What choice do we have? I can't run on this leg and I don't know any healing spells. I could use the silver rose, but with its limited reserves, I'd rather not waste it on something as trivial as a sprained ankle."

I could still hear Rowena off to my left, still searching blindly for us through the fog. "Artie, go!"

"No," he said stubbornly. "I won't leave you to Rowena's mercy."

"I'll be fine. She won't see me in the fog. Please, Artie."

He took my hand, his brow crinkled in concern. "Get to Maude's house. I'll be back as soon as I can." He touched a strand of my hair. "Stay safe, Penelope." He then took off back the way we came, calling, "Race you back to town, Ro!"

"That's it, Arthur! Prepare to be strangled!" Rowena dashed after Artie. She passed by so close, that I had to take a step back on my good foot, to avoid a collision. If Rowena noticed my presence, she didn't show it.

"Ah, but I thought your high and mighty friends in Kelton Castle frowned upon that. Naughty, naughty, Ro. You'll get in *trouble*." Artie's voice had started to fade, but I could still hear the singsong note on the last word.

I giggled. Artie definitely knew how to lift my spirits. I stood there until I could no longer hear them. Then, I started the slow and painful journey of walking the twenty feet to Maude's door with a sprained ankle.

About halfway there, I stopped to rest. My ankle was swelling badly. I reached into my bag, searching for a container of water, when my hand brushed against Lupine's paper. Turning the drawing over, I found two words, written in an unfamiliar hand.

Squinting, I read, "Gideon, *Entalen.*" Immediately, I was bathed in a green glow of magic. It was like nothing I'd ever experienced before. The magic seemed to be coming from the paper, not me. It felt ancient and powerful. It enveloped me in a sense of well-being, like someone I loved was giving me a hug. Somehow, I knew nothing would harm me as long as this mysterious force was present. The green light began to fade, but the feeling remained.

Several seconds passed, before I shook my head, as if awaking from a dream. I stretched, feeling incredibly refreshed, when I realized that my ankle no longer hurt.

"Did Lupine know I would get injured and need a healing spell?" I muttered to myself. I looked back at the paper. "Who's Gideon?"

"Gideon? I didn't know that you two had met."

Turning, I found Cadmus standing beside me. "Cadmus? What are you doing here?"

"I was looking for you. I saw Artie run by with Rowena not far behind. When I didn't see you, I got worried. So, how do you know Gideon?"

"I don't. I have no idea who he is."

"Oh! Then, never mind," Cadmus said, starting for the house. "Come on, inside before Rowena returns. Mag and Artie should be along soon."

"Hold on, Cadmus," I said, darting in front of him. "Who is Gideon? Where's Mag?"

"What happened to your ankle?" he countered.

We stared each other down, neither one of us even blinking. Finally,

I couldn't take it anymore and said, "I sprained my ankle. Artie's distracting Rowena, giving me time to get to the house. The spell that healed me had Gideon's name in it. Happy, you little furball?"

Cadmus didn't look insulted by my last comment, in fact, he even chuckled. "I guess I deserved that. To tell you the truth, Penelope, thanks to my lion form, nobody has ever called me out like that. It's kind of refreshing."

I snapped my fingers to gain his attention. "Cadmus, focus. Mag and Gideon."

He sighed. "Unless you already know about Gideon, I can't tell you anything. I'm sorry."

"But, Cadmus."

"No. Now, drop it."

I didn't like it, but I knew better than to ask. I wouldn't get any more information from him.

"What about Mag? Where did she disappear to?"

"Ah, something I *can* answer. She went to find the highest point in Tealeaf. She'll be down soon."

"Cadmus, what aren't you telling me?"

He hesitated, before saying, "Oh, Penelope, haven't you noticed? Look around. What's missing?"

Frowning, I did as he said. At first, I didn't see anything. Nothing was missing. I could see Maude's old house, the distant tree line, the bright sunlight shining down on us. Wait.

"The fog… it's gone!"

CHAPTER FIVE

HEARTLESS HARTFORD

"Mag did it!" I cried. "She got rid of the fog."

"Yes, yes, she did," Cadmus said distractedly. "Penelope, I really think we should head inside and wait for Mag and Artie. If we're lucky, we can hold out for reinforcements."

"Reinforcements? Cadmus, Tealeaf is isolated from the rest of Alsmora. The only ones here are you, me, Mag, Artie, and Rowena. Lupine might be around here somewhere, if we can find him. I think between the five of us, we can easily stay ahead of her."

"No, Penelope, you don't understand."

A burst of fire shot into the air. "Mag," I whispered. For a split second, I was torn between helping my friends or waiting in safety with Cadmus. The choice was obvious. I turned on my heel and ran back the way Artie and I came.

"Penelope! Come back!" Cadmus called.

I ignored him and kept running. I didn't make it far, before Cadmus, now lion-sized, leapt in front of me, blocking my path.

"Listen!" he said. "Mag uncovered something when she burned away the fog."

"And what was that?" I wasn't trying to be rude, but I was sure that burst of fire meant that Mag and Artie were in danger. I bounced on the balls of my feet anxiously.

Cadmus growled and stalked closer. He stopped, his face an inch from mine. I stopped bouncing. No matter how much I trusted Cadmus, he was still a lion.

We stood there, staring at each other, until Cadmus smiled. "I'm glad to see I got your attention, Penelope. You can't just go running off into Tealeaf like that. It's too dangerous."

"Why?"

"Better to show you." He gestured to his back. "Hop on."

"Cadmus—"

"I'm a lion, Penelope. I can easily carry you."

I hesitated, before I climbed onto his back. Cadmus clearly wouldn't let me search for Mag and Artie, until he showed me whatever had spooked him. And I could never outrun him while he was in lion form. I would humor him for now.

Once I was settled on Cadmus's back, he took off toward the trees. I had to throw my arms around his neck to keep from falling.

He didn't seem to notice as he dodged the trees with ease. I had to keep ducking branches.

"Cadmus! Slow down!"

He ignored me. We burst out of the trees and into a clearing.

"Cadmus, stop!" I yelled, pulling hard on his mane.

He stopped, but I almost went sailing over his head. I managed to keep my seat, but immediately wished I hadn't.

There was a low rumbling, deep in Cadmus's throat.

That can't be good, I thought and scrambled from his back. We were standing next to a lone tree, which I quickly hid behind.

Cadmus shook his massive head and walked toward me. "You're lucky you did that to me and not another lion. Any other cat would have clawed you to shreds." He stopped in front of me.

I looked at his razor-sharp claws and gulped.

Cadmus continued, "I forgive you this time, Penelope, because you didn't know any better, but never do that again. That hurt."

"Sorry. I promise."

"Good. We're here, by the way. If you hadn't stopped me, we probably would have run right past it."

I stared at him incredulously. "Then, why did you growl at me?"

"I don't like having my fur pulled."

"Fair enough, but why…?"

"Penelope, we can either stand here arguing all day or we can do what we came to do and move on. Now, do you recognize the place or not?"

Looking around, I realized we were in the same clearing as before. I was standing next to the same, strange tree that Mag couldn't approach. The colorful, round objects were swaying in the breeze.

"Why are we here?" I asked.

"Two reasons. One, do you still have the thing I knocked out of the tree?"

"Yes," I said, reaching into my bag and rummaging around. My fingers closed on the object. It felt a little like a ball of string, but I knew better. *My* magic had twisted and warped this tree when I was a child. I was amazed it was still alive after all this time. I pulled out the item and stared in wonder at all. It was a ball of yarn.

"I have no idea why it grows yarn balls," Cadmus said. "This tree has been here for years. As far as I know, it's always been like that."

"Eight years," I said quietly, "back when the golden dragon first attacked Tealeaf. Cadmus, I did this. I caused this tree to sprout yarn balls. My magic was unstable and unpredictable. It happened while I was unconscious. I must have somehow created the barrier at that time. I didn't mean to. I simply had too much magic. It kept bursting out of me at random."

Cadmus touched my arm with his giant paw. "It's an amazing feat of magic, Penelope, but the other reason we're up here."

"I'm listening." I tossed the yarn up and caught it.

"Over there," Cadmus said, nodding out across the valley.

I turned and immediately dropped my yarn. Beyond the hill, it was chaos in silver and blue. At first, I just thought it was a bunch of harmless flowers, but no. It was moving in our direction. I was looking at a group of people, all wearing Alsmora's royal colors.

"Queen Alana's soldiers," I whispered, watching as at least a hundred troops marched toward Tealeaf. "What are they doing here?"

"I was hoping you could tell me," Cadmus said. "The fog seems to have been shielding their approach. When Mag and I saw them, we rushed back to find you and Artie. Mag should have already rescued him from Rowena's clutches. Now that you know what we're up against, we need to return to Maude's house. Hopefully, we can make it back without anyone noticing."

"This is insane," I said. "There's no way the soldiers could have assembled so quickly. The fog was only up for about thirty minutes."

"They worked fast," Cadmus said. "We can't worry about the details. We need to head back, now."

Nodding, I grabbed the yarn and boosted myself onto Cadmus back. As he raced off, I had an idea. "Cadmus, those are Queen Alana's soldiers, right?"

"They seem to be. Why?"

"Well, she knows what we're up to, that we're trying to defeat the golden dragon. Maybe she sent her army to help us! I'm sure if we talk to them, we'll find that it was all one big misunderstanding."

Cadmus didn't say anything until we were in the forest again. "And what if it isn't a misunderstanding?" he asked quietly. "It's been a week since you left Kelton Castle, Penelope. A lot could have changed since then."

"You're wrong," I said stubbornly. "Queen Alana is an old friend of my mom's. She wouldn't betray us like this."

"Maybe they're not after you."

That shut me up. We continued on in silence as I sat on Cadmus's back, wondering. What if the soldiers were here searching for Malcolm and not for me? I had to find him and fast. He was accused of starting a fire inside Kelton Castle. I didn't believe it. My brother was innocent.

"Penelope?" Cadmus said. "Penelope. We're here and we've got company."

I jerked my head up and immediately grinned. Swinging myself off of Cadmus, I ran to meet my friends. Mag and Artie were standing with their backs to us. It looked as if they had just arrived. Artie's hair was windswept and he had a small cut on his arm, while Mag was still in dragon form. They looked up as I hurried toward them. Mag became human once more.

Throwing my arms around them in a group hug, I said, "I'm happy to see you two! I was so worried."

"We're fine, Pen," Artie said, hugging me back. "I'm glad to see your ankle is better." He pulled away and looked me straight in the eye, his expression serious. "Rowena cornered me by the fountain, but Mag came to my rescue. She swept down from the sky and landed in front of me. I jumped on, but Rowena threw a knife." Artie smiled ruefully. "She nicked my arm, but we managed to escape."

"Won't she chase us back here?" I asked.

Mag snorted, shoving me away. "Humans, so emotional," she muttered. "You don't have to worry about Rowena. I've already taken care of her."

"Do I want to know?"

She shrugged. "As I took off, my tail *accidentally* swung and hit Rowena. I may have knocked her out for a bit. Oh, don't look at me like that, Penelope. She's still alive."

I sighed, shaking my head. Sometimes, there was no reasoning with Mag.

"So, what do we do now?" Artie asked, nodding toward the rest of Tealeaf. "Mag showed me the soldiers from the air. We're completely surrounded."

My eyes widened. "Completely? I thought they were only by the one hill. How are we going to get out of here?"

Mag and Cadmus exchanged a look.

"Should we tell them?" Cadmus asked quietly.

"I think so," Mag said. "Aldrich might kill me, but there's no way around it. We can't stay here and, thanks to the soldiers, we can't fly. They'll just try and shoot us down. There's only one way out now. Shall we go set it up, Cadmus?"

"That would probably be for the best."

"What are you two talking about?" I said.

Mag didn't seem to hear me. She walked straight past both me and Artie and headed into Maude's house, Cadmus at her heels. Before Artie or I could do anything, the door slammed shut behind them.

We were left alone outside.

"What just happened?"

Artie shrugged. "No idea. Pen, listen, about Rowena…"

I took his hand. "Artie! I'm so sorry! I forgot about your arm. Here, let me look!"

"It's fine, Pen. It's a tiny scratch."

"Are you sure?"

"Positive," he said, pulling me toward the door. "We don't want to linger out here too long. Trust me. Rowena's still out there."

"Leaving so soon?"

Artie and I spun around to find Rowena standing behind us. Her hair was a tangled mess, her eyes flashed with anger, and there was a red bump on the top of her head, no doubt where Mag had struck Rowena with her tail. She was brandishing a knife. It was stained with blood. Artie's blood.

We backed up slowly, toward the house.

Rowena followed us, glaring at Artie. Her gaze never wavered from her prey.

Artie's grip tightened on my hand. "Rowena! Long time, no see! How have you been?"

"Oh, perfect, except for the fact that your wretched dragon knocked me out!"

"Rowena, if you'd let me explain," Artie began, but she cut him off.

"Do you know how long I've been waiting to capture you, Quick?" She didn't wait for a response, before snapping, "Too long. I have searched and searched all over Alsmora, with nary a word about you, *Arthur*. I was beginning to lose hope of ever finding you. Then, I followed the soldiers to Tealeaf and you fell into my lap. If only *Captain* Bogg, could see me now."

"Malcolm!" I gasped. I couldn't stop myself.

Rowena rounded on me. Her voice lowered to a growl. "*You* know Malcolm Bogg? Who are you?"

Artie and I had backed up so far, we were pressed flat against the front door. As I reached for the doorknob, my heart sank. The door opened outwards, toward us. We were well and truly trapped. Rowena waited. Clearing my throat, I said, "I'm Queen Alana's niece… Hazel. She knew I was stopping by Tealeaf on my way to see her. She asked me to check out the place, in case I found her missing guard."

"Is that so?" Rowena said. "Queen Alana's niece just so happens to be traveling with a known thief. Why don't you tell me who you really are, *Hazel*?"

"Leave her alone," Artie said, taking a step forward. "It's me you want, not her."

"Artie," I whispered, placing my hand on his shoulder, ready to pull him back.

"What's the matter, Arthur?" Rowena taunted, as she removed a set of handcuffs from her belt. She jangled them threateningly. "Is this another of your thief friends?"

Bum-ba-ba! Ba-bum!

No. Not the drums. Not now.

Rowena frowned and turned. Artie seized the moment to leap into action. He lunged forward and seized her wrist. I fumbled for my amulet, as the two struggled for the knife.

"Beredan!" I yelled. Ropes materialized from the ruby and wrapped themselves around Rowena. Her eyes widened as she started to fall. Artie, now in possession of the knife, quickly shoved it into my shaking hands and caught Rowena, laying her gently on the ground.

I saw Artie turn toward me, just as I slumped against the wall. Everything was muted silver again.

"Penelope!" he cried, rushing to my side. "Are you all right?"

I blinked several times, until the world's color returned. "Thanks," I mumbled as Artie helped me up.

Ba-bum! Bum-ba-ba-bum!

"Penelope," he said urgently. "Those drums, it can only be the soldiers approaching. We need to get Mag and Cadmus and leave now."

I glanced at Rowena. "What about her?"

Before Artie could answer, the door opened, revealing Cadmus.

"Penelope, Artie, what's taking you so long? Mag and I are ready." He stopped when he saw Rowena bound on the ground. "Okay," he said slowly. "I'm not even going to ask."

Bum-ba! Ba-ba-bum!

The drums were getting closer.

"Cadmus, would you go get Mag?" I said anxiously. "We have to get Rowena inside quickly. We can't leave her outside with the soldiers on the way."

He nodded. "One moment."

Cadmus trotted back into the house. Seconds later, Mag came running back out.

"What's going on?" she said. "Cadmus said something about a bound guard."

"Rowena Hartford," Artie said. "The two of you met when your tail collided with her head."

"Oh, right. Good times."

Rowena strained against the ropes, her expression murderous.

"She's been chasing me since my first visit to Silent Stream."

"But you're innocent," I protested.

Three years ago, Artie and his friend Ben had been passing through the city of Silent Stream. They were accused of a robbery they hadn't committed. Artie and Ben had barely managed to escape.

Artie snorted. "Do you think she cares? To her, I'm simply one more thief to catch."

Ba-ba-bum! Ba-bum!

"We're out of time," Cadmus said, as Mag picked up Rowena with ease. "We have to go now."

"Cadmus, take Penelope and Artie through. I'll drop her inside," Mag inclined her head toward Rowena, "and then I'll hold *him* off."

She disappeared inside with the bound Rowena.

"Who…?"

BA-BUM-BUM! BUM-BA-BUM!

I looked up. Those weren't drums. On the horizon, flying right toward us, was the golden dragon, the one responsible for the destruction of Tealeaf. Below him, marching straight for Maude's house, were the soldiers Cadmus and I had spotted earlier.

Artie whistled softly. "We're never going to get out of this."

"Don't be so sure," Cadmus said. "Come."

Artie and I followed him to the door, as Mag stepped out again.

"Mag, no," I said, grabbing her arm. "You can't take on the golden dragon and all those soldiers by yourself."

She smiled, revealing her fangs. "I'm a dragon guardian, Penelope. Watch me."

"Good luck!" Rowena called bitterly from inside. "I hope the golden dragon tears you to pieces, whoever he is."

"Don't you know his identity, Rowena?" Artie said. "You came into Tealeaf with the soldiers."

Rowena let out a bark of laughter. "Me, with the golden dragon? As if, Quick. No, he may think I'm working with him, but I'm really investigating the magical barrier that's appeared around Kelton Castle."

My blood ran cold. "Magical barrier?" I repeated. "What magical barrier? What's happened to Kelton Castle?"

Rowena shrugged. "No idea, Hazel. Or, should I say *Penelope.* That's why I'm investigating. I'm sure the golden dragon is behind it. That's why I followed him to Tealeaf. I'll tell you what, though. If you free me and tell me how you know Malcolm Bogg, maybe I won't arrest you, even if you are traveling with a known thief."

I glanced at Artie, Mag, and Cadmus. Mag was standing in the doorway, staring at Rowena suspiciously. Artie and Cadmus had similar looks of distrust on their faces.

Given how Rowena had chased Artie and cornered both of us in front of the house, I didn't exactly trust her either. But I couldn't think about that now. The golden dragon and his soldiers were almost at the door.

Turning away from Rowena, I said, "How are we getting out of here?

You too, Mag. We're not leaving you behind."

"This way," Cadmus said, heading for a nearby bookcase. He muttered something I couldn't make out. There was a small click and the bookcase slid away, revealing an entrance.

Cadmus stepped through. Mag, with some reluctance, followed.

Artie approached the opening. "This looks like one of my sister's tunnels. When did Sylvia have time to visit Maude's house?" He offered me his hand. "I'll ask her later. Come on, Pen. We have to go."

I started forward, but stopped when I saw Rowena. I couldn't leave her. Taking the knife Artie had shoved into my hands, I began to cut the guard free.

"You're actually helping me?" Rowena said, smirking. "I knew you would. Why would you side with that filthy thief anyway, *Pen*? By helping me, you've chosen the side of justice."

I could feel my blood boiling at her words. Nobody called me 'Pen.' Nobody, except Artie. And who was Rowena to talk about justice, after chasing Artie halfway across Alsmora?

"I'm not doing this for you," I snapped, as I continued to saw through the ropes. "Nor am I doing this for a misplaced sense of justice, like you seem to have."

"Then, why are you doing it?" Rowena sneered.

"I can't leave you here," I said simply. "If I did, I'd be no better than the golden dragon. He destroyed Tealeaf. My home. I wouldn't put it past him to try and demolish Maude's house, once and for all. You'd be killed if that happened."

I finished freeing Rowena and pulled her to her feet. "Leave, Rowena. Leave and never come back to Tealeaf. I don't know where you're going, but if you ever attempt to hurt Artie again, I won't be so lenient next time. Now, get out of Maude's house."

With that, I followed Artie through the secret passageway. As I crossed the threshold, the bookcase slid between us and Rowena. My last view of my beloved Tealeaf was Rowena slipping away into the night, while the golden dragon set fire to the house.

Chapter Six

Heartfelt Hartford

I stood there shaking, trying to regain my composure, but all I could see was the house being consumed by flames. Two dim torches flanked the bookcase door, giving out barely enough light to see. I had no idea how long I'd stood there, fighting back tears, when Artie suddenly slipped his hand into mine. Startled, I turned toward him, Rowena's knife clattering to the floor between us. I could just see my friend in the semi-darkness.

"I'm sorry about Maude's house."

"Me too." I would miss that old, broken-down cottage. At least I still had the picture I drew for Maude when I was eight. I gasped as I remembered what was written on the back of the paper.

"Pen, what is it?" Artie said.

I held it out to him. "Lupine had me search Maude's house for this. Any idea what it means?"

"Gideon, *Entalen,*" he read. A bright green light flashed. I blinked in surprise, but Artie didn't seem to notice. He flipped the paper over and saw my picture. He smiled. "Nice drawing. Sorry, Penelope. I have no idea what this means."

"Right…" I said, still confused by the green light. "Where are Mag and Cadmus?"

As if my words had summoned her, Mag suddenly appeared out of the darkness. "There you two are. We're waiting for you downstairs."

"Downstairs?" I couldn't see more than two feet ahead. If there were stairs in front of us, it was lucky that Artie and I hadn't fallen down them.

"Yes, downstairs," Mag said impatiently. "Cadmus is waiting. He says there's someone he wants us to meet." As she turned on her heels and marched off, muttering about what she'd like to do to the golden dragon, her hair burst into flames. I watched as the light cast faint shadows on the wall.

"Penelope," Artie said. "What have we gotten ourselves into?"

I shrugged. His guess was as good as mine. I seized one of the dim torches on the wall and, after Artie had picked up Rowena's knife, we hurried after Mag.

We made our way down the spiral stairs. Mag was a distant beacon of light. I could hear the slow drip of water in the distance.

"I can't believe all of this is right under Maude's house," I whispered, my voice echoing slightly. I put my free hand on the wall. Damp.

"It could be under all of Tealeaf, as far as we know," Artie said. He tucked the knife into his belt beside his own silver dagger. "Pen, any chance you could make that fire bigger? I can't see anything except you."

"Why, Artie?" I teased. "Don't you like seeing me?"

"Of course I do," he stammered. "It's just, um…"

I laughed, squeezing his hand. "I'm joking, Artie. Be ready to catch me in case I collapse from the spell." Before Artie could say anything, I placed my hand on my amulet and said, *"Funner."*

As expected, my vision turned silver, but, like before, it was a muted silver. I leaned against Artie for support. Despite my silver vision being seemingly weaker, it was still disorienting. I was shaking so badly, I almost dropped my lit torch.

"Pen!" Artie cried, taking the torch from me, despite the heat. I smiled gratefully at him, before sinking to the nearest step and closing my eyes.

I felt drained, as if I'd run a mile. Suddenly, without warning, Artie pulled me into a tight embrace. Smiling slightly, I wrapped my arms around him and breathed deeply. After several minutes, I opened my eyes and found everything was back in perfect color. The dull, muted silver was gone. Artie was still hugging me. I wished we could have stayed like that forever, but I knew we couldn't. The golden dragon and the soldiers were probably trying to find their way inside at that very moment.

"Artie," I said, softly. "We've got to go."

Slowly, he withdrew his arms and gazed deeply into my eyes. "He can't get in, Pen. The golden dragon can't possibly get into a burning house, let alone find the secret entrance. We're safe."

"Maybe you're right," I said. "I can't see the golden dragon working out the hidden puzzle of the bookcase, even if he did get inside Maude's house. No, I'm more concerned with what's at the bottom of these stairs."

Artie took my hand once more. "There's no sense worrying. We'll face whatever it is together. Come on, let's go find Mag before she gets into more trouble."

I laughed. "True. We can't let her go hitting more potential friends with her tail."

Artie laughed as well. "It doesn't make a good first impression, does it?"

Still chortling, we found Mag waiting for us at the bottom of the winding stairs. Her hair was still on fire and she was gazing down a long hallway. Cadmus was nowhere to be seen. Artie and I stopped laughing at once.

"Mag?" I asked. "Are you okay?"

"Yeah, I'm fine," she said distractedly. "It's just that…" She shook her head. "I'm sorry. I think we made a terrible mistake."

"What are you talking about?" Artie said.

"We're in the headquarters of the Storm Knights," she said. "I've known about them for a while, thanks to Aldrich. Cadmus learned of them from his father, Grrwrath."

"What are the Storm Knights?"

"They were created a hundred years ago, during the golden dragon's rise to power. Once he was defeated, the organization was disbanded. I'd heard rumors that they were forming again, now that our golden friend has resurfaced."

"But, Mag, what does that have to do with us?" Artie asked. "We don't know anything about these Storm Knights."

"We've already met their second-in-command," Mag said, the flames in her hair crackling ominously. "She went to report to her leader. I saw her when I came down the stairs. Cadmus is with her now."

Before we could ask any more questions, we heard footsteps coming down the long hallway. Artie and I turned and saw a small group walking toward us. Cadmus was at the front, slightly apart from the other two: a knight and a girl with gray eyes, long flowing brown hair, and a welcoming smile. She was wearing a green dress, with the golden chain of a necklace visible around her neck.

Rowena.

We stood there, our mouths hanging open in shock. Rowena escaped into the night. How did she get down here so quickly? And why did she change her clothes?

Shaking off my surprise, I stepped protectively in front of Artie. I wouldn't let Rowena hurt him. Not again. "What are you doing here?" I demanded.

Rowena didn't move, but the knight lowered his weapon and pointed it directly at me. Artie drew his silver knife and leapt forward to my defense. I grabbed the sword strapped to my belt, when Cadmus cried, "Stop!" He was back in lion size and his voice rang across the hall.

Everyone turned to look at him. Cadmus crossed the room to stand by Mag, Artie, and me. He was an impressive sight with his black and gray fur rippling in the torchlight. "Calm down," he whispered to us. "They're not here to harm us." In a louder voice, he said, "Miss Hartford, my apologizes. My friends are simply confused as to your identity."

Rowena's welcoming smile had been replaced with a haughty look, but at Cadmus's words, she relaxed and did something I never thought Rowena would do. She laughed. She laughed so hard and for so long, that she had to put her hand on a nearby wall to steady herself. Once her chuckles had finally subsided, she waved her hand at the knight and said, "At ease. This is all one big misunderstanding."

As her guard stepped aside, Rowena said, "Welcome to the Storm Knights' headquarters. I'm sorry for the rude reception, but we were not expecting visitors. Won't you please join us?" She gestured down the hallway.

"We're not going anywhere with you, Rowena," Artie said. "Not after everything you've done to me."

"Arthur Quick, I believe?" Rowena said.

He nodded.

Rowena sighed. "Despite what you may think, I am not Rowena."

Artie's eyes widened in realization. Mag and I, however, started in surprise. Even the flames in Mag's hair died out. It fell flat on her head.

I was the first to find my voice. "If you're not Rowena, who are you?"

"Ah, Penelope Bogg. The one we've all heard about. It's a pleasure to meet you."

I didn't return the compliment.

"Where are my manners?" not-Rowena continued. "My name is Fiona. Fiona Hartford. I'm Rowena's twin sister."

* * *

Between Mag, Artie, and me, it was hard to tell who was the most startled. Mag was looking between Fiona and the exit, obviously planning out a possible escape route. Artie gazed at Fiona suspiciously, while fingering the handle of his knife. I studied the knight. Who was he? Was he friends with Malcolm?

Clearing my throat, I said, "It's, um, nice to meet you too, Fiona. What is this place? How do you know about us?"

Fiona stared at us incredulously. "You don't know? How do you not know?"

"Know what?" I asked, perplexed.

Fiona glanced at the knight and said, "You can leave us. I want to talk to our guests in private."

"Lady Fiona?"

"That's an order, David," Fiona said. "We don't have time to argue. Go and check on the secret passageway between Stormfall and Tealeaf."

David hesitated, before striding back up the hallway and out of sight.

Once we were alone with Fiona, Artie said, "Are you sure you're not Rowena?"

"Quite sure. Why?"

"Because the way you spoke to that guard reminded me of her."

Fiona laughed again and her whole face lit up. Rowena would look so much nicer if she laughed as well.

"True. We can both look rather frightening when we want to. But, believe me, I am definitely Fiona."

"Until now, I forgot Rowena had a twin sister," Artie said. "You don't chase me like she does."

Fiona shook her head. "I don't persecute the innocent, Arthur. I know it wasn't your fault. It was a long time ago. Blaming you would accomplish nothing."

"Please, call me Artie. Sorry I didn't recognize you sooner."

"What is this place?" I said again, louder.

"Stormfall," Mag said quietly. "Aldrich told me about it, but I never thought I'd see it for myself."

"But what is Stormfall?"

Mag shook her head, either unwilling or unable to speak.

"Stormfall is the Storm Knights' base," Fiona explained. "We've spent the last week preparing, ever since Aldrich alerted us."

"You know my grandfather?" Mag asked.

"Of course," she said. "I've met him. He told me all about you three."

"He did?"

"Yes. I know that Mag is a dragon guardian, Penelope is a witch, and Artie is a thief, though a reluctant one."

"If you know that I'm an unwilling thief," Artie said, "then how does Rowena not realize it? She was there the same day as you."

Fiona sighed. "What you have to understand about Rowena is that she is obsessed with catching thieves. Nothing else matters to her. Not her friends and certainly not her family. I haven't seen her in years."

"But why would she go after Artie?" I asked. "He's the kindest and gentlest thief I know."

"That doesn't matter to Rowena," Fiona said. "As long as someone was once a thief, she'll pursue them relentlessly, even if they no longer steal." Her voice dropped and she turned away. "Enough about my sister. Let me give you a tour of Stormfall. Cadmus has seen only the front gate."

"Your guards wouldn't let me go any further," Cadmus said. "They seemed to think I was dangerous."

"Well, you *can* grow into the size of a lion," Fiona said, leading us down the hall. "You can't be too careful."

Cadmus snorted, but didn't say anything.

* * *

We walked in silence, until we reached the end of the hallway. As we emerged into a bright light, I gasped. A gigantic city was resting right beneath Tealeaf.

"Welcome to Stormfall," Fiona said.

Stormfall was protected by high stone walls that glistened like silver. An opening in the cavern roof let in light. I couldn't see much of the town itself, except for the tops of some tall buildings. A small gatehouse set in the wall blocked our access inside.

"How is something like this under my hometown? I don't remember ever seeing anything like Stormfall and I lived half my life in Tealeaf."

Fiona smiled slightly. "The opening is actually an illusion. It imitates the light outside. A very clever witch set it up for us years ago. No, I'm afraid the only way in or out is to know where to look. Maude's bookcase, the lake by Dewdrop Village, the Elnora Oak in Vanguard Forest, even a simple rock at the oasis."

My head swam as Fiona rattled off all these locations, until she mentioned one in particular.

"The oasis?" I turned to Mag and Artie. "Now, why does that sound familiar?"

Artie and Mag frowned at me as they both thought it over. Mag's eyes brightened and she said, "Grandfather!"

"Of course!" Artie said. "Now I remember!"

Cadmus and Fiona both looked confused.

"We were at an oasis and ran into Aldrich," I said. "He tapped a rock by the water's edge and a secret passageway appeared. Aldrich entered and closed the tunnel, before we could get a good look inside."

Fiona smiled. "One of our newer members set it up. She's really talented at creating tunnels. Only yesterday, she told me she had secret passageways hidden all over Alsmora."

An idea started to form at the back of my mind. I wasn't sure what it was exactly, but those tunnels sounded familiar.

Artie looked troubled as well. He opened his mouth to speak, when—

"Lady Fiona."

We all turned to see the guard, David, approach us.

"David, status report."

"The golden dragon and his men have *not* broken into the passageway yet. In fact, they seem to have disappeared."

Fiona frowned. "Where are they? Why did the golden dragon leave Tealeaf? He wouldn't just vanish, especially when—" Fiona glanced sideways at me, before turning back to David. "Anything else?"

The guard looked at us, as well. "This is really for your ears only, Lady Fiona." He leaned in and whispered something to her.

I was watching them both curiously, when I caught a mumbled word. I froze.

Malcolm.

"Thank you, David," Fiona said, turning to us. She was white and shaking.

"Fiona, what's wrong?"

"We have to get through the wall and into Stormfall. There's a serious matter that requires my attention." She took a deep breath. "Please, we need to hurry."

Before we could say anything, she strode off through the gate. David followed.

CHAPTER SEVEN

REPORTS AND REAPPEARANCES

The gatehouse guard waved us through and we stepped into a familiar village. It was like walking into a copy of Tealeaf, albeit an intact and glistening facsimile of my home. Houses, shops, and landmarks matched the town above, but everything was bright and shining in the afternoon sun. It was a cleaner and more idealized version of Tealeaf.

Fiona was speaking to David, who nodded and raced off, disappearing around a corner.

"I've sent David ahead to alert Commander Ashcroft," Fiona said. "We have to hurry." And she sped off down the street.

I exchanged looks with Artie, Mag, and Cadmus, before running after her.

"Fiona! Slow down!"

"We can't stop now," she called over her shoulder. "We have to talk to the Storm Knight leader, High Commander Jasper Ashcroft. He'll know what to do."

"Is that a vote of confidence, Fiona? I never knew you thought so highly of me."

Fiona stopped in the middle of the street. In front of us was a man with black hair and a curly mustache. He had appeared so suddenly that I was almost sure he had materialized out of thin air. He smiled warmly, all the way up to his deep blue eyes. He was dressed in a crisp, red uniform with brass buttons.

"Please, come inside," he said, waving us into a nearby building. We all filed into what looked like a small office. The man left the door ajar.

"Commander Ashcroft," Fiona said. "I'd like you to meet Penelope Bogg, Mag Everett, Artie Quick, and Cadmus. Everyone, this is High Commander Jasper Ashcroft."

"Hello," I said. "It's a pleasure, sir."

"Likewise." He nodded, still smiling, before turning back to Fiona. "We need to talk. David burst in and gave me a very breathless report. He said something about a wolf."

"Yes, Commander. We received word from our agent, Lupine. He sent us an update. The news is bleak."

"Lupine?" I said, startled. "He's here?"

"He was. He left about fifteen minutes before you arrived."

I looked at Mag and Artie. Why was a wolf an agent of the Storm Knights?

Fiona continued her report to Ashcroft. "Lupine states that the guards are still searching for Malcolm Bogg."

My heart sank at these words.

"He also brings grave tidings from Kelton. A magical barrier has been placed around the castle and surrounding village."

"Rowena said the same thing," I chimed in. "But is it to protect

Queen Alana and the villagers or to keep them trapped?"

Fiona shook her head. "Lupine didn't go into details."

"No offense to your agent, Fiona," Cadmus said, "but I think I'll head over to Kelton Castle and check on matters myself."

Fiona nodded. "Thank you, Cadmus."

Shrinking down to house cat size, Cadmus turned to leave, when he stopped and looked back. "I'll see what I can find out about Lydia. I'm sure she's fine." He didn't sound convinced.

Unable to speak, I nodded gratefully. Last I'd heard, Lydia had been attacked by the golden dragon. I hadn't received any news of my sister since.

"Thank you," I whispered.

Cadmus smiled sadly, before he headed out the open door and ran to the gatehouse, disappearing the way we came.

Turning my back to the others, I tried to wipe my eyes discreetly. Artie quietly clasped my hand. Once I was composed, I took a deep breath, ready to face everyone again.

I found Ashcroft shaking his head. "The Gilded Lions. I hate it when they show up."

"Hey, that cat happens to be a good friend of mine," Mag said.

"Well then, I hope you can understand him, because I sure can't." Ashcroft rolled his eyes. "All these lions ever do is meow and roar at me, before running off again."

"I didn't know they were called the Gilded Lions," Artie said.

"Fiona can understand animals," Ashcroft explained. "She got the name from their leader, a big brute name Grrwrath."

Fiona cleared her throat. "Commander Ashcroft, Kelton Castle."

"Yes! Of course! What did you learn about the queen, Fiona? Where is Alana in all this?"

"Nobody seems to know," she said. "Some are saying Queen Alana's ill, others claim that she was killed the night of the gala in the ensuing fire. Still others think she's been taken hostage by the golden dragon."

"Regardless of the reason, this will prove difficult for our plans," Ashcroft said thoughtfully. "We need the Queen's help if we are to defeat the golden dragon. We can't do it on our own." He sighed. "I hope Alana is all right."

"Cadmus the lion just went to investigate the situation, sir," Fiona said.

Ashcroft nodded. "It's a start. Fiona, I want you to be at the base at all times, until he returns. Why we use animals as our informants, I'll never know."

Fiona smiled. "Because no one ever suspects an animal spy?"

Ashcroft laughed. "There is that." He turned to us. "Now, what to do with a dragon, a thief, and a witch?"

We all exchanged confused glances.

"Do?" Mag finally said. "What do you mean? We're just trying to get to Cherry Grove to find Maude."

"But *she,*" Ashcroft pointed at me, "is the Silver Rose. The one of silver hair, the one foretold to bring down the golden dragon once and for all."

"Still misquoting me as always, huh, Commander?" a new voice said.

Grinning, I turned to find a woman standing in the doorway. She had wild, white hair, blue eyes, and a purple lizard on her shoulder.

"Hello, Penelope," Mad Maude said. "It's good to see you again."

Cissy chirped in agreement.

Chapter Eight

A Tale of the Past

"Maude!" I cried excitedly, throwing my arms around her in a hug. "How are you? When did you get here?"

"Just now," she said, smiling at me. Cissy leapt from Maude's shoulder to mine, chittering a greeting.

I laughed. "Nice to see you too, Cissy."

She trilled happily.

"Maude," Mag cut in, "what is going on? A wolf leads Penelope to your old house, soldiers invade Tealeaf, and we have to beat a hasty retreat underground to Stormfall! *What is going on?*"

Maude began, of all things, to cackle. "Brilliant! You three have had an adventure-and-a-half just to get here!" She continued laughing.

Cissy shook her head and chittered at Maude, almost like she was scolding her.

"How did you get here?" Artie asked. "We were on our way to Cherry Grove to see you."

Before Maude could answer, Commander Ashcroft cleared his throat. "While this has been a touching reunion, we do have pressing matters to discuss."

Maude grinned. "Oh, yeah. And what's that, Ashy?"

Ashcroft's bottom jaw quivered, but whether it was from amusement or anger, I wasn't sure.

"You're the same as ever, Maude," he finally said.

"Thank you."

"That wasn't… oh, never mind. Would you kindly explain your cryptic remark? You're not going back on your prediction, are you, old friend?"

"Hmm? Oh, we're old friends, now? What was my *cryptic remark,* as you put it?"

"I think what Commander Ashcroft means," Fiona piped up, "is that you contradicted him about Penelope being destined to defeat the golden dragon."

"Ah, Fiona Hartford, is it?" Maude asked pleasantly. "I wasn't sure if it was you or your sister." She lowered her voice a fraction, but we could all clearly hear her. "I've always liked you more than Rowena."

"Uh, thank you."

"Now, Penelope, do you know why you're called the Silver Rose?" Maude said.

"It's because I was born with silver hair, isn't it? It means I'm the only one who can defeat the golden dragon. At least, that's what everyone keeps telling me."

Maude tsked, obviously annoyed. "That's not what I said at all. Whoever I told it to missed the point."

"And that is?" Mag said.

Cissy climbed up Maude's shoulder and chittered in her ear, scolding her again.

"All right, all right," Maude said. "You know best, as always." She turned to the rest of us. "Cissy is threatening to never speak to me again, unless I tell you everything."

Ashcroft groaned softly. "Headache," he murmured. "Maude has given me a headache. Again." He sighed and said, "Fiona, we'll continue this in my office. You three," he nodded toward us, "stay with Maude and try to make some sense out of her ramblings."

Muttering about raving lunatics, he headed further into the building, toward a backroom. Fiona gave us a reassuring smile, before she followed.

Once the door had closed behind them, Artie said, "Back to my original question. How did you get here?"

"Flew, naturally. How else?"

Mag looked at her sharply. "I didn't know you could fly, Maude."

"*I* can't."

We waited for Maude to continue, but when she didn't, I decided to change the subject. "What was with that argument you had with Commander Ashcroft? Am I destined to defeat the golden dragon or not?"

Maude sighed dramatically, suddenly looking much older and grayer. Cissy's tail drooped sadly. After several minutes of the two of them staring long and hard at each other, Maude said, quite bitterly, "You never should have told Gideon."

Cissy grumbled.

"Fine," Maude said, rolling her eyes. "*I* never should have told Gideon."

I frowned. There was that name again. "Who's Gideon?"

Maude didn't answer, but continued to argue with the lizard. "I was perfectly happy living in Gideon's domain, but then you, Cissy, decided that you wanted to leave."

Cissy chirped and shook her head.

Maude waved her hand dismissively. "Yes, your brother. Of course you wanted to see your brother and get his advice. But, because of that, Gideon asked where we were going. I told him about my vision of a silver-haired girl fighting the golden dragon. He passed the information to Alice and she panicked when her daughter was born with silver hair. That's why she magically changed Penelope's hair brown. So, really Cissy, it's your fault that *everyone* learned about my little prediction."

Cissy turned her back on Maude and stalked toward me. She scampered up my shoulder and spoke in a high-pitched voice, right in my ear. All I heard was chittering.

"Whoa, Cissy. I didn't follow any of that. Start from the beginning. Who is Gideon and what does he have to do with me and my mom?"

Cissy sighed and chittered at Maude, rolling her eyes, the argument already forgotten.

Maude smiled. "They can't understand you. I think you'd better show them."

Cissy nodded, before she jumped to the ground and scurried outside. She closed her eyes. Maude shepherded us to the open door.

Frowning, I started to ask, "What is going on?" when a movement from Cissy caught my attention. I looked back and stared in shock. Mag and Artie had similar expressions of disbelief.

Cissy was growing at a rapid rate. One moment she was the size of a normal lizard, now she was Lupine's size, now lion Cadmus's, but it didn't stop there. As her size continued to increase, her claws sharpened into dangerous talons and her teeth became fangs. Wings sprouted on her back. Finally, she stopped growing. She was the size of a large, two-story house. Cissy opened her eyes to reveal violet irises. She smiled.

We stepped onto the street and gawked.

"I don't believe it," Mag whispered. "It can't be."

"Cissy," I breathed. "You were a *dragon* this whole time?"

"Yes," she said in a rich, musical voice, more fitting to her current size. "I'm sorry for deceiving you, but I was indeed hatched a dragon."

"Why didn't you tell us sooner?" Artie asked. "This is amazing!"

Maude smiled. "Thank you for that assessment, Artie, but Cess couldn't reveal her identity. Too risky."

"Wait a moment," Mag said, her eyes narrowing. "Cess? You don't mean…?"

"Yes," the purple dragon said. "My real name isn't Cissy. I am Cessala. I fought the golden imposter a century ago. And Maude here helped. She is a witch and my friend. Together, we saved Alsmora."

* * *

Mag was the first to find her voice. "Aunt Cessala? Where have you been all these years?"

"*Aunt* Cessala?" I asked. "You two are related?"

"Through my dad, yes. He's Cessala's older brother."

"Why have you never mentioned this before?" Artie asked, looking between the two dragons.

"I didn't mention it, because my aunt and I have never met." Mag shook her head at the older dragon. "We thought you were dead."

Cessala winced. "I'm sorry, Mag. I promise we can catch up later, but for now, we need to focus. Penelope needs training before she can face the golden dragon."

"Hold up," I said, "I have a few questions first. How are you both a dragon and a lizard, Cessala? I thought all dragons had human forms."

"Not necessarily," she said. "Maude figured it out."

Maude cackled. "Indeed. It was in my younger days, when I worked for Queen Rebecca at Kelton Castle. I was so surprised when a full-grown dragon appeared, begging for help."

"I didn't beg," Cessala muttered.

"My dear Cess, what do you call flying through a thunderstorm and crash landing in front of Kelton? You were gasping by the time I got to you."

"I call that asking for help, not begging," Cessala said primly.

"Whatever, you overgrown lizard," Maude said. "Where was I?"

"How Cessala is both a dragon and a lizard," Artie prompted.

"Right, right," Maude said, getting a dreamy look on her face. "Oh, how I remember that day."

"Maude, focus," Mag said, snapping her fingers under the old witch's nose. "We don't have all day."

She sighed. "So pushy. Fine, the condensed version is this: when the trolls stormed Elton Castle, they killed King Cecil and Queen Winona. Princess Rebecca, however, managed to escape. As she fled, the golden dragon flew to the topmost tower and roared his victory to the world."

"Golden imposter, more like," Cessala mumbled.

Maude ignored her. "For a while, the golden dragon controlled all of Alsmora. He and a dozen ferocious followers would frequently fly out and terrorize villagers, simply for the fun of it. Nobody could stop them. Rebecca, by this time, had made it to an unused ruin of a castle she dubbed Kelton. Admittedly, she wasn't very creative with names.

"She tried to hold everyone together, but she was a young and inexperienced queen, who had just started to learn her royal responsibilities. There was mass hysteria in the streets, people panicking left, right, and center. It was a mess. I was good friends with Rebecca at the time and did my best to advise her.

"One morning, I was taking a walk, trying to calm myself after an infuriating meeting with Rebecca and her two advisors, Alexander and Victoria.

"As I fumed, I heard the swish of wings and looked up. A purple dragon was circling Kelton Castle. At first, I thought we were under attack from one of the golden dragon's lieutenants, but then I noticed the jerky way she was descending."

"Injured my wing," Cessala said ruefully.

"Really?" Mag said. "Me too. Aneurin's poison."

"Pierced by an arrow, right before I reached Kelton Castle," Cessala said bitterly. "I lost my way, got disoriented by a recent storm, and wound up too close to a battlement. I later found out that Alexander shot the arrow."

"Who's Alexander?" I asked.

"A royal guard," Maude explained. "He helped Rebecca escape Elton Castle. Alexander was always protective of her. So, it came as no surprise when he brought down Cessala. After Cess crashed, I approached her cautiously and she begged me for help."

"Asked, Maude!"

"Right, asked for help. I couldn't ignore an injured dragon, but the whole of Kelton Castle was on edge from recent attacks. Alexander and Victoria were coming and the dragon was lying helplessly on the ground. I did the only thing I could think of. I used all my power and transformed the dragon into another animal, a lizard."

"First off, Maude, that was painful," Cessala said. "Second, why a lizard? Why not any other animal?"

Maude shrugged. "I panicked. You were still a reptile, after all. When the others arrived, all they saw was an injured purple lizard, so I was able to bring Cess back to the castle with nobody the wiser.

"Any other questions?"

Yes, I wanted to say. *Plenty.* But before I could voice any of them, Fiona exited the inner office and joined us outside. She did not look happy.

"What's wrong, Fiona?" Cessala asked.

"Oh, hello, Cessala. It's good to see you back in dragon form. It's nothing." Fiona sighed. "Just a slight disagreement with Commander Ashcroft. It's not serious." She shook her head and smiled. "Come on. Let's get everyone settled in Stormfall for the night. The golden dragon is gone for now, but none of you are going anywhere, at least not until morning."

"That doesn't sound ominous," Artie muttered as we followed Fiona further into the Storm Knight base.

Chapter Nine

A Friend From Kelton

Twilight was falling as we stepped into the main square of Stormfall. Like the town above, there were houses and shops encircling the square. There was even a fountain in the center, but that's where the similarities to Tealeaf ended. Whereas the statue on Tealeaf's fountain was shaped like a mermaid, Stormfall's was of a regal-looking dragon.

"Maude, Cessala, could I talk to you for a moment?" Fiona asked tensely. "In private? It won't take long."

"Of course," Cessala said. She, Maude, and Fiona stepped out of earshot.

"I can't believe it's him," Mag murmured, not even looking at the departing trio. She nodded toward the statue. "Dad. It's a good likeness."

I thought I saw a tear at the corner of Mag's eye. I reached out and squeezed her shoulder comfortingly. Artie went to her other side and took her hand.

"Thank you, Penelope, Artie," she said quietly.

"You must miss him very much," I said. "What happened to him?"

"He disappeared without a trace eight years ago." The tears were flowing freely now.

"I'm sorry."

"How did a statue of your dad wind up in Stormfall?" Artie asked.

"Dad helped form the Storm Knights," Mag said, wiping her eyes. "They're named after him. When he vanished, the Knights honored him with a statue. Aunt Cessala and I both lost a great deal that day."

"Oh, Mag," I began, when two warriors, David and a redheaded man, walked into the square. They froze when they saw us. I held my breath as their gaze lingered on Artie. What if they knew he was a thief? But, as they approached, I could see that they were both smiling.

"Forget it," Mag muttered.

"Oh! It's you three!" David said warmly. "Penelope, Mag, and Artie, right?"

"That's right," I said, smiling back. "And you're David." I glanced at the redheaded guard. Now that he was closer, I could see that his hair was more orange than red. "I don't think we've met."

He held out his hand to each of us in turn. "Patrick Redmore," he said.

"You look familiar, Patrick. Do I know you?" I had a faint memory of when Malcolm first become a royal guard. He introduced me to his new partner, a guard with ginger red hair.

Patrick looked surprised, then thoughtful. "Wait a second. Penelope? Penelope... Bogg? Yes. Yes, I remember you now. You're Malcolm's younger sister, aren't you?"

"I am. And you're Malcolm's partner in the royal guards, right?"

He nodded, considered me for a moment, then laughed. "I can't believe you're in Stormfall, Penelope! I remember when Mal introduced us. When did you get here?"

"Earlier today. The golden dragon attacked Tealeaf and we rushed into Maude's secret passageway to escape him."

"That explains it," David said.

"Explains what?" Mag asked.

"Why we found signs of recent magic in Tealeaf," David said. "We thought it was Maude activating the bookcase entrance, but the signatures didn't match."

He and Patrick exchanged troubled looks.

"Was there something wrong with the bookcase?" I asked nervously. "Can the golden dragon use that entrance to track us somehow?"

"Not that I'm aware of," Patrick said. "The magic on the bookcase is rather a complicated spell. Maude, David, and one of our newer members set it up."

"This new member…" Artie began, when Mag cut him off.

"What kind of magic?"

"The spell allows me to detect magical signatures," David said. "It's important for the Storm Knights to know who is coming and going from the base at all times."

"But not everyone has magic," Artie protested.

"On the contrary," David said, "all humans *have* magic, but not everyone is *capable* of harnessing it. Whether you use your magic or not, I can still tell who's been near Stormfall. There was that odd one, though…"

"What odd one?"

Before David could continue, Fiona, Maude, and Cissy in her lizard form reappeared from around the corner.

"Well, it's been decided," Fiona said. "Penelope, you'll start your training with Maude and Cessala tomorrow. Until then, follow me to your rooms, please. You'll be staying at my house tonight. Weird things tend to happen on the streets of Stormfall when the moon is out. David, Patrick, Commander Ashcroft would like to see you both."

As we separated, I saw the two guards watching us closely and I wondered, what made a magical signature odd?

* * *

A few hours later, I lay awake, staring up at the ceiling of my borrowed bedroom in Fiona's house. Mag and Artie were down the hall. My mind raced. It hardly seemed real. One moment, I was a handmaiden in Kelton Castle and now, I was actually in the Storm Knights' base.

How could everything have changed so quickly?

I sighed. I wasn't going to get to sleep anytime soon, that was certain. I decided to explore the room. I swung my legs off the bed and looked around.

It was a small space, with the bed in one corner and a desk in another. A window sat above the desk, showing the night sky, even though I was underground. I remembered what Fiona had said about the cavern roof being an illusion. Next to the bed was a wardrobe. It was full of clothes that were in my size. I decided not to question it. They were probably magically enchanted to always fit the occupant. A bathroom with a tub connected to my room.

Gingerly, I pulled off my torn and tattered handmaiden dress that I'd been wearing since Queen Alana's gala. I'd never had time to change. Fifteen minutes later, I came out fully bathed and riffled through the clothes. They were all extravagant. Finally, I pulled on the plainest dress I could find. It was dark blue, with little silver flowers embroidered into the skirt. As I walked, the skirt swished and the flowers seemed to shimmer.

A knock sounded at the door, causing me to jump. I glanced out the window. The moon was high and bright in the sky. Who could possibly be calling at this time of night?

The knock became louder and more insistent as I hurried to answer. Whoever it was would wake up everyone in Stormfall if they kept pounding.

I yanked open the door and I found Mag and Artie standing on the threshold. "Come in," I said breathlessly.

As they swept past me, I could see that Artie had new clothes as well. He was in a long-sleeved green shirt and brown pants. A new green cloak was tied around his neck. Like my new dress, Artie's clothes seemed to shimmer as he walked. He turned as he entered the room and I saw both his silver dagger and Rowena's knife tucked into his belt.

Mag was still wearing her old, red cloak. I looked at it curiously. It never seemed to get dirty.

I glanced out into the hallway, but all seemed quiet. Fiona hadn't stirred. Closing the door, I turned to my friends. "You can't sleep either?"

Artie shook his head. "No. Too much has happened that we need to talk about. Why did David find an odd magical signature? What makes it odd?"

"I think we should go back to the bookcase and check it ourselves," Mag said. "We can't sit here all night. There's too much to do."

"There's one tiny flaw in your plan, Mag," I said. "We're not supposed to leave the house, remember? Fiona said strange things happen in Stormfall at night. Plus, we don't know our way around. We'll never be able to find it in the dark."

Mag smirked. "Stop thinking so negatively, Penelope. You have a tracking spell, don't you? And we can handle anything that may be lurking in the shadows. What are you two afraid of?"

"Maude and Cessala's disapproval," I said.

"Commander Ashcroft kicking us out of Stormfall," Artie added.

"Running into wild animals."

"Said wild animals being more dangerous underground than above."

"Using too much magic, so you have to carry me back."

"All right, all right, I get it," Mag said. She suddenly grinned. "Could you handle all that?"

Artie and I exchanged a mystified look.

"I suppose we could. Pen?"

"Well, I doubt Ashcroft would expel us from Stormfall," I said slowly. "Maude and Cessala wouldn't be too upset. They'll most likely see it as a great adventure. And any animals would probably think twice before attacking a dragon. I just don't want to faint on you."

"You usually recover within a minute or two, anyway," Mag said.

"Now, if there aren't any more problems, let's go."

"But—"

"Penelope, as my mom used to say, 'Think of the worst thing that could happen. If you can handle that, you should be fine.'"

I couldn't argue with that logic and Artie didn't raise any other objections, so after checking to make sure Fiona was still asleep, we stepped out into the dark hallway. We made it out the front door and onto the street without incident.

We'd been walking for about a minute in the direction of the gatehouse, when Artie whispered, "Any chance you could turn us invisible?"

"Artie, there's no one here."

"I know, but better safe than sorry. One of the key skills a thief can have is to remain hidden. Someone might come across us, before we have time to hide."

"I thought you didn't like being a thief," I teased him.

He smiled. "I may not steal from innocents, but I remember every lesson my dear parents taught me on the thieving arts."

We reached the end of the street and peered around the corner. Fiona had guided us from the gatehouse to her home, but everything looked different in the dark. Even my knowledge of Tealeaf didn't help. There was no gatehouse above.

"No invisibility," Mag said, "at least for the moment. I'll be able to hear and smell anyone coming our way. Our biggest problem is finding our way out of Stormfall. I have no idea how to get from here to the bookcase. A tracking spell would probably be our best bet."

"What was your plan if I'd stayed in my room? Wander around aimlessly, hoping you'd find the exit?"

"Most likely."

"You never cease to amaze me, Mag," I said, shaking my head.

"Are you going to use the spell or not?"

"Fine." Placing my hand on my amulet, I imagined an arrow pointing us in the right direction. *"Endoraken."*

For a split second, a blue tracking arrow appeared, before the muted silver flashed in front of my eyes again. It was gone in an instant. I groped for Artie's hand to steady myself.

Mag said something to Artie and I felt his grip tighten.

"Pen! We have to move! Now!"

Before I could respond, Mag and Artie had hustled me around the corner and into the shadows.

"Somebody's coming," Mag whispered. "It's faint, but I can hear them."

As we stood, hardly daring to breathe, the silhouette of a girl slowly came into view.

"Who's there?" the newcomer called.

I breathed a sigh of relief as I recognized the voice.

"Fiona!" My wooziness gone, I stepped forward, smiling. "What are you doing here? I thought you went to bed hours ago."

She blinked in confusion, before she smiled as well. "I did go to sleep, but something woke me up… uh, Penelope."

"Sorry, that was us," Artie said, as he and Mag came out of hiding behind me. "Mag and I were knocking on Pen's door. We convinced her to go on this little excursion."

Fiona's eyes widened in surprise when she saw Artie. As I watched, her expression became guarded and neutral. I gazed at her curiously, wondering what was wrong.

We stood there awkwardly, until Fiona cleared her throat and said, "Where were you three going?"

"To the gatehouse," Mag said. "And we have to go now. Which way, Penelope?"

"Over there," I said, pointing toward the right. The tracking arrow had reappeared.

Mag turned to leave, but Fiona darted in front of her. "Could I speak to Arth- Artie, please?"

He shrugged. "I guess so. I'll be right back."

Artie followed Fiona about ten feet away. Mag snorted. I glanced at her and found her glaring at Stormfall's second-in-command. "There's something off about Fiona, Penelope."

"I know what you mean," I said. "Fiona seems absent-minded. Maybe she's stressed out? I'm worried about her."

"Thank you for your concern, but it's not necessary. I'm perfectly all right."

The voice came from behind us. Eyes wide, Mag and I turned and found… Fiona?!

I looked back at Artie and saw him talking to Fiona, but Fiona was also standing beside me and Mag.

Mag and I stared at each other in horror. *"Rowena!"* we cried in unison.

"What's wrong?" Fiona said.

Neither of us answered as we scrambled toward Artie. Rowena glanced up and sneered.

"Artie, run!" I cried. "That's Rowena!"

To Artie's credit, he tried to escape. The moment I said Rowena's name, he sprang away from her. But, before he could go more than two steps, she seized Artie's arm, yanked him back toward her, and grabbed her knife from his belt, pressing it against his throat.

"Not so fast, *Quick!*" she spat, panting slightly. "You're not getting away from me that easily."

"Rowena," Artie said calmly. More calmly than I would be in that situation. "Let me go. I wasn't the one who killed your father."

"Artie's right, Rowena," Fiona said. "Yes, Dad was killed when we were nine, but it's been ten years. We may never know the murderer's identity, but you have to move on. You can't take your anger out on Artie anymore, Ro."

While Fiona was talking, Mag and I were edging closer to the angry royal guard. Rowena seemed to falter when her sister called her *Ro* and even dropped the knife slightly away from Artie. That was all Mag needed. As soon as the knife moved, she leapt forward and starting wrestling Rowena for the weapon. Artie ducked as the knife swung wildly over his head. He stumbled toward me.

"Artie! Are you all right?" I grabbed his arms to steady him.

"I'm fine," he said. "Thanks to you, Mag, and Fiona. I never thought Rowena would try something like this."

"And she might try again, if you stick around," Fiona said. She hadn't taken her eyes off Rowena. "Take Mag and go. Do whatever you came to do. I'll find you later. For now, I need to have a word with my sister."

"Wait, Fiona!"

"Don't hang around and don't worry," she said, turning to us. Her eyes were glowing. "I know what I'm doing. Just grab your friend, before things get messy. Good luck. Now, *go!*"

At Fiona's signal, Mag shoved Rowena aside and together, the three of us darted away into the night. We didn't look back.

Chapter Ten

A Saturation of Color

"Mag, slow down!" I panted, as we ran down another street. The dragon statue was nearby. We had to be close to the gatehouse.

"Can't, Penelope, sorry!" she called back. "You didn't get a good look at the sisters, did you?"

"A good look?" Artie repeated. "Mag, of course we saw them. It was kind of hard to miss Rowena when she had a knife to my throat!"

"No," she said. "After that, when Rowena lowered her weapon."

I frowned, thinking. Did I notice anything? "Fiona's eyes glowed," I said, "but it could have been a trick of the light."

Artie's eyes widened. "They glowed? But it can't be. Fiona and Rowena aren't… they can't be… are they?"

"I think so," Mag said. "Wait until I tell Aldrich. He's going to *love* this."

"What are you two talking about?" I said.

"I'll explain later," Artie promised. "For now, we have to keep moving."

Reluctantly, I nodded.

We continued toward the statue, but before we could go too far, my magical tracking arrow suddenly started pointing in the opposite direction, right at Mag and Artie. I stopped and my friends stopped with me.

"Pen? What's wrong?"

"You don't see the arrow, do you?"

They shook their heads.

"Only the one who cast the spell can see it," Mag said, her hair bursting into flames again. Her eyes darted back and forth, scanning for danger, for Rowena. "We have to go. Which way to the gatehouse?"

I pointed to a building just past the dragon statue. "It's over there, but forget about that. My tracking spell is pointing straight at you two."

"Ah," Mag said, the flames dying down slightly. "This complicates matters."

"Complicates?" I said, bristling. "Of course it complicates matters. My friends are keeping secrets about Fiona and Rowena! Who are the sisters? Why were Fiona's eyes glowing? Why did Rowena accuse Artie of killing her father? What do you have to do with any of this, Mag?" I took a deep breath. When I spoke again, my voice was much softer and urgent. "I need answers and my reveal spell is showing me where I can get them."

Mag and Artie exchanged knowing glances. When they turned back to me, their faces were set.

"All right," Artie said, "we'll tell you, but could we keep walking? Fiona and Rowena are not to be trifled with."

I nodded and the magical arrow once again pointed us to the left. Nobody spoke as we slipped through the gatehouse, which had been left unguarded, much to my surprise.

We stepped into the stone hallway on the outskirts of Stormfall.

Retracing our steps from earlier, we found the stairs and started to climb up to the bookcase, Mag's hair giving us light.

I turned to Artie expectantly. He nodded.

"Ten years ago," he began bitterly, "when I was six, my dad decided it would be a good idea to take Sylvia and me out thieving. At that age, I was young, impressionable, and willing to do anything to please my father." He sighed and shook his head. "We went to this quaint, little lakeside town called Dewdrop Village. Absolutely beautiful, not too far away from the Quick Hideout.

"My time in Dewdrop was profitable. I stole more in those three days than I ever have in the decade since. Nobody ever suspected that the cute little children they were cooing over were skilled pickpockets. They would reach out and pat one of us on the head, while the other would deftly swipe their valuables. Our dad was so proud.

"When we left Dewdrop Village, the townspeople were much poorer than when we arrived. Dad, Sylvia, and I had to go by the lake on our way home. A man and two nine-year-old girls were playing near the water's edge, climbing into the nearby trees and diving into the water.

"As we passed the family, a cloaked figure burst out of the trees, wielding a knife. I couldn't hear exactly what they said, but there was a short altercation and the man fell, stabbed. One of the girls screamed as the cloaked figure fled, dropping the knife as he went.

"Dad rushed to help, but the man was already dead. He ushered the two girls toward me and Sylvia and told us to look after them."

"Fiona and Rowena," I said.

Artie nodded. "Yes. Fiona started crying for her father, asking over and over why this had happened. Rowena stood by herself, not crying, not screaming, just glaring in my dad's direction, like he was to blame."

"Why was Mr. Hartford killed?"

He shrugged. "No idea, but there's a strong possibility that the cloaked figure was a thief. Rowena picked up the knife the assailant dropped. It's the same type of dagger used in my father's organization."

I shuddered. "Was that…?"

"Yes. The knife Rowena threatened me with is the one that killed her father. I think she's hoping to use it on the murderer one day."

We lapsed into thoughtful silence as we continued up the spiral stairs. We were nearing the bookcase.

"Will Rowena ever leave you alone, Artie?" I finally asked.

"Doubtful," he said. "That wasn't my first run-in with Rowena since her father died and it probably won't be the last. She recognizes me from that day. She knows I didn't do it, but she needs to take her anger out on someone. And I'm an easy target. I'm not holed up in the Quick Hideout, like Dad and Sylvia."

"What about you, Mag? How do you fit in?"

"Let's just say the sisters have an interesting heritage and leave it at that. I don't like to talk about it."

We reached the top of the stairs and faced the bookcase. The secret door was closed. Artie and I looked at Mag.

She blinked innocently at us. "What?"

"Aren't you going to open the door?" Artie asked.

"Ah, that," she said, looking away. "I may have forgotten to tell you. Cadmus knows how to open it, not me."

"You don't know how to get inside?"

"Oh, I never said that," she said. "I'm pretty sure I can get us in. We just have to find the right book. That'll cause the secret door to spring open. It's enchanted to keep everyone out, until the right book is pulled."

"Okay," Artie said. "So, find it."

"Well, that's the problem. Have you seen the bookcase?"

I looked around. All the books' spines were facing away from us.

"The books," I said. "We can't see their titles."

"That's right," Mag said. "Start pulling." And she seized a random book from the top shelf.

Riding the Storm: Ten Foolproof Ways to Find and Surf on Lightning Bolts.

"Nope, not that one," Mag said, tossing it aside.

I caught it, before it fell down the stairs. "Mag, be careful!"

She shrugged. "We're in a hurry, Penelope. I'm sorry if I'm not gentle with your precious tomes, but let's face it, Maude's weird books aren't all that important."

"Mag! How can you say that? Books are windows into the past and the future. They are special…"

Artie took my hand, cutting me off. "I agree with you, Pen," he said. "But now's not the time." Raising his voice slightly, he continued, "Mag, the more noise you make throwing those books, the more likely it's going to attract Rowena's attention and the sooner she'll arrive. Why don't we just stack the books on the ground? It'll be faster and quieter."

Mag and I looked at each other for a moment, before we grudgingly said in unison, "Agreed."

We all got to work checking the books. There were three shelves. Mag took the top, Artie the middle, and I had the bottom.

"What book are we looking for?" I said, staring down at the bright yellow book I was holding. *Magic Snacks, Magic Attacks: The Ultimate Guide for All Your Magical Food Attack Needs!*

Mag frowned. "Green, I think. No, blue. Definitely blue. The front had something to do with wolves."

"Wait a second," I said, my eyes widening. "I remember that book! I read it when I was little. I spilled tea on it when I was eight. There! I see it! Two to your right, Artie."

He pulled out the book and showed it to me. The cover was dark blue and showed a gray wolf howling at a full moon, but no title. The author was C.M. Aude.

"C.M. Aude?" Mag said, smiling. "Cessala and Maude."

"This has to be it," I said, "but why is the secret doorway still closed?"

"Under normal circumstances, it would open," a voice behind us said. "But thanks to the golden dragon's fire, the extra security measures have activated. I can help open it, if you like."

Mag, Artie, and I all turned.

"David?" I said, squinting at him in the low light from the torches. "What are you doing here?"

"I followed you," he said. "Patrick and I were on guard duty, when

Fiona reported that her sister had entered Stormfall. She sent me to find you, in case Rowena had gotten to you first."

"Rowena escaped from Fiona?" I asked nervously.

"Rowena is determined and brutal," David said. "We found Fiona exhausted on the floor, close to collapse. Patrick stayed behind to take her to the infirmary. I figured you might need some magical assistance."

Mag's claws slid out as she balled her fists. She didn't seem to notice. "How do you know it was Fiona and not Rowena?"

"The sister we found had the silver crescent necklace," David said. "Fiona was the last to have it and she would never willingly give it to Rowena."

"I saw Fiona wearing a necklace when we arrived," I said, "but Rowena could have stolen it since then."

"No, she couldn't," Artie said, shaking his head. "Not the silver crescent necklace. It's immune to being stolen. I can't believe Fiona has it. The silver crescent is a legend among thieves."

Mag tilted her head in confusion. "You've lost me there, Artie."

"That particular necklace happens to be unique," he explained. "There's a powerful protection spell on it. Anyone who tries to steal it would find themselves experiencing a nasty electrical shock."

I winced. "Definitely a good incentive to stay away from it."

"Yeah," Artie said, his eyes glazed. "Just imagine how valuable that piece of jewelry is. If a thief could lay his hands on it and bypass the shock, he could make a fortune selling it." He snapped to attention and laughed awkwardly. "Not that I would try, of course."

"Of course," I said, amused. Artie was too honest a thief to try something like that. I turned to David. "So, Fiona is safely in the infirmary and Rowena is hiding somewhere in Stormfall. I don't envy you telling Commander Ashcroft."

"Fiona said she would do that," David said. "Luckily, Ashcroft knows the difference between the two sisters. Fiona won't need the silver crescent necklace to prove her identity."

We all stared at him.

"But you said Fiona has it."

"She did," David said, reaching into his pocket. He pulled out a small, wrapped bundle. "Fiona wanted you to have it, Penelope."

He handed it to me. I breathed a sigh of relief when there was no electric shock. I slowly removed the cloth.

I was looking at a simple, elegant golden chain with a crescent moon charm hanging off of it. I ran my finger down the length of the charm, before slipping it over my head.

"Thank you, David," I said, smiling up at him. "Fiona is beyond generous."

He grinned back. "You got that right. I'd be careful, though. If Rowena sees you with the necklace, she'll think you stole it. She doesn't know about its unique properties, at least according to Fiona."

Mag rolled her eyes. "Great gift, David."

"We'd better hurry and figure out how to open the secret door," Artie said. He held up the book by C.M. Aude. "What are the extra security measures and what do they have to do with this book?"

"Ever since the golden dragon destroyed Tealeaf the first time, Maude's been worried that he'd return and finish the job. And how does a dragon best destroy?"

"Fire," Mag muttered sullenly.

"That's right. The extra security is designed to keep Stormfall from catching on fire."

"How do we get out then?" I didn't relish the thought of being stuck inside Stormfall with Rowena.

"We have to check the stability of the house," David said. "We can't risk any potential fire hazard, after all. A simple reveal spell will do. If it's too dangerous, the bookcase will glow red. Blue means safety. Would you like me to do it?"

"I have used this spell before, David," I said. "It leaves me seeing silver, but that's nothing new." I smiled reassuringly and placed my hand on my amulet. *"Endoraken."*

I had barely finished saying the word, when something strange happened. Instead of the bookcase turning either red or blue, every other color around me became deeper, stronger. It was like everything was saturated and dripping with color, overloading my senses. I collapsed, shaking.

"Pen? What's wrong?"

Turning to Artie, I gasped. He was glowing bright green. Mag was deep red.

"Pen, talk to us," Artie said, reaching for me.

I felt a jolt as he took my hand. Closing my eyes, I took a couple of deep breaths.

"Penelope. Penelope."

"Artie?" I murmured. "Is that you?"

"I am not your companion. I am not Arthur. My name is Gideon. I can't maintain this connection for long. We have to talk, Penelope. I have the answers you seek."

"But I don't know you," I whispered.

"Your mom does. Come to Vanguard Forest. I'll be waiting."

When I opened my eyes again, I found myself flat on the floor, staring up at the ceiling. Mag and Artie were kneeling over me.

"Pen! You're awake!" Artie said, helping me up.

"What happened?"

"You collapsed," Mag said, "for about five minutes."

I turned away, my head pounding, Gideon's words echoing in my mind. *I'll be waiting.*

A slight chirping caught my attention and I looked up. David had disappeared and Maude and Cissy were standing in his place.

"Out for a midnight stroll?" Maude said, smiling. "I can't blame you. Stormfall can be claustrophobic even at the best of times."

Cissy chittered in agreement.

"Or was there another reason?" Maude continued, her eyes sparkling. "Something daring and magical, perhaps?"

"We were trying to get into your house, so we could detect magical signatures. David said he found a strange one."

"And you were wondering what made a magical signature strange, correct?"

"Yes."

"Admirable," she said. "Really admirable, but now's not the time to practice magic."

"Why?" Artie asked.

"Arthur Quick! I will get you!"

"Of course," he muttered.

"Rowena's on her way," Maude said. "I've already talked to Fiona and Ashcroft. They've given us permission to leave."

"Where are we going?"

"I think Mag knows."

She grimaced slightly. "While you were unconscious, Penelope, David ran to get help. He returned long enough to give me Ashcroft's message. Artie was too busy trying to help you to notice."

"What did he say?"

Mag took a deep breath. "The Storm Knights are sending us to Elton Castle. They got word that the golden dragon is after Hugo."

Chapter Eleven

Tender Memories

"Hugo?" I cried. "Why would the golden dragon go after Hugo? He's harmless."

Hugo was a troll, but unlike his more violent brethren, he was a librarian. He lived in Elton Castle, the former capital of Alsmora, as an unofficial caretaker. He had already taken great strides to restore the once proud ruins to their former glory. It was nowhere near perfect, but at least the library was usable.

"The golden dragon probably wants to finish the job he started a hundred years ago," Mag said. "Anything left standing from his first war with Alsmora has to go. He loves nothing better than mindless destruction. Look at his recent actions in Tealeaf. But we'll show him. We can ambush him at Elton Castle and he won't even see it coming!… And we can save Hugo, too, naturally."

"Naturally," Artie said, "but the golden dragon has a head start, Mag. We'll never get to Elton Castle before him."

Mag seemed to turn rather deaf at that moment and didn't answer.

"I wouldn't worry about Hugo," Maude said. "He may be peaceful, but he can also look after himself."

"So, Hugo is completely safe?" I asked. "Nothing and nobody can harm him?"

Maude shook her head. "Far from it. The golden dragon will attempt to kill that lovable troll, but only if he can find him. It's unlikely that will happen, though. Hugo knows all the best hiding spots and secret passageways."

Cissy chittered impatiently.

"All right. Keep your scales on," Maude said. "Everyone into the house. It's too cramped in here. No room for Cessala to spread her wings."

"Maude, I hate to break it to you, but we're stuck behind this bookcase," I said. "The extra security measures are still in place."

Maude laughed. "The security measures? I forgot those were still up! Dear me, no wonder the bookcase is glowing blue. At least we know the danger has passed. Safety first, after all. Well, you satisfied both requirements. You pulled the right book from the shelf and you confirmed that my house is safe. Just say the passcode and we can get out of here."

"Passcode?"

"David didn't tell you? The bookcase glowing only alerts you to possible danger. You still have to use the correct spell to open it."

"But I—"

"Open it, Penelope. *Open* it."

Realization dawned as I stared at Maude. "Oh…" Placing my hand on my amulet, I said, *"Anoffen."*

The bookcase swung open with a small click. Early morning sunlight streamed in, dazzling me. I blinked the spots out of my eyes. My silver vision was nowhere to be seen. I was puzzled, but pleased.

Mag, Maude, and Cissy stepped through the opening, but I paused and looked back down into the darkness cloaking Stormfall. We couldn't just leave everyone, not with Rowena on the loose.

"Pen," Artie said, taking my hand. "We have to go."

"But…"

"Rowena is after me. Stormfall will be a lot safer once I leave. Trust me, it won't take her long to discover that we've gone."

"What about Fiona, David, and the others?"

"They'll have to fend for themselves, at least until Rowena picks up my trail. We can't worry about that. Our job is to find Hugo. If the golden dragon has him, all is lost. Hugo is an expert historian. He's the only one who can tell us more about Elton Castle. He might even know some long buried secret, something that will allow us to defeat the golden dragon once and for all. Please, Pen. We have to go, before it's too late."

There really was no other choice.

"Lead the way." Pushing my doubts aside, I walked out of the secret passageway, hand-in-hand with Artie.

* * *

The house was gone, completely ravaged by the golden dragon's fire, which had burned itself out. The walls, the roof, almost everything was destroyed beyond recognition. The bookcase was the only thing still intact. Maude was standing by herself in what was once a room, now exposed to the elements. Mag and Cissy were nowhere to be seen.

"Maude."

"I haven't been back here in years," she said quietly. "I'd almost forgotten, well, everything about this place." She picked up a cracked blue teacup with a sunflower painted on the side. The same one she used the first day I visited her house. It had somehow survived the fire. Maude sighed and set it gently back on the ground. She turned away, but I could see tears in her eyes.

"Oh, Maude," I whispered, hugging her.

"Thank you, my dear."

We stayed like that until Maude's tears subsided. When we broke apart, she was smiling sadly. "I'll be fine, Penelope. It's just emotional being back."

"I understand, Maude, I really do. More than I can say." How I wished I could go back to that carefree time, back before the golden dragon attacked. Back before I lost the only life I ever knew.

I blinked as Artie took my hand. I may have lost Tealeaf, but I had gained friends in Mag and Artie. Friends I wouldn't trade for anything.

"Dragon fire," he said grimly. "It destroys everything it touches, or burns for years, like in the Blue Rose Swamp. Once the fire consumed all the fuel in Maude's house, it went out on its own."

"You know your infernos," Maude said approvingly. "Most dragons can regulate their fire, so this won't happen. However, I think it's safe to say that the golden dragon intended to kill us." She sighed. "I'll have to warn Ashcroft not to use this secret passageway anymore. At least the bookcase door itself is magically protected. Come on. We should go."

"Where are we going?"

"Outside, of course. Mag and Cessala are waiting."

* * *

The early morning was quiet as Maude, Artie, and I stepped out of the rubble. All the soldiers were gone, along with the golden dragon, leaving only some trampled earth and the lingering smell of fire. The gray, predawn light illuminated the two dragons standing before me: one red, one purple.

"It's about time you showed up," Mag grumbled as we approached. "My wings are starting to go numb. It's cold out here!"

Cessala smiled. "It's been a while since Mag and I were both in dragon form. She's a bit put out."

"Oh, yes," Mag said, rolling her eyes. "I love freezing my wings off, while Hugo is in danger! It's not like every second counts!"

Cessala sighed. "Calm yourself, Mag. There's more to it than that. I think we're going to have to tell them, Maude. They have a right to know."

"Tell us what?" I said, frowning.

"There's a magical barrier surrounding Kelton Castle," Maude said. "It's been up for two days and since then, nobody has entered and exited."

"We know," Artie said. "Rowena told us. Rather kind of her to relay the information, really. I wonder if she's starting to like me."

I laughed. "Probably shouldn't get your hopes up."

"The spell that created the barrier is powerful," Cessala continued, ignoring us. "More powerful than any spell we've seen in recent years. We think the golden dragon is searching for a way to break through and seize control of Alsmora from Queen Alana. The Elton Castle library has the largest collection of books in all the land. Think what he can do with that kind of intelligence."

"What about Hugo?" Mag demanded. "He's a scholar. Surely, he knows how to break the barrier. Both he and the books are in danger!"

"I agree with Mag," Artie said. "Either the golden dragon takes the books and kills Hugo or he'll burn the books and capture Hugo. He won't want that knowledge floating around for us to find."

"Well, then," I said, gazing out at the brilliant sunrise barely peeking out over the horizon. "We'd better get to Elton Castle and find Hugo, before it's too late."

Chapter Twelve

Wildling

While Mag, Artie, and Cessala prepared to leave for Elton Castle, I pulled Maude aside and said, "What can you tell me about a wolf named Lupine? He had me search your house for this." I held out my old drawing with the spell on the back.

Gideon, *Entalen.*

Maude's eyes widened and she muttered, "Gideon, awake." Clearing her throat, she said, "I have many friends, Penelope. I can't remember all of them. This Lupine was probably a local wolf who wanted your help."

But this explanation didn't explain my connection to Lupine.

"Maude, I think I know him."

She raised an eyebrow. "Oh?"

"I think Lupine was one of those wolf puppies I saved when I was eight. He must be."

Maude seemed to relax. "Well, isn't that splendid! Lupine has a good friend in you, Penelope. Now, speaking of wolves." She pointed at the book in my other hand, the one by C.M. Aude. The wolf on the cover seemed to shimmer. "Keep that safe. It's the key to opening the bookcase door, whether the extra security spell is active or not. Without it, our enemies will never be able to find the Storm Knights' base."

"What about the Storm Knights? Can they still leave?"

"Not through here," Maude said. "But don't worry. There are other entrances and exits scattered all throughout Alsmora. Now, to business. What has David told you about detecting magical signatures?"

"Not much. Just that he has a spell to detect them. He hasn't gone into any detail."

"I'll teach you," Maude promised. "Though, if your little demonstration earlier is any indication, it won't take long."

"Demonstration?"

"Your opening the bookcase door was most impressive. But enough of that. We have to get going. We still have to land for the night."

"I thought we were heading straight to Elton Castle."

"Cessala hasn't flown in years. There's no way we can make such a long trip by nightfall. We should be there by tomorrow."

"Tomorrow! Hugo could be captured or dead by then!"

"Fear not, Penelope," she said. "Hugo is safe for now. He's not an idiot. He'll hide when the golden dragon comes calling. Our gaudy golden friend isn't exactly quiet. Hugo will hear him long before he arrives."

"The golden dragon could still steal the books."

"Ah. Now, that is a problem," Maude said. "Hugo will try to save as many books as possible, but he's just one troll. There are only so many books he can carry. Hugo won't give them up easily, though. No, I estimate that we have a few days before the golden dragon strikes. I'll let you know when to start worrying."

"Pen? Maude? Are you ready to go?"

We looked over and saw Artie standing beside Mag and Cessala. Both dragons had supplies strapped to their backs, courtesy of the Storm Knights. Cessala was bearing it all patiently, passing the time with a dreamy look on her face, watching the clouds go by. Mag was pacing back and forth, swinging her tail to and fro. She almost hit Artie in the face when she turned suddenly. He ducked. His expression clearly said, *hurry.*

Trying not to laugh, I headed off in Mag and Artie's direction. The moment she saw me, Mag said, *"Finally!* Come on, let's go. We need to leave for Elton Castle, *now.* I can't wait to sink my claws into that pretender golden dragon."

"Calm yourself, Mag," Cessala said gently, not taking her eyes off the clouds. "We'll get there when we get there."

"That's not good enough!" Mag growled.

"Maude already explained everything to me," I said. "She's assured me that Hugo will be fine, at least for now."

"How long can he last, though?"

"Hugo is a troll," Artie said. "He may not look it, what with his reading glasses and romance novels, but he is incredibly strong."

The three of us exchanged worried glances.

Mag began pacing again. "All right. We'll stop for the night, but I don't like it. I feel as if the golden dragon is going to do something terrible to Elton Castle while we're not looking."

She had a point. The last time the golden dragon visited the old capital of Alsmora, the castle wound up in ruins.

Artie and I climbed onto Mag's back. Maude jumped lightly onto Cessala, who looked up sleepily and said, "Oh, we're leaving now?"

Maude smiled and patted Cessala on the neck. "Yes, old friend. Time to go."

"Right," she said, stretching her wings. "I haven't done this for a while. I might be a bit rusty." She leapt into the air.

Once they were far enough away, Artie muttered, "Cessala isn't exactly rash about anything, is she?"

"You got that right," Mag said. She snorted. "It's very un-dragon-like."

"I don't think that's a word. Come on. Let's catch up with them. I don't want my teachers to get away."

"It should be a word," Mag said, spreading her wings. She took off into the sky after Maude and Cessala. The purple dragon and eccentric witch glided serenely along, looking as if they hadn't a care in the world. Cessala yawned.

"Ah, there you are. What took you so long?"

"Long?" Mag said. She turned to me, her eyes flashing with annoyance. When she looked back at the older dragon, I knew we were in for a tirade. Artie and I both covered our ears, but we could still hear Mag.

"What is wrong with you? Are you a dragon or not? I don't understand you, Aunt Cessala. You and Maude were the first to defeat the golden dragon! Why aren't you doing anything? Don't just float there! He's back and trying to destroy Alsmora again! Get mean! Get angry! Show me

what you were like when you fought that imposter a hundred years ago! He's not even a real dragon! He's just some human pretending!"

When Mag finished, she was breathing heavily. I could feel her rumbling beneath me and I was afraid she was going to shoot out fire. Before she could, however, Cessala spoke.

"You're right, Mag. I have changed in the last hundred years. I used to be more like you. Brash, confrontational, thinking I knew everything. But I'm older and wiser now." Her eyelids drooped. "I've also spent too much time as a lizard. Do you know what that does to you?"

My eyes widened. "Lizards are cold-blooded, aren't they, Cessala?"

"They are," she said. "It's taking a bit to wear off."

"Wear off?" Mag repeated harshly. "What are you talking about?"

"Don't you get it, Mag?" Artie said. "Lizards can't produce their own heat. They become sleepy when they're cold."

Mag narrowed her eyes. "You're saying that once you warm up, you'll be more alert, right?"

"Correct," Cessala said. "Have you ever seen a lizard just sitting out on a rock, sunbathing? Well, that's because they can't maintain their body temperatures on their own. They need an outside source to help keep them regulated. I've gone from a six-inch lizard to a massive dragon in the space of a minute. Sure, as a dragon I have fire, but it's going to take a bit for my internal heat to stabilize." Her stomach rumbled with hunger. "Speaking of which, it's time for breakfast. Maude, will you be all right until I get back?"

The witch nodded, stood precariously on Cessala's back, and leapt nimbly onto the airborne Mag.

"Maude!" Mag yelled, as our new passenger made herself comfortable sitting behind Artie. "What was that?"

"Cess has to hunt."

"I'll meet up with you later!" Cessala called. "Don't worry. I'll be as discreet as possible."

"You always are," Maude said, as the purple dragon flew away.

The moment she had disappeared, Artie and I turned to look at Maude.

"Why does she need to hunt now?"

"Because she's hungry."

"You know what we mean, Maude," Artie said. "Does Cessala's hunger have anything to do with her sudden return to dragon form?"

"Dragons do need to eat more than lizards."

"I don't get it," Mag said. "Why didn't you turn Cessala into a human, like the rest of the dragons? We don't have that kind of problem when we switch back and forth."

"Bringing an injured lizard back to Kelton Castle was easier to explain than an injured human," Maude said. "The issue is that Cissy needs less energy than Cessala, so whenever she becomes a dragon again, Cessala is lethargic and starving."

"What happens when her stomach is full and she changes back into a lizard?" I asked.

Maude shrugged. "She's very hyperactive. In those instances, she's not only warm from her internal fire, but she also needs to scurry around everywhere, trying to burn off all that extra energy."

We fell silent as Mag flew us further and further north. I watched as the scenery rapidly changed beneath us and still Cessala didn't return. At midday, I started to get worried.

"Maude?" I said tentatively.

"Hmm?"

"Do you think we should have waited for Cessala?"

Maude stretched and looked around. "Nah. Cess is fine." She closed her eyes for a moment and took a deep breath. When she opened them again, she smiled and jerked her head off to the east. "She should be here any minute."

Artie and I looked expectantly in that direction. Except for a bird flying nearby, the sky was empty.

"Uh, Maude?" Artie said. "I don't think— Pen, do you hear that?"

I tilted my head and suddenly heard it as well. We locked eyes. "That can't be good."

A low, rumbling roar was echoing around us. As we all turned, a purple shape came zooming toward us: Cessala.

I started to relax. The roar must have come from her.

"Cessala, over here!" I called.

But she wasn't alone. A dark, shadowy figure was flying after her.

The pursuer was gaining on Cessala. He was almost on top of her, when Cessala quickly whirled, whipped her tail through the air, and whacked him in the jaw. This caused him to sail backwards through the air. The pursuer stopped and hovered, shaking his head. That's when I saw what we were up against.

It was a black dragon, with vacant white eyes that stood out in stark contrast to the rest of his body. Thick tendrils of gray mist curled and twisted around him, like some cruel parody of an embrace. His image was warped and distorted, so he appeared more beast than dragon.

The mist sparked with what looked like mini lightning bolts. The black dragon roared in pain as he continued to fly after Cessala.

Mag halted in midair, seemingly frozen to the spot. Her breath came in shallow gasps and I worried that she might lose concentration and return to human form. The only thing keeping us in the air was the sporadic beat of her wings.

"Mag," I said, shaking her shoulder.

She didn't respond.

"Mag!"

She shook her head and looked around. When she finally focused on me, I could see the panic in her eyes.

"It's happening again!"

"What?"

"The blank, white eyes. The lightning mist that controls your every move." I could feel a shiver run down her spine. "The last time this happened was a hundred years ago. I never thought I'd see it for myself. That dragon has gone wild!"

Cessala swooped in beside us and yelled, "Mag, move!"

"But... shouldn't we help him? I think I remember him from Dragon Valley. He doesn't know what he's doing."

"Mag," Cessala said sternly. "Remember the mission. We have to find and save Hugo before it's too late. The golden dragon sent this wildling as an obstacle in our path."

Above us, the wildling screamed in pain again as another miniature lightning bolt flared out of the mist. Mag, Artie, and I winced in sympathy.

Cessala continued, "I know it's tempting, Mag, but you can't fix every wildling. Believe me, we've tried. Most of them are too far gone."

Maude nodded sadly in agreement.

"Mag, take Penelope and Artie and head straight for Elton Castle. Find Hugo. Protect him from the golden dragon at all costs. Maude and I will draw the wildling away, giving you time to escape. We'll incapacitate him and meet you at Elton Castle as soon as we can."

Maude stood and stretched. "Oh, it's been so long since we had a good chase with a brainwashed dragon." She hopped off Mag and onto Cessala.

"Wait!" Mag cried. She glanced back at me and Artie. I could see the desperation in her eyes. She turned back to her aunt. "He's innocent! You can't—"

Growling, Cessala darted forward until she and Mag were nose-to-nose. "Can't? Can't what, Mag? Leave him like this? We can and we will. The fate of Alsmora depends on us finding Hugo before the golden dragon does. If that means sacrificing one wildling who's beyond saving, so be it."

Before we could say anything else, Cessala had spun around to face the wild dragon.

"Hey, wildling!" she called. "What's the matter? Can't handle a bit of lightning?" And with that, she dove for the ground.

The black dragon snorted and, without even looking at us, took off after Maude and Cessala. The lightning mist was still sparking with electricity, but at least the wildling was no longer screaming in pain.

"I think I like Cessala better when she's half-asleep," Artie said.

"This isn't right," Mag said. "He's innocent."

"Are you sure about that, Mag?" I asked. "He's gaining on them."

Cessala and Maude had flown far in a short amount of time, but the black dragon was rapidly closing the distance.

Mag looked between the way to Elton Castle and our retreating teachers for a moment, before she said, "Orders or not, I can't abandon my friend. There has to be a way to save him."

"Do what you have to do, Mag. I'm sure Hugo will understand."

Tears of gratitude welled in Mag's eyes. "Thank you."

She turned to face Maude, Cessala, and the wildling, who were fighting in midair above a small forest.

Taking a deep breath, Mag flattened herself and took off like an arrow in flight. I squeaked in surprise and threw my arms around her neck in a vain attempt to hold on. It was no good. The force of the wind ripped my arms away from her and pushed me against Artie.

"*Bechulen,*" I gasped. A protective bubble formed around the three of us. It was completely transparent, except for the glittering blue pulses of energy at the edges of the bubble. I breathed a sigh of relief as the wind died down, my magic stopping the worst of it.

Luckily, my spell didn't seem to prevent Mag from flying. I could still feel the air rushing past, but at a much gentler speed.

"That was quick thinking, Pen," Artie said.

"Thanks. This should hold, at least for now."

We scooted forward until we were back to where we had started.

"Not that I don't trust your magic, Pen, but if it's okay with you…" Artie reached past me and put his arms around Mag's neck. I was now safely in between my two friends and, to be honest, I didn't mind.

"Everything all right back there?" Mag called from the front.

"We're fine," I said. "Right, Artie?"

"Never better."

As I smiled at Artie and he smiled back, it suddenly dawned on me. "Artie!"

"What?" he said, starting to withdraw his arms.

"You're okay, Artie." I grabbed his hand excitedly. I couldn't explain why, but I didn't want him to let go. Staring straight into his eyes, I said, "My silver vision!"

He looked taken aback. "What about it?"

"It's gone! I cast that protection spell and my vision never changed color. It's been slowly weakening since Tealeaf!"

He frowned. "What does that mean?"

"No idea."

There was a roar off to our left and Artie and I looked over at the nearby forest. My heart almost stopped. Cessala and the black dragon were fighting high above, locked in combat. Maude was holding on doggedly, muttering under her breath. A bright, white light kept flashing around them. As we watched, the wildling raked Cessala across the flank and she and Maude went down, down, down, falling into the trees.

Chapter Thirteen

Fire and Ash

"NO!" Mag cried. She dived toward the trees, but we didn't see any sign of Maude or Cessala.

"Mag! Mag! Calm down!"

"Calm down?" she yelled back. "Maude and Cessala are probably… they might be…"

"I don't think they're dead, Mag," Artie said. He was squinting at the ground. "Think positively."

"Positively!" Mag demanded. "They fell hundreds of feet!" She was interrupted when another roar caused us all to look up. The wildling.

"Mag, I know you're worried about Maude and Cessala," I said. "So are we. But Artie and I can't fly. You can. You deal with the wildling. We'll go down and check on them."

"Leave it to us," Artie promised.

Before Mag could argue, Artie and I, still holding hands, jumped from her back.

"Are you two crazy?" Mag shouted.

"Protection bubble!" I called back as we raced toward the ground.

"Pen, are you sure this will work?" Artie asked as the wind rushed past us.

"Pretty sure," I said. But I had a moment of doubt. What if I couldn't control this thing?

As the ground hurried up to meet us, I grabbed my amulet and shouted, *"Lanasan!"* Instantly, our bubble slowed and we began to sink gently to the ground.

"Good thinking, Pen."

"Thanks." I directed the bubble toward the forest, where it popped a couple of inches above the grass. We touched down on the ground safely. "Where are Maude and Cessala?" I didn't see them anywhere.

"There," Artie said, pointing.

I looked over and saw Maude lying facedown, spreadeagled in a pile of leaves, but no Cessala.

We rushed to her side, just as the black dragon roared above us. Mag roared in response. Artie and I quickened our pace. When we reached her, I saw that Maude was unconscious.

Together, Artie and I turned her over so she was lying on her back. Her breathing was shallow.

"Maude, Maude, wake up!" I cried, bending over the old witch. She didn't stir. Frantically, I searched my pockets for something, anything that might help. The only thing I found was my old, crumpled drawing from Maude's house. I was about to toss it aside, when I saw the words written on the back.

Gideon, *Entalen.*

Entalen. Awake.

Fumbling in my excitement, I placed one hand on my amulet and the other on Maude's shoulder.

"Entalen."

A few tense moments passed. Then, Maude began to glow green. Her eyes flew open. I jumped back in surprise as she started to cough. Artie, thinking quickly, handed her a canteen of water.

"Thanks," she said, once her coughing fit had subsided. "That wildling caught us off guard. How did you revive me, Penelope?"

"I used a spell. *Entalen.*" I whispered, staring at my hands. They were glowing green as well.

"How did Lupine know?" Maude murmured.

"Know what?"

"How did he know you would need Gideon's spell?"

"We can talk about that later," Artie said. "For now, we need to find Cessala and help Mag. Where is Cessala, Maude?"

"Right here," she said, reaching into her pocket and pulling out a tiny, purple lizard.

"Cissy," I said, relieved. "We're glad to see you! What happened?"

After shaking her head, Cissy started chittering excitedly, pointing at the black dragon above, who was still fighting Mag. When Cissy finished, she gazed up at us, expectantly.

Artie and I stared back helplessly, neither of us understanding a word she had said.

"In short," Maude said. "The wildling got the better of us and forced us to the ground. Cess reverted back to lizard form before we landed and I conjured a shield around us. It took the brunt of the damage, but knocked me out in the process."

I patted Maude on the shoulder, my hand still glittering with the strange green energy. Out of the corner of my eye, I thought I saw the bushes rustle slightly. Someone or something was watching us. Turning to Cissy, I asked, "Can you still fly?"

Cissy stared at me for a moment before she transformed back into Cessala. "For now."

"Good. Could you fly me up there? I can't let Mag fight alone."

"I'm coming with you, Pen."

"No, Artie. Wait here with Maude."

"Oh? And why am I staying?" Maude asked, her eyebrows raised.

Nodding toward the bushes, I whispered, "I believe we have company." In a louder voice, "Maude, you're still dazed after your fall. You were barely breathing when we found you. Stay here and rest. Artie will look after you. Cessala and I can handle this."

"I can't stay with you long," Cessala said. She indicated a nasty scratch on her leg. "The wildling got me. I can only take you to Mag before I have to return to the ground."

"I understand."

"Pen, don't do this," Artie said. "You're throwing yourself into a dragon fight. It's too dangerous."

"I know what I'm doing, Artie." At least, I hoped I did.

Before anyone could talk me out of it, I hopped onto Cessala's back and she spread her wings.

"I'll be back soon," Cessala promised. In a whisper, "Try to survive against whatever is lurking in the bushes until I get back."

"Just get out of here, you scaly lizard," Maude said, shooing us away. "Artie and I will be all right for a few minutes."

Artie glanced up at me. "I can't convince you to stay, so good luck, Pen."

"Thanks, Artie."

Cessala slowly took off into the air. Her leg must have still been bothering her.

"I'm so sorry I'm asking you to do this, Cessala," I said as the wind rushed past us. "I wish I could do something."

"Actually, Penelope, you can," she said, glancing back at me. "I know a healing spell. *Abselen.* As a dragon, I can't use human magic. I would appreciate your help."

"Of course, Cessala." I placed my hand on my amulet. *"Abselen."* There was a flash of green light and the injury on Cessala's leg vanished.

"Thank you," she said, gratefully. "Let's go save my niece from the wilding, shall we?"

Mag and the black dragon had separated and were circling each other. As we soared toward them, I heard a high-pitched cry down below.

"Artie! Maude!" I yelled. My heart pounding, I scanned the ground, but I couldn't see anything. Maude and Artie were on their own.

"Penelope," Cessala said. "I know what you're thinking, but they should be fine, at least for now. You're here to help Mag against the black dragon. I don't think she can hold out much longer."

I hesitated for a moment, torn between my friends. One was miles away and possibly fine, while the other was closer and fighting for her life against the wildling. Even from here, I could see that she was covered in burns, bites, and scratches.

I tore my gaze away from the ground and said, "Mag."

Cessala gave me a sympathetic look, before speeding toward the battle. The black dragon's back was facing us. Mag, however, saw us coming.

Her eyes widened. "Penelope? Cessala? What are you doing here? Get back, before you get hurt!"

"Watch out!" I cried, as the wildling breathed fire, right at Mag.

She dodged, but not fast enough. Mag hissed in pain as a stream of blue engulfed her right wing. She tucked her left wing into her body, held the other one out, and spun in midair to extinguish the flames.

"Why was that fire blue?" I asked Cessala.

"Blue fire is hotter than red," she said grimly. "The golden dragon's magic is making the wildling stronger than average."

"Can we save him?"

Cessala sighed. "When Maude and I were first fighting the golden dragon, he sent hordes of wildlings after us. Most of those dragons had been my friends. We tried everything to turn them back to normal. We saved a few, but not all. We couldn't get to them all before they disappeared. We still don't know why they vanished. It is possible to save this wildling, but I don't know if we have the time. Hugo needs us."

Mag flew up beside us, wincing in pain. "We need a way to stop the wildling. Any ideas?"

"First off, we should try to fix that wing of yours," Cessala said. "Penelope."

"On it. *Abse—*" but I didn't get any further. The black dragon had swooped in for a new attack.

"Penelope, jump!" Cessala cried.

"What?"

"Just do it! Jump onto Mag's back. I'll distract him."

The black dragon swiped at Mag, but Cessala was there to stop him. She slammed her tail right into the wildling's side. "GO!"

Feeling like Maude, I scrambled from Cessala's back and leapt onto Mag's. She winced as I stumbled and stepped on her burnt wing.

"Sorry," I said, wincing with her.

"It's fine," she gasped, but I could hear the distress in her voice.

The moment I was clear of Cessala, she took off, the wildling right on her tail.

Mag started after them.

"Wait, Mag! Your wing!"

"What about it?" she snapped. "We have to help her. Save your spells, Penelope. We can't waste any time."

"Rest a moment," I said soothingly. "I assure you, Mag. We're not wasting time."

"Fine, but hurry up, will you?"

"Abselen."

The burned membrane of the wing started to glow green. Within seconds, all her injuries had disappeared.

Mag flexed her wing as she turned delightedly toward me. "Thanks, Penelope."

"No problem."

I frowned. No silver vision and my magic was green instead of blue. As soon as we were back on the ground, I would have to ask Maude why it had changed.

"Penelope? You still with me?"

I started in surprise and found Mag watching me, her expression worried. I tried to laugh it off. "I'm fine, Mag. Really. Come on, let's go help Cessala."

Mag gave me one last, curious look, before she dived toward her aunt and the wildling. They were scratching and clawing each other above the trees. I glanced at the ground, but there was no sign of Maude and Artie.

As we approached the two dragons, I realized that Mag and I were at a serious disadvantage. The black dragon wasn't showing any sign of fatigue, while Mag had already been scratched, clawed, and burnt. Despite my healing spell, she was still flying slower than usual.

I wasn't doing much better. Sure, my silver vision wasn't affecting me at the moment, but I could feel a slight pain building up behind my eyes. After everything I had been through in the last few days, I was ready to collapse. I shook my head. I couldn't think of that now. We had to stop this wildling, before things got even more out of control.

But what could Mag and I do in our exhausted state? The black dragon would attack the moment he saw us.

And then I knew.

"Mag, do you trust me?" I asked.

"Of course, Penelope."

"Perfect." I took a deep breath. *"Aun evas comren."* There was a flash of green and Mag and I blinked out of the color spectrum.

This spell was a strange one. All the color would drain from our bodies, leaving us black and white. From our perspective, we could see each other. For everyone else, we were invisible.

Mag, now in black and white, turned to grin at me. "Good thinking, Penelope. Time for the element of surprise." And she slammed directly into the black dragon.

The force jolted me to the side, where I was barely able to keep my seat. As I struggled to rise, Mag tore the wildling from her aunt. Cessala, for her part, looked confused, before her nostrils flared.

"Ah, I get it," she said. "Invisibility. I have to go check on Maude and Artie. Good luck."

As soon as Cessala was gone, Mag went on the attack. She breathed fire right at the wildling.

"Mag!" I yelled. She was aiming straight for his wing.

The black dragon dodged. The fire missed him by inches.

Mag snapped her jaws shut, ending the stream. "What, Penelope?"

"You can't aim for his wing, Mag! He's your friend!"

"So? He did the exact same thing to me!"

"That's not the point, Mag, and you know it."

Mag grumbled under her breath, her amber eyes shining brighter than usual.

Our argument was cut short as the wildling renewed his attack. Like Cessala, his nostrils were flared. We would have to hurry. We couldn't use invisibility to dodge forever. Eventually, he would find us with his other senses.

Mag rammed her head right into the wildling's stomach and I winced in sympathy as he struggled to catch his breath. I wished I could heal him, just like I did with Mag's wing.

Wait. Heal? That was it! Cessala had said that the black dragon was beyond help, but I did have that strange green magic. It had already helped both Mag and Cessala. Maybe it could heal the wildling, too!

"Mag," I said, standing. "Do me a favor and don't attack the black dragon."

"Penelope…"

Before Mag could protest, I leapt from her back, right onto the wildling. For a split second, there was absolutely nothing between me and the ground below. Then, I went through the gray lightning mist and landed on the black dragon.

He immediately roared and tried to throw me off, but I held on.

The mist condensed, thickening around me like an oppressive shroud. A lightning bolt arced straight toward me. There was nowhere to hide, so I did the only thing I could.

"Bechulen!"

My magical shield sprang up between me and the lighting, just in time. It bounced off the glittering surface harmlessly, but the force of the blow had shattered both the shield and my concentration. I knew I didn't have enough energy to stop another attack, but I still had one more trick up my sleeve.

Mag was flying next to us. "Penelope, get off the wildling! Are you trying to get yourself killed?"

"No. I can do this." Taking my amulet in one hand, I reached out mentally to the green healing magic. I could feel the energy pulsating at the back of my mind, waiting to be used. Focusing on the wildling, I said, "*Abselen.*"

The green light of my magic seeped into the dragon's scales. A moment passed before his white eyes darkened to bright blue. At the same time, a raw, primal scream erupted from the gray mist. I watched in terror as lightning spiraled in midair, right in Mag's path.

She dodged, but one of the bolts zapped her on the tip of her tail. Mag cried out in surprise and pain, but otherwise seemed fine.

The gray mist evaporated, leaving the sky clear once again.

"Who? What?" the black dragon said, dazed. "Where am I?" He turned his head and noticed me on his back. "Who are you?"

"I'll explain once we're on the ground." I sat back, shaking. I could still smell the electricity in the air.

The dragon hesitated, before beginning his descent. Mag followed.

"What's your name?"

"I'm Ash… I think. I had the weirdest dream."

I had wanted to wait until we were safely on the ground, but looking at the poor, lost dragon, I said, "My name is Penelope and it wasn't a dream, Ash."

A clicking from the ground caught my attention. I looked down and my heart almost stopped. I now knew what had attacked Artie and Maude. A *yikty,* a giant magical scorpion, was scuttling into view.

CHAPTER FOURTEEN

DRAGON'S RESOLVE

Mag drew level with me and Ash. "Penelope," she said, "did you see that?"

"I did. Why did it have to be scorpions?"

"Bad experience with *yikties*?" Ash asked.

"Experiences. Plural. Let's see, I've been beaten, taunted, and paralyzed, and that was on a good day." I shuddered. "Ugh. I absolutely hate them."

"What about you?" Mag said to Ash. "Have you ever dealt with *yikties*?"

If Ash noticed her icy tone, it didn't vex him. His voice was quite calm as he said, "No, but my brother was attacked recently. I returned home to Dragon Valley to check on him, but Venn was fine by then. I was on my way to Kelton Castle to study the barrier when a bright light shined in my eyes. Next thing I know, Penelope is on my back."

Mag faltered in midair. "Wait a second. Venn is your brother? Ash, is that you?"

"Mag?"

The two dragons stared disbelievingly at each other, before they both started babbling.

"I thought that was you, but I couldn't be sure! You've been away from Dragon Valley for years! Where have you been, Ash?"

"Living amongst humans, trying to learn their ways. Is it true that you're the fabled dragon guardian, Mag?"

"I am. Why did you attack us? How did Penelope turn you back to normal?"

Holding up my hands, I said, "Time out, you two. We should go help Artie, Maude, and Cessala, before you have your cozy catch-up."

Mag rolled her eyes. "You're no fun, Penelope. Fine. Scorpions first."

Both dragons dived. I was amazed at Ash's speed as he tucked his wings in and plummeted to the ground faster than Mag.

"Ash!" I yelled, as the ground rushed to meet us. He pulled up at the last minute. I tried to calm my racing heart as Ash glided over the trees. When he turned to look at me, there was a foolish grin plastered on his face.

"That was great!"

"Yeah," I said shakily, making a mental note to never fly with Ash again.

Mag caught up seconds later. Her head was tilted as she considered him. "Impressive, Ash. Then again, you always were a fast flier."

He beamed.

We started scanning the ground. There was no sign of our friends or the *yikty*. I caught a glimpse of a gray blur, but when it didn't reappear, I decided it must have been a trick of the light.

"Nothing," I sighed. "Where are they?"

"Maybe right next to you."

Startled, I almost fell off Ash as I turned. Cessala was hovering beside us, Maude and Artie safely on her back.

"Weren't you just on the ground?"

"We were," Maude said. "But things were getting a bit complicated down there."

"What?"

"Look down," Artie said. "The place is swarming with *yikties.*"

Together, Mag, Ash, and I glanced at the ground. A moment ago, there had been a single scorpion. Now, the forest floor was covered in a scuttling mass of black-armored arachnids.

"Where did they all come from?" I said, my mouth dry.

"Don't know," Cessala said. "It's like they're multiplying from the trees themselves. We need to get out of here, now."

"No," Ash said. He was still staring at the scorpions far below.

"No? Ash, what do you mean no?"

"I'm not going with you," he said. "I'll stay behind and distract the *yikties,* so you can get away." He turned to look at me. "Go. I can handle this."

"Ash, I… we can't ask you…"

He grinned. "You don't have to."

"Penelope," Mag said, flying up beside us. She was so close, her wing brushed Ash's. "We should go. He's made up his mind. Come with me."

I looked between the two dragons. I knew the right answer, but it didn't make it any easier. With a nod, I carefully stood and stepped onto Mag's back.

"Good luck, Ash."

He smiled sadly. "Thanks, Penelope. Sorry for attacking you earlier." With one last look at all of us, Ash dived for the ground. Once he was close enough, he breathed fire on the scorpions.

"That is one brave dragon," Artie said.

"Brave, but foolish," Cessala said. "I'm glad you somehow found a way to save him, but too much fire will burn down the entire forest." She and Maude exchanged worried glances. Then, abruptly, "Artie, off my back."

"What?"

"Get on Mag's back, behind Penelope. Now."

Mag glided toward Cessala and the same process ensued. Like me, Artie clambered over, but he wasn't too graceful. As he gingerly stepped onto her back, Mag shifted slightly and his foot slipped. He made a wild grab for my hand but missed. Instead, he latched onto her wing.

"A little help!" Artie hung by his fingertips, hundreds of feet in the air. Ash's fire began to lap at the trees beneath us.

"Hold on, Artie!" I threw myself forward and reached for his hand. Just as our fingers brushed, however, Mag jerked forward. The force of the momentum tore me away from Artie and caused him to almost go sailing into the fire. He managed to hold onto Mag's wing with one hand.

"Mag!" I exclaimed. "What happened?"

"Not my fault," she muttered. "It's Ash's fire."

"Ash's fire?" I repeated as I grabbed Artie's hand and pulled with all my might. He was too heavy.

Frowning, I placed my hand on my amulet and said, *"Ohen."*

A green light engulfed Artie and he gently floated onto Mag's back beside me. I hugged him tightly. We were both breathing heavily. After several minutes, we broke apart. Artie slumped back in relief. I turned to the others. Maude and Cessala had drifted away, their gaze focused on the ground.

"What about Ash's fire?" I asked.

"Look," Cessala said.

Artie and I looked down and our eyes widened. Ash's fire, which had still been tiny moments before, was now rapidly spreading throughout the forest.

"The fire is affecting the air currents," Mag explained. "Cessala and I can't hold steady paths, not with the fire and air mixing beneath us."

"What can we do?" I asked. "We can't let the forest burn down."

"That's where we come in," Maude said. "Artie was telling us that Mag used back fire to save a swamp."

"Don't remind me," Mag muttered.

I patted her on the shoulder. Mag and her friend Venn had been the cause of that particular fire. It had taken eight years, but Mag had finally fixed her mistake when she stopped the Blue Rose Swamp fire with more fire. The two competing infernos had burned through the available oxygen, extinguishing both conflagrations.

Mag took a deep breath. "I'm ready. Let's stop this fire before it's too late."

"No, Mag," Cessala said. "Take Penelope and Artie and fly them to safety. Head for Elton Castle. And we mean it this time. No detours.

We'll meet you there in a few days."

"But…"

"No buts, Mag, we don't have the time," Cessala said sternly.

Slowly, Mag grinned. "Well, Aunt Cessala, it's nice to see you regain your dragon spirit."

Cessala grinned as well. "I never lost it. Go, now. We'll help Ash."

As they turned to leave, Maude called out to me, "Oh, and Penelope, before you try any major spells, remember the three R's: rest, mediate, and friends."

"Meditate? Friends? But, Maude, those don't…"

"Try not to need any spells before we get there! But if you absolutely must, the three R's should help. Toodles!"

And with that, Cessala and Mad Maude flew off to stop the fire and save the forest.

Chapter Fifteen

Dreams of the Past

I was amazed at how fast the fire spread. Smoke obscured most of the forest and the sky above. Our path to Elton Castle had disappeared.

Artie and I began to cough, our eyes streaming.

"Bec- Bechulen," I croaked as Mag flew through a particularly dense patch of smog. Instantly, my glittering bluish-green shield formed around us.

"Thanks, Pen," Artie said, clearing his throat. "If that's how fast Mag and Venn's fire spread at the Blue Rose Swamp, I'm not surprised it burned for years. Dragon fire really is deadly."

"You got that right," Mag said. Even she seemed grateful for the shield's protection. "I know Ash meant well, burning the *yikties,* but that was far too reckless."

"At least Maude and Cessala are here to temper his enthusiasm," I said. "Mag, how do we get to Elton Castle from here?"

She snorted. "That's easy, Penelope. Just head north."

"Okay. Which way is north?"

Mag opened her mouth, stopped, and frowned. "Um. Well. You see, with the smoke…" She sighed. "I'll know just as soon as we break through to some clear sky. Right now, I barely know which way is up and which is down."

That didn't exactly fill me with confidence.

"Anything we can do to help, Mag?"

She shook her head. "Unless you two can fly, no. Go to sleep. I'll wake you if anything happens. You haven't slept much in the last couple of days, Penelope."

I started to argue. Why should I go to sleep? I could help Mag keep a lookout for any *yikties* that escaped Maude, Cessala, and Ash. Perhaps I could…

I didn't have time to finish that thought. Mag had started to sing. It was slow and lilting and my eyelids began to droop.

"No fair," I murmured drowsily and fell asleep.

* * *

When I opened my eyes, I felt as if I were floating. At first, I didn't think this was strange, because I was sitting on a dragon, but as I became more aware of my surroundings, the floating sensation faded and I realized that I was completely alone. Mag and Artie were nowhere in sight.

"Mag? Artie?" I stood up unsteadily. It was then that I noticed that I was on the ground. *Don't panic,* I told myself, as I looked around. Nothing but the grassy hill I was standing on, some trees, and a peaceful river snaking its way down below. A castle was visible above the trees. *Mag and Artie got me off her back and they decided to let me sleep. We must be near Elton Castle.*

Still, that didn't explain why both of my friends were gone.

"Hello?" I called. "Anyone there? I'm awake. Hello?"

The only answer I got was the sound of birds chirping.

This was getting ridiculous. It wasn't like them to disappear on me. They didn't even leave any supplies. Had they dropped me off and flown away again?

It was as I was standing there, lost in thought, that I saw it. A flash of movement to my right.

Turning eagerly, I was about to call out, when the words died on my lips. My friends hadn't returned. Instead, a young blonde woman was standing beside the river, her back to me.

As I stepped closer, I noticed that the girl was wearing an old-fashioned, dark blue dress with white lace around the neck, sleeves, and hem. She looked out of place, as if she belonged to a different time.

"Hello," I said, walking up to her. "My name is Penelope Bogg. I'm looking for my friends, Mag and Artie. Have you seen them?"

The girl didn't answer. She didn't even look at me. Maybe she was deaf.

"Miss? Can you hear me?" I hesitated, before I waved my hand in front of her face. Nothing. She continued to stare out into the water, completely ignoring me.

That settled it. I must be invisible. But then, why couldn't she hear me? And why was I in color?

I was trying to decide what to do when a voice behind me yelled, "Rebecca! There you are!"

Turning, I saw a teenage boy in old-fashioned clothes hurrying toward us. He wore a long, purple tunic, with black breeches. A purple cloak was fastened to his right shoulder with the aid of a gold brooch. As he got closer, I could see that he was slightly taller than the girl, with black hair and brown eyes.

"I'm glad you're here," I said, relieved. "I think your friend needs some help. She can't see or hear me."

"Where have you been?" the boy demanded, brushing past me without a second glance.

"Hey!" I protested, reaching out to tap him on the shoulder. Instead, my hand went through the boy, like he wasn't even there.

I stared at my hands in shock, trying to work out what had happened. One thing I knew, though. This wasn't my doing. I didn't know any spells that made people transparent.

Those two could be ghosts, I thought. *Or, maybe I'm dreaming.*

I looked up at Elton Castle. It was better than I remembered. It was bright and colorful and completely intact. Nobody would mistake it for a pile of ruins.

The blonde girl was named Rebecca, same as Queen Alana's grandmother. That couldn't be a coincidence. Given her age, which I guessed to be around sixteen, Rebecca would be a princess right now.

There was no doubt in my mind. This had to be a scene from the past and, since I didn't know any time travel spells, I had to be dreaming.

"I've been here, Mir," Rebecca said, not taking her eyes off the water. "It's much more peaceful away from the castle. I can finally slow down and think."

"Uh huh," he said, yawning. "Whatever you say, Bec. Listen." His eyes lit up eagerly. "Have you heard the announcement?"

Rebecca sighed and made eye contact with him. "Mir, really, it's none of our business."

He rolled his eyes. "Sure, it isn't. But you have heard the rumors, haven't you?"

"I have," she admitted reluctantly.

"It's about time they decided," he said, beginning to pace excitedly. "I've been telling them that they should start my training. Took them long enough."

"Mir," Rebecca said sternly, grabbing his arm and swinging him around to face her. "Mom and Dad are the best king and queen Alsmora has ever had. They'll choose a successor when they're ready. Until then, be patient."

"That's the problem with you, Bec," Mir said, yanking his arm back. "You have no sense of urgency. Don't you want to rule Alsmora? Have servants? Tell other people what to do?"

Rebecca's eyes flashed. Even in a dream, I took a step back, fearful that I would become trapped in her gaze. Her voice lowered. "*Have servants? Tell other people what to do?* Mir! You. Are. A. Prince. You already do that!"

"Ah," he said, lowering his voice as well. "But I can still be overruled by you, Mom, and Dad."

A tense silence followed. I glanced nervously between the two royal siblings. Mir glared at his sister, while Rebecca stared coolly back.

"Very well," Mir said silkily. "I'll wait, just as you say, dear sister. But when they declare me king, I hope you remember what you said to me today. I have a long memory."

Without another word, Mir turned on his heel and stormed off. Rebecca turned back toward the water, her shoulders slumping.

I took a step forward to comfort her, before I remembered that she couldn't see or hear me.

"I appreciate the thought, Penelope, but it has been over a hundred years."

Rebecca turned to face me.

I almost fainted right then and there, causing me to wonder what would happen if I passed out in a dream. "What? How?" I gasped.

A table with a tea set appeared out of nowhere. Rebecca gestured me to one of the two chairs. "Please, sit. We have much to discuss."

Chapter Sixteen

A Dragon and a Dream

I slowly sank into the nearest chair, unable to take my eyes off Rebecca. I couldn't believe I was talking to the former queen of Alsmora, even if it was a dream.

Rebecca sat down, moving a small, blue book off to the side, and started to arrange the tea set. "Tea, Penelope?"

"No, thank you," I said. "Are you really Queen Rebecca?"

She smiled as she poured herself some tea. "I'm the projection of Rebecca from when she was alive. The real Rebecca moved on a long time ago. I am her memory."

"You're a ghost?"

"That's one name for what I am. Just know that anything I say or do is what the real Rebecca would have done."

My head began to ache, but I contented myself with knowing that I was talking to some form of Rebecca. "What are you doing here? What am I doing here?"

She sipped her tea and considered me. "We had to talk and we finally had the means to do so."

"What?"

"The necklace," she said. "The silver crescent necklace. You're wearing it, aren't you?"

I touched the necklace. My amulet thudded gently against it.

"I'm tied to the crescent," Rebecca explained. "We can only talk when you wear it and even then, only in dreams. As a memory, I can't manifest into the real world, at least not easily. Maybe if I focused."

She closed her eyes and grimaced. Opening her eyes, she sighed. "It's not going to work, I'm afraid."

"Let me see if I understand this correctly," I said. "We're in a dream, I can't talk to you in the real world, and you wanted to meet me. Why?"

"You needed to see my memory," she said. "I know you're trying to defeat the golden dragon and I want to help."

I sat bolt upright. "You can tell me who the golden dragon is? Oh, thank you, Rebecca! That'll make it so much easier to stop him if we know his human identity."

"I can't tell you, Penelope," Rebecca said quietly. "I don't know myself. I never knew. I don't think even Maude or Cessala ever found out. No, I showed you this memory because this is the day it started. The last day I saw Mir and the day my world fell apart."

The peaceful valley around us suddenly changed. Instead of brilliant sunshine, it was now night. I could see a fire burning brightly through the trees.

"Rebecca, what's happening?"

"That night," she said. "That horrible night a hundred years ago, when I became an orphan. My whole family died the same day I had my conversation with Mir. I spent my entire life trying to discover how it happened. I now pass the task to you. The golden dragon is responsible for this, I just know it. Start your search there and help me avenge my dear parents and brother. Please, Penelope."

"Rebecca, I don't know," I said. "Stopping the golden dragon is one thing, but revenge?"

Everything around me began to fade and I started to feel lightheaded.

"The dream is ending. Find the truth, Penelope. That's all I ask. I'm always around if you want to talk. Just have Mag sing as you fall asleep. Her powers will lead your spirit straight back to me, but only in your dreams. I'll be there to guide you. Now, wake up."

* * *

"Wake up, Penelope!"

I opened my eyes and found myself on the ground. It was nighttime. The only illumination were the stars twinkling overhead. Artie was staring down at me.

"Pen! You're awake!" He held out his hand and pulled me to my feet. I looked around. We seemed to be in a forest glade. Artie continued, "You were asleep for a long time."

"You were also muttering something about Rebecca," Mag said, walking up to us. She was back in human form. "Would that be Queen Rebecca, by any chance?"

"Yes," I said and told them about my conversation with the late ruler. "She said I can talk to her anytime I want, as long as I'm wearing the silver crescent necklace and you sing me to sleep, Mag."

She let out a great whooshing breath. "Rebecca truly wants me to sing to you? Why me?"

Artie and I exchanged puzzled looks.

"It's probably because you sang Pen to sleep while we were in the air," Artie said. "Remember what Aldrich said last week in Dragon Valley. Your music is imbued with an ancient magic only dragons can control."

"Yeah, but what if I have to do it in some public town square?" She grimaced. "That would be way too embarrassing."

I smiled. "Mag, do you suffer from stage fright?"

"No! I have no problem fighting in front of others!"

"How about when you're not fighting?"

Mag blushed and looked away. "It's not like… you see, one day… aarrgh! I can't talk to you people right now!" She stormed across the glade and sat down on a tree stump, her arms crossed and back to us.

Shaking my head, I turned to Artie, "What happened while I was in the dream? Where are we?"

"On the outskirts of Elton Castle. Mag insisted on walking from here, rather than flying."

"Any particular reason why? I thought she wanted to make a grand entrance and take out the golden dragon in a blaze of glory."

Artie shrugged. "I think Mag was hoping to catch him off guard with the element of surprise. He'll never see us coming if we're on foot."

"It still seems odd for Mag," I said. "I hope nothing's wrong."

I gazed out across the glade toward the river. Near the water's edge, Mag was sitting on her tree stump, her head thrown back as she watched the stars in the sky. The wind picked up, causing me to shiver.

"Mag?"

"Hmm?"

"It's getting cold. Why don't we head over to Elton Castle and spend the night with Hugo? He'll love the company and we can ask him about the silver crescent necklace. We can get an early start in the morning. We still have to find a good hiding place for him and his books."

"You two go ahead," she said, without turning. "I think I'll stay here for a bit longer. I'll meet you at the castle."

"Mag, is anything wrong?"

"I'm fine, Penelope. I'll see you in a bit." She still wouldn't look at me.

"This isn't about you singing or possibly having stage fright, is it? Because I was joking about that."

Mag finally looked up. To my surprise, her amber eyes were bright with tears, so bright they were almost white. When she spoke, however, Mag was her usual gruff self. "It's nothing, Penelope. I'm simply tired from flying. I'll meet you at Elton Castle later."

Artie placed a hand on my shoulder. "Come on, Pen. Let's go find Hugo." He whispered in my ear, "Give Mag some space."

"All right," I said reluctantly. "See you soon, Mag."

She turned away as Artie and I started the long walk to Elton Castle.

"Artie, did you notice anything strange about Mag?"

"You mean the way she dismissed us? Now that you mention it, yeah. She seemed fine in the air, but after she landed, she became very quiet. That was an hour ago. I wonder…"

"Wonder, what? Please, Artie, tell me everything."

He sighed. "Once I got you off her back, Mag immediately walked away from us and stared at Elton Castle. She didn't say a word, not until you woke up and even then, I sensed she was holding something back. Why didn't she land right next to Elton? It's not completely demolished yet, so we know the golden dragon isn't here. It's not like we have to be careful, right?"

"I don't know," I said. "Didn't the golden dragon leave before us? What's taking him so long? Maude and Cessala said the imposter would be going after Hugo and the books. Maybe they were wrong."

I glanced up at the sky, but the golden dragon was nowhere to be seen.

We arrived at the bridge spanning the river, which separated us from Elton Castle. I was half expecting to see the resident goblin and crocodile who guarded the crossing: Tarboone and Little Darling.

The first time we met them, we were trying to explore Elton Castle and the surrounding area. I had been partially across the bridge, when a crocodile burst from the water, a goblin on her back. The goblin had dismounted and introduced himself as Tarboone and the crocodile as Little Darling. They wouldn't let us pass until we told them our names, which Artie was reluctant to do.

Now we had no problem getting over the bridge. No goblin or crocodile stopped us this time.

"That was disappointing," Artie said. "Not that I want Tarboone and

Little Darling to waylay us like last time, but I do miss them."

"I know. I was looking forward to seeing them too. I hope they're all right."

A hoarse laugh interrupted us. It was coming from beneath the bridge.

"I'm *so* touched, you two. I didn't know you cared."

Smiling, Artie and I scrambled down the muddy bank. There, standing on the riverside was Tarboone. He was disheveled and soaking wet, but he still looked the same. The goblin was three feet tall, with pale skin, pointed ears, and fiery red hair.

"Hello, Tarboone."

"How long have you been waiting? Why are you wet?"

"Good to see you, Penelope, Artie," he said, grinning up at us. "I got here moments before you. The reason I'm wet is because Little Darling threw me in the river."

I blinked in surprise. "Why would she do that?"

Tarboone shrugged. "No idea. I think she was trying to protect me. Hey, where's Mag?"

"Where's Little Darling?" I countered.

"Off at the castle," Tarboone said. "Mag?"

"Off in a clearing."

We stared at each other for a moment, before Tarboone burst out laughing again. "Oh, perfect! What's Mag up to in the glade? I think I'll go pay her a visit." He started to leave, then turned back, his expression serious. "Watch yourselves around Elton Castle. There's been a chill in the air these last few days. It's unnatural."

Tarboone walked away.

"What do you mean *unnatural?*" Artie called after him. "Tarboone?"

The goblin raised his hand in farewell, but didn't say anything.

I shook my head in mild bemusement. It was so hard to get answers out of him. "What do you think, Artie? Should we go help Hugo and Little Darling against this unnatural chill or head back to Mag?"

Artie looked back and forth, between Tarboone's retreating back and the distant ruins of the castle. "Elton," he said. "Mag can take care of herself. If the golden dragon appears, Hugo will need our help."

I glanced in Mag's direction, before nodding. "You're right. Hugo first. Let's go."

Chapter Seventeen

A Troll and a Crocodile

The moon was high as we approached Elton Castle. The ruins looked imposing in the moonlight, but I knew within those walls was our dear friend Hugo. We had to find him.

That was easier said than done. Elton Castle was massive.

All was quiet as we neared the front doors. Not even the wind stirred. I shivered. Tarboone wasn't kidding. There was a cold sense of foreboding in the still night air.

Artie and I stood on the threshold of the castle, the oak doors towering above us. Neither of us knocked. The silence stretched.

Bam!

A deafening bang had come from within Elton Castle, reverberating outside. A symphony of birds, squirrels, chipmunks, and other woodland animals rose as one, chittering and squawking at the noise.

"What was that?" Artie said, raising his voice so he could be heard.

We got out answer when a side door burst open, revealing a troll with reading glasses perched on top of his head.

Hugo!

He was carrying an armload of books and was hurrying away from the castle. Behind him was a crocodile pulling a cart full of ancient-looking scrolls.

"I think we found Hugo and Little Darling."

"They're definitely in a hurry." I stepped forward and called, "Hugo! Little Darling! Over here!"

They both turned, but far from looking delighted, Hugo's expression was one of fear.

"Penelope, Artie, behind you!"

Looking back, I caught a glimpse of a tree falling, before Artie yanked me out of the way. *"Oof!"* I gasped as I landed painfully on my side.

The tree slammed into the ground where I had been standing moments before. Dirt, dust, and leaves flew everywhere. Choking, my eyes watering from the debris, I saw a huge figure stride into view. I couldn't see who it was, but he picked up the tree with ease.

"Stand still and take it like a witch," our attacker growled. He raised the tree higher.

With cries of alarm, Artie and I rolled over and scrambled to our feet, just ahead of the second strike. That's when I saw who we were up against.

"Laborc," I said.

The corners of his mouth twisted upward in a malicious grin. "Miss me?"

Laborc was a troll. Like Hugo, he was about eight feet tall, had hard scaly-looking skin, a greenish hue, and arms and legs like tree trunks. But whereas Hugo was wearing a neat little blue vest with red accents, black slacks, and a blue cloak with gold stars, Laborc had an ill-fitting steel plate over his chest and a grimy pair of brown pants.

"What are you doing here?" Artie demanded.

Laborc smiled, revealing, pointed fangs. He hefted the tree over his shoulder and countered, "What brings two tiny humans to troll territory?"

"Elton Castle doesn't belong to you," I said boldly. "This was the first capital of Alsmora. It's Hugo's home."

"Exactly. Hugo may be a disgraced troll, but he's still a troll. That makes the castle ours."

Off in the distance, Hugo was frantically flipping through books. He looked up a couple of times as if to make sure Laborc wasn't beating us to a pulp.

"I'm curious, Laborc," I said. "Hugo's lived in Elton Castle for years and you haven't tried taking over. Why now?"

The cruel troll laughed. "You really are dense. I haven't had the power to take Elton Castle for my own until now."

"Meaning that you work for the golden dragon," Artie said. He took my hand and the two of us began to back up. Laborc stalked toward us.

"Of course," he said. "How else would I have the power to seize Elton? The only obstacle in our way was Hugo, and now, you. No matter. This won't take long." He raised the tree.

Quick as a flash, Artie whipped out his knife and I drew my sword. Dropping Artie's hand, I said, "Bad news, Laborc. There are two of us and only one of you."

To my surprise, he didn't attack, but bellowed at the top of his lungs.

At first, nothing happened. He just stood there, weapon raised, not moving. Artie and I glanced at each other, confused.

"Sorry, Laborc, it looks like your little ploy didn't work," I said.

There was a mighty crash from the forest, followed by a second. It sounded as if someone was knocking down trees.

That can't be good, I thought, watching the tree line apprehensively. With a thunderous roar, a whole horde of trolls flooded out into the open.

My mouth went dry as I looked at the mass of trolls, some of whom were armed with wooden spears. There were too many of them. Now we knew what Little Darling was protecting Tarboone from. I glanced hopefully at Hugo, but he was still flipping through his books, apparently too focused on his task to notice. Little Darling thrashed her tail, but even that didn't help. Hugo was nose-deep in a book.

"I think you stand corrected, Bogg," Laborc gloated. "Trolls, attack!"

The horde let loose a battle cry, which caused a murder of crows to abandon a nearby tree. One of the birds broke away and headed straight for Hugo, but I had no time to focus on that as the trolls came rushing toward me and Artie.

Together, we ducked as a troll swung a club right at our heads. I deflected the club, at the same time Artie stabbed another troll in the leg with his knife.

"Nice one, Artie!" I called.

"Thanks. Pen, to your left!"

I spun around and stopped a troll who was aiming for my stomach with a spear. I blocked him, metal clanging against wood, but the troll was too strong. Sneering, he pushed against our interlocked weapons, forcing me back. My sword was the only thing preventing the troll from impaling me. I couldn't even reach for my amulet, because I needed both hands on the hilt. My arms were shaking.

Squawk!

The troll and I both looked up as a crow landed on his head and began to peck him mercilessly.

Startled, the troll withdrew his spear and flailed it wildly in the crow's general direction. My feathery ally dodged easily.

I stood off to the side, panting.

The bird cried in pain as the spear grazed his wing. I tightened my grip on my sword and slashed at the troll. He stumbled back, right into the river. He roared and clawed at the bank, but the current swept him away.

"Good riddance," the crow said, landing on my shoulder.

"Milo?"

We had met Milo recently in Silent Stream, while gathering supplies. He had annoyed everyone with his constant yammering. The last I'd seen him was at Maude's house in Cherry Grove.

"Hello, Penelope. Long time, no see. Hugo wanted me to deliver a message. Can't give it to you if you're dead."

"Gee, thanks."

Milo continued. "He said to use the spell, *Brinze.* No idea what it does."

"I'm sure I'll find out. Hold on, Milo. *Abselen.*"

His wing glowed green for a moment. When the light faded, he was healed.

Milo flexed his wing. "Thanks," he crowed delightedly.

"Don't mention it," I said and turned back to the rest of the battle. My heart sank. Artie was fighting several trolls at once, but I could see him tiring. He wouldn't be able to last much longer. More trolls had replaced the ones we had already defeated.

"Milo. Get Mag. She's in the glade across the river."

He nodded and flew off at once.

"Hurry, Mag," I whispered, when a troll nearly struck me with his sword. I quickly blocked it. Deciding that I had nothing to lose, I placed my hand on my amulet and shouted, *"Brinze!"*

For one scary moment, nothing happened. A gentle breeze wafted through the air, but besides that, everything else was the same. The battle still raged on around me. Then, the wind picked up. It began to gust faster and faster, until it turned into a full-out gale. Everyone stopped fighting to stare.

Hurricane level winds begin whipping around the clearing, sucking up every troll in its path, except for Hugo. Incredibly, I was still on my feet, as was Artie. I made my way to him, as every troll unlucky enough to be caught in the tempest was carried off by the wind and dropped in the river.

The wind died down, leaving everything calm once more.

"That was amazing, Pen!" Artie said. "I didn't know you had power over wind."

"Neither did I," I said, rubbing my temples. My head was pounding like it was about to split open. The strain of controlling the wind had been almost too much.

Closing my eyes, I leaned against Artie for support. He wrapped his arms around me in a tight embrace.

Time seemed to stand still as he held me. A magical spark surged between us.

When I opened my eyes, I smiled up at Artie. "Thank you."

"For what?"

"For being you."

Artie blushed.

Milo darted up to us and said, "Mag's on her way, but I think you two have bigger problems at the moment."

He pointed with his wing and my heart dropped. The trolls were clumsily climbing out of the river and they did not look happy.

"Oh, this is not good," Artie said.

"Understatement of the century," I muttered. I tried to step forward, but my knees buckled. I was still too weak from the spell.

"Pen," Artie said, putting his arm around my shoulders. He was the only thing keeping me upright. "Look."

There seemed to be a commotion down by the river. All the trolls were turning and attacking something hidden in the trees. I couldn't see what it was, but I could hear it growling fiercely.

I shivered. With any luck, I'd never have to face that monster.

"Penelope, Artie, welcome," Hugo called.

I tore my eyes from the scene below. Hugo was striding up to us. Little Darling was not far behind, pulling the book cart. Milo fluttered gently onto her back.

"Hugo, good to see you! Thanks for the wind spell. I thought we were done for when those trolls attacked."

Hugo smiled. "I'm just glad I found it in time. As you can see, I had a lot of books to search through."

"No offense," Milo said, spreading his wings, "but I'm going to go check out the fun over there. Be back soon. Where is Mag? She said she'd be here in a minute."

Before we could say anything, Milo shook his head and flew off, leaving Artie and I with the bookish troll and the faithful cart crocodile.

"Are you well, Penelope?" Hugo asked, squinting at me in concern.

"I'm fine, Hugo. Just used a bit too much magic."

I held my amulet up for him to see. The silver crescent necklace, caught in the amulet's chain, came up with it.

Eyes wide, Hugo opened his mouth to speak, when the fight by the river reached a fevered pitch. As one, every troll had bellowed defiantly at their mysterious opponent. I grinned when I saw who it was. Definitely not a monster.

A red dragon was battling her way through the onslaught of trolls. They tried to overwhelm her with sheer force of numbers, but she batted them brutally aside, sending them sailing into the river or onto the rocks with sickening crunches. The remaining trolls broke and fled until only the red dragon was left standing. She snorted and flew up, landing on the spires of Elton Castle.

"Mag?"

She turned toward us. Her eyes were completely white.

CHAPTER EIGHTEEN

THE SILVER MOON

Laborc and his army had scattered. It was just two humans, a troll, and a crocodile facing an angry dragon.

"Mag? Mag, are you all right?"

She roared. She didn't seem able to speak.

"Mag!"

"Pen, what are you doing?" Artie cried, pulling me down.

"Trying to calm her," I said, yanking my arm away. "We have to help Mag!"

"Penelope," Artie said, stepping in front of me, forcing me to look at him. "I think Mag has gone wild!"

It took several seconds for me to register his words. Mag, gone wild? There was no possible way that could be true. But even as I denied it, I looked at her. Her eyes were like Ash's when he was a wildling: blank and white.

I looked for the Mag I knew. She had to be in there somewhere, but all I could feel from her was anger.

"Don't lose hope, Penelope," Hugo said quietly. "Milo told me you helped Ash when he was a wildling. What did you do for him?

"I jumped on his back and used *Abselen.* But how do I get to the top of the tower to use it on Mag?"

"Simple," Tarboone said, as he emerged from the trees. "You have to scale the battlements."

"Tarboone! Where have you been? What happened to Mag? You were with her. How did she turn wild?"

"All in good time, Penelope. As for the problem at hand, if I were you, I would hurry and calm her down. Wild dragons are notorious for starting fires. I wouldn't want to be in the way when Mag starts throwing fireballs, would you?"

"But…"

"He's right, Pen," Artie said. "Let's save Mag first, then we can question Tarboone."

I looked between dragon and goblin. I wanted answers and Tarboone was clearly the one to give them to me, but I couldn't leave Mag like this. She was my friend.

"Hugo, what's the quickest way into the tower?"

"Side door," he said. "Little Darling and I escaped with the books right before Laborc and the other trolls arrived. I locked the door, but I can open it for you."

"I'll come with you, Pen," Artie said. "Mag's my friend, too."

I smiled. "Thanks, Artie."

"Little Darling and I will stay here," Tarboone said. He was watching Mag warily. "We'll look after your books, Hugo."

"I appreciate it, Tarboone. Thank you."

"Go!"

With Mag still roaring in the background, Artie, Hugo, and I raced to the side door. We found a large boulder blocking our path, jamming the door in place.

"Ah," I said. "This is how you locked the door, Hugo."

He shrugged. "Best I could do on short notice." He stepped forward and picked up the rock, his muscles rippling, before throwing it to the side.

"Impressive." I darted inside and found myself at the base of a circular tower. It was bare, except for a staircase spiraling upward and a door off to my right.

"The door leads to the rest of the castle, the stairs to Mag," Hugo said as he and Artie came in. "I can't go up. The whole tower is unstable while Mag sits on top. If she shifts her weight too much, everything could come crashing down. I'm sorry, but it's up to you two. Be careful."

I gave Hugo a quick hug. "You're amazing. Thank you."

He patted me clumsily on the shoulder. "Happy to help. Now, go."

I released him and Artie and I started up the stairs. Artie went first. As he put his weight on the wooden step, I heard a creak. Hugo wasn't kidding about the tower being unstable. Artie started to climb. A few seconds later, I followed.

Slowly but surely, we inched our way up. I had no idea how long we spent on those stairs. My only measure of time was when we passed by a window. The night sky was lightening to gray. Dawn was approaching.

We were about halfway up when the tower began to shake. Artie and

I were forced to steady ourselves on the wall to keep our balance.

"Mag," Artie said.

"We need to hurry. There's no telling…"

The tower began rocking again, more violently this time. I grabbed Artie's hand for support as I heard a loud *crack!* under my feet. The wooden step was breaking!

"Artie!" I cried as I started to drop.

"Penelope!" With a huge heave, Artie pulled me onto the higher step with him. "You all right?"

"Ye-es," I said, as the wood clattered to the ground far below. Without thinking, I rested my head against his chest. "That was so scary. I thought I was going to fall."

"You've dealt with worse threats than that, Pen," Artie said, giving me a quick pat on the back.

I smiled as I pulled away. "Dragons, scorpions, evil thieves, sea serpents, werewolves. I've faced them all, but somehow, there's nothing as frightening as gravity."

Taking a deep breath, I looked around and suddenly realized that Artie was on the step above mine. "Weren't we just…?"

"I climbed up," he explained. "I didn't want that step to give way too."

"Good call." I glanced up at the top of the tower. We still had a long way to go.

"We could use magic," Artie suggested. "A simple 'up' spell would do it."

I grimaced. "After summoning that hurricane, I would prefer not to risk it. What if I dropped one of us? No, Artie. We have to think of another way."

"Like what? Mag could leave her perch at any time. We *need* to risk it." He squeezed my hand. "Trust me."

I didn't like it. I still felt weak and shaky after my earlier spell and almost falling, but Artie was right. We had to do this. For Mag.

"Ohen."

To my surprise, Artie said it with me. He stared into my eyes and new strength flooded into me. We began to hover several inches above the step.

"Artie, don't. You won't be able to stand if you keep giving me your energy."

"I'm a mundane, Pen," he said. "I can't use magic. You need my strength more than I do."

As we talked, we rose right up to the top of the tower. We landed on the highest step and the spell broke. Artie immediately collapsed into me.

"Artie!" I cried, lowering him to the ground. "Why?"

He smiled sleepily. "When a magical and a mundane are as emotionally close as we are, Pen, the mundane can give up his strength for the magical. As long as I have energy, you'll never run out of magic. Penelope." He sighed as he drifted off to sleep.

Standing, I wiped the tears from my eyes, stunned by his sacrifice. When I found my voice, I said, "Artie, I know you can't hear me, but don't *ever* do that to me again. I won't have you weakened for my sake."

He snored softly.

The step we were on was more like a platform. It was so close to the roof, that I had to stoop. Light streamed in from a trapdoor in the ceiling. It was open and I could see Mag perched right above me.

Glancing between Artie and the trapdoor, I chose the trapdoor. Artie couldn't help me now. I would get him before heading back down.

I hoisted myself onto the roof. Mag was balanced precariously, her claws gripping the slanted spire. I ducked as her tail whipped over my head.

"Mag! It's me, Penelope!" I took a step forward and felt myself sliding on the slick tiles. I reached out to steady myself and found my hand on the tip of Mag's tail. She turned to look at me and I saw her white eyes.

I gulped. "Mag?"

At my voice, her eyes reverted to amber.

"Mag!"

"Penelope," she grunted. "I'm turning wild. Run!"

"No! I'm not leaving! I'm here to heal you!" I fumbled for my amulet. *"Abselen!"*

There was a flash of greenish-blue light. At first, nothing happened. Then, Mag's whole body shuddered. Her eyes were slowly becoming white.

"Why isn't this working?" I said desperately.

"We're... too close to... the golden dragon," Mag panted. "He's... near... Elton Castle. Penelope, I need... the silver crescent."

"What?"

"Just hand it over," Mag pleaded. "Please. Hurry. I'm… fighting it, but… there isn't much time." With a grimace, she transformed, her image flickering between her two forms, before settling on human. She teetered on the edge of the roof. I reached out and steadied her so she wouldn't fall.

"It's okay, Mag," I said gently. With one hand, I dropped the silver crescent around her neck.

A tense moment passed as I waited. Mag opened her eyes. Amber once more.

"Thank you, Penelope," she said weakly.

"Mag! You had us worried."

"I know. I'm sorry," she said, straightening. "I'll explain everything on the ground." Her wings sprang out of her back. "I think I can get us down."

"Let me grab Artie," I said, hurrying to the trapdoor. I dropped down, just as Artie started to stir.

"Pen?" he rasped. "Did you save Mag?"

"I did. Let's get you out of here."

It took a few minutes, but I got him on his feet. For someone who recently had his energy drained, Artie was quite steady.

"That was fast. I was only gone for five minutes."

He shrugged. "I've done this before for Sylvia. It doesn't take long to recover. I once gave her all my energy and was back up within half an hour. She says my hard head protects me from injuries, even the magical ones."

I laughed, but I couldn't help but wonder at Artie. He said that he could give energy to witches or wizards he was close to. So far, he mentioned two: me and Sylvia. Sylvia was his sister, but how was I included in this list? Artie and I had only known each other for a few weeks. An eventful few weeks, but still…

Artie was watching me curiously. Clearing my throat, I said, "Well, you seem to be back to normal now. Come on, Mag's waiting."

As we started for the roof, I heard a faint howling below us. It sounded familiar. "Go on without me, Artie," I said. "Tell Mag I'll be there soon. I need to check something."

He nodded and disappeared through the trapdoor. I approached the side of the platform and looked down. At the base of the stairs stood Lupine.

CHAPTER NINETEEN

A DISPLACED PRINCE

I was about to call down to Lupine, when a flash of light engulfed the lone wolf. As I blinked the spots out of my eyes, I saw someone walk away, toward the inner door, and he didn't look like a large canine.

Lupine? I had seen a wolf, hadn't I? Then, why did the departing figure leave on two legs?

"Penelope?"

I glanced up and saw both Artie and Mag, in dragon form, staring down at me from the open trapdoor. They looked concerned.

"Are you okay?"

"I'm fine," I said brightly, a little too brightly, but neither Mag nor Artie seemed to notice. With one last glance at the inner door, I climbed to the roof and joined my friends.

"Finally," Mag said when I was standing beside her. "I've been on this tower far too long."

"Care to explain?" Artie said. "One moment, you were fine by the river and the next, you're roaring on top of this spire."

Mag winced. "Let's just say that the silver crescent is a big help and we'll leave it at that. I need to talk to Hugo."

"Well," I said, looking down at the ground. "It's only fifty feet."

"Oh, please. Give me a challenge," Mag said.

We climbed onto her back.

"You sure you're up for this, Mag?" I asked nervously, looking down at the sheer drop.

She turned to look at us. The necklace was sparkling around her neck. "Of course. Hold on."

Before Artie and I were ready, she extended her wings and leapt off the roof.

For a dragon who had almost gone wild, Mag glided calmly and smoothly to the ground. She landed next to Tarboone, who was now alone. Hugo, Little Darling, and the book cart had disappeared.

"Mag!" he said. "Good to see you calmed down. I hope our earlier talk was helpful."

Mag glared at him as she returned to human form. "Our talk? You mean, when you showed up in the glade and told me to 'head straight for Penelope'? I was turning wild, Tarboone! The last thing I wanted to do was hurt Penelope or Artie."

The goblin grinned. "But you didn't. I knew you wouldn't hurt your friends, Mag. You're stronger than you think."

"Strong! The golden dragon nearly mind controlled me! He did mind control me! I could feel his anger and rage worming its way into my brain, until I wanted to burn everyone and everything around me!" Mag shuddered and I could see tears sliding down her face. When she spoke again, her voice was a faint whisper, "If it wasn't for Penelope and the silver crescent, I would be a mindless husk serving the golden dragon."

"Exactly," Tarboone said.

Everyone stared at him.

"You and Penelope are linked through the dragon guardian bond. Your connection, your *friendship,* is what saved you, Mag. The necklace simply provided the focus you needed. Never forget that you two, no, you *three,* are much stronger together than you are apart."

Mag sniffled, the tears still falling. She wiped them away fiercely. "But I was weak! I'm a dragon guardian, sworn to protect Penelope against the golden imposter! Instead, I became his puppet! I don't deserve to be a guardian!"

She reached for the silver crescent, as if to yank it off.

"Hey," I said, taking Mag's hand, stopping her from ripping the necklace away. "None of that. It wasn't your fault you were mind controlled. We didn't know how to stop it before. You're safe now. He can't hurt you anymore."

"What if the golden dragon tries again?"

Artie took her other hand. "Then you'll fight him off again. You're a dragon guardian, Mag, chosen by magic itself to aid Penelope in her quest. You can do this."

"You're our friend, Mag," I said. "We can't do this without you."

We wrapped our arms around Mag in a group hug. I don't know how long we stood huddled together. When we finally broke apart, she didn't reach for the silver crescent. It stayed glittering around her neck.

"Thank you."

I smiled reassuringly at her, before addressing Tarboone, "Do you know where Hugo is? We need to talk to him."

"He took Little Darling and her cart inside. Hugo wants to put every book back in its proper place." He rolled his eyes. "Come on. We can catch him in the library."

As we started for the tower door again, I heard a rustling in the bushes. By the time I looked though, it had gone. There was nothing. Not even the wind.

When I turned back to my friends, it was to find Artie staring in the same direction.

"What was that?"

I shrugged. "No idea."

Mag and Tarboone didn't seem to notice. They were almost to the door. I made a split-second decision.

"Mag, Artie and I need to check on something. We'll be along in a minute."

She gave us a curious look, before following Tarboone inside.

"What are you thinking?" Artie said. "That we'll find something in the bushes?"

"I saw Lupine in the tower."

"He's here?"

"Yes. Artie, I… I…"

"You what, Pen?" Artie said gently.

I took a deep breath. "I saw Lupine transform. He's a human."

"Are you sure?"

"Positive. One moment he was a wolf, the next, he was a human, walking into Elton Castle."

"He's a werewolf?"

"I don't see how. He doesn't look or act like the one werewolf we've met."

"True. Aatto's a menace. I never want to meet him again."

A week ago, Mag, Artie, and I had been traveling through a small village called Wolf Bay. While there, a werewolf, a half-man, half-wolf monster, had attacked Artie. He hadn't been turned, but it was a near miss.

"I think Lupine's just a wolf with a human form. The dragons can look human. Why not a wolf?"

"I don't know," Artie said thoughtfully. "Something still doesn't feel right."

As we talked, we searched the bushes at the edge of the tree line. I doubted Lupine was still there, but he might have left a paw print or two to track later.

Artie parted a bush and leapt back in surprise. "Penelope! I found someone!"

"Lupine?"

"No, not Lupine," he said. "Not unless I'm looking at him as a human."

At the base of a tree was a teenage boy with shaggy, black hair. He was so pale, he seemed to emit an unearthly glow. His eyes were closed, as if in a deep sleep.

"We should get him back to the castle," Artie said. "We can't leave him like this."

"Wait," I said, frowning.

"What's wrong?"

I took Artie's arm and dragged him off to the side. "I recognize him," I whispered.

"You do? Is he an old friend?"

"No. I only saw him recently. Artie, that's Mir."

His eyes widened. "Queen Rebecca's brother? I thought he died during the troll attack. How did he survive and why is he still a teenager?"

"No idea." I hesitated. I knew we had to get him inside, but something about Mir's behavior in Rebecca's memory was off-putting. He seemed a bit too eager to become king.

Despite my uneasiness, I knelt next to the prince and shook his shoulder. "Mir? Mir, wake up."

Slowly, he opened his eyes. They were a deep brown. "Where am I?" he said. "Who are you?"

"Penelope and Artie," I said. "We're in front of Elton Castle. You're Prince Mir, I presume?"

"I am. Are you new to the castle?"

"No," Artie said, "we've been here before."

"Oh, well." Mir stood and stretched. "You must be here to see my father, King Cecil. I was heading that way myself. I'll take you to him."

"Mir," I said. "What's the last thing you remember before waking up?"

"I was talking to Rebecca. Our parents are going to make a big announcement today and I wanted to let her know." He glanced around, confused. "I saw her a few minutes ago. Where is she?"

Artie and I exchanged a glance. This would be painful.

"Mir," I said gently. "About Rebecca and your parents…"

"Oh? Did my dear mother and father send you to find me?"

"No," Artie said. "We've never spoken to them, but Penelope knows Rebecca."

"Yes?"

I sighed. This was getting us nowhere. I would just have to break it to him. "Mir, your sister and parents aren't around anymore. King Cecil and Queen Winona died in a troll attack a hundred years ago. Rebecca's gone, too."

Mir stumbled back. "What? No! I left Rebecca by the river! Mother and Father are waiting for us in the castle! They can't be dead!"

I reached out to steady him. For a split second, I thought I saw hatred flashing in his eyes, but I blinked and it was gone. I must have imagined it. Pushing my doubts aside, I smiled and said, "Maybe we should head inside Elton Castle, Mir. We might find a clue as to what happened."

"Yes," he said distractedly. "Yes, let's go. I have to know." He marched off toward the castle.

Artie leaned in and whispered, "I can see what you mean, Pen. He's very intense."

"You got that right. In Rebecca's memory, he seemed almost eager for his parents to die and leave him the throne. Now, he's remorseful."

"Grief can hit us all in different ways," Artie said as we started after Mir. "Maybe he didn't realize how much he loved his family until they were gone."

"Maybe," I said, "but something seems off."

We caught up to Mir at the castle's main doors.

"Why won't these open?" he said, pounding on the wood. "Where are the servants? They should have arrived promptly to my summons."

"Elton Castle has been abandoned for a century," Artie said. "The only one who lives here now is Hugo. You can usually find him in the library."

"Well, why didn't you say so earlier?" Mir snapped. "Come on. I know where to find the side door."

He rounded the corner, his expression like a dark storm cloud.

I shook my head. "What do you think of his grief now?"

"It could still be there," Artie said. "Just under that princely attitude of his."

Before we could follow Mir again, the front doors were thrown open to reveal Tarboone and Little Darling, now cart-free, standing on the threshold.

"Who was pounding on the door?" Tarboone asked.

"Not us," I said. "We heard a rustling in the bushes and found Prince Mir unconscious. We woke him up. He was the one pounding."

Tarboone frowned. "Prince Mir?"

"Queen Rebecca's younger brother. He's still alive."

Tarboone's eyes widened and Little Darling swished her tail in agitation. "Rebecca's brother? Not possible. He must be in his hundreds by now."

"Try teens," Artie said. "He can't be more than fifteen or sixteen."

"This complicates matters," Tarboone said thoughtfully.

"How?"

"Who's the rightful ruler of Alsmora? Alana, Queen Rebecca's granddaughter, or Mir, Queen Rebecca's brother. This will be interesting, especially if he tries to take the throne."

"We'd better talk to Hugo," I said. "He's a scholar. He must have some idea who inherits."

Artie and I stepped inside, past the goblin and crocodile. Without anyone even touching them, the doors swung shut behind us. The sound echoed throughout the quiet halls of the old castle.

CHAPTER TWENTY

SORROW AND HOPE

Elton Castle was big and deserted. The entryway itself could easily fit Mag in dragon form and she was ten feet tall. Time and the troll attack had not been kind. It had probably been impressive a hundred years ago, but now everything was in ruins. Grime covered every surface and a chandelier was lying smashed at the foot of a cracked marble staircase.

I stepped forward, but I wasn't looking where I was going and tripped over a worn and faded rug. "Ow!" I wasn't really hurt, except for my pride.

"You okay, Pen?"

"I'm fine." I was about to scramble to my feet, when I saw the paw print in the dust.

"Lupine."

"That wolf has been hanging around lately," Tarboone said. "Little Darling and I saw him when he first arrived. He's harmless."

"Do you know where he is? I want to ask him about this." I pulled out the ragged piece of paper I'd retrieved from Maude's.

Tarboone leaned forward. After one glance, he froze, gaping at the two words written there.

Gideon, *Entalen.*

"We think it says, 'Gideon, awake,'" Artie said, "but we're no closer to understanding it. Who is Gideon? What is he awakening from?"

Tarboone sighed. "I'm not the best person to ask. All I know is that Gideon suffered a tragedy sixteen years ago and became a recluse. Nobody but his closest friends and family have seen him since. It's a shame. He used to be really popular. As a sign of respect, nobody talks about him. We value his privacy. Everyone would love to see him again, though. If anyone can convince him to rejoin Alsmora, it'll be Olivia."

Off to our right, a door banged open and a harassed-looking Mag came stalking out of the library, followed by Hugo. Bringing up the rear was Mir.

"Olivia?"

Tarboone didn't answer as he and Little Darling slipped out the front door. Mag made a beeline for me.

"Penelope, tell this… *prince* that Hugo and I are *not* his servants." Smoke curled from her nostrils.

"You are living in *my* castle," Mir said, flicking a dust particle from his sleeve. "My castle, my rules."

"You just woke up!" Mag snapped. "Besides, this castle has been abandoned for a century! If anything, this is Hugo's castle!"

Hugo held up his hands. "If we could please calm down."

"What are you even doing in my castle?" Mir demanded. "Trolls destroyed my home and killed my family. How could the people of Alsmora give Elton to this… this… thing?!"

"Enough!" I yelled, stepping in between Mag and Mir. "Mag, we found Mir passed out at the base of a tree. He has no idea what's going on. Be nice."

Mag rolled her eyes and turned away.

"Thank you, minion—"

"As for you," I interrupted, glaring at Mir. "You may have been born a prince, but that does *not* give you the right to treat my friends like servants. This is Hugo's home now. He restored the ruined library. You should be thanking him."

Mir gaped at me, his face deathly white and his hands balled into fists. I doubted anyone had ever spoken to him like that before.

A moment elapsed and then Mir smiled. It didn't quite reach his eyes. His hands unclenched. "You're right, Penelope. Forgive me. I haven't been myself lately. It all started earlier today, I mean, a hundred years ago. I was just so excited for my father's announcement that I've been snapping at everyone. I'm sorry. Truly, humbly sorry. Would you all, please, help me to restore Elton Castle? With any luck, it will at least be habitable by the time I start my reign."

Nobody moved or spoke as we all stared at Mir. Mir didn't seem to notice. He was too busy studying the chandelier, probably trying to figure out how to reattach it.

I sighed. I couldn't let him live in this delusion any longer. "Mir, you can't be king."

"Why not?" he said, without even looking up. "You said Rebecca and my parents are dead. I'm the only one left. I'm the new sovereign."

"We already have a monarch," Artie said. "Queen Alana."

"What! I disappeared for a century and you found a new ruler?"

I was working out how to let him down gently, when Mag growled, strode up to Mir, and spun him around to face her.

"Hey! You can't—"

"Listen up, you pompous prince," Mag said. "Rebecca didn't die in the troll attack. She escaped and started a family. Her *granddaughter* is Queen Alana."

"Ah," Mir said. "I guess that means I can't be king, after all." He shrugged Mag off and walked, seemingly dejected, toward the doors.

"Mir? Where are you going?"

"To the gardens," he said vaguely. "I have a lot to think about."

As Mir reached the door, he looked back. His eyes flashed green and brown. I blinked and they were green once more. It must have been a trick of the light. Still, I felt uneasy.

Once Mir had gone, Hugo sighed. "Poor kid. I feel sorry for him."

"Sorry?" Mag snorted. "Hugo, he was horrible! Way too entitled, bossy, and a thief."

"A thief?" Artie said. "Come on, Mag, you've traveled with me long enough to know that it's only stealing if it's not yours. Mir did live in the castle."

"Oh, yeah? Then, why did he try and take this?" Mag held up the silver crescent. "He tried to yank it away from me the moment he saw it. I barely managed to stop him. He's lucky he didn't get shocked!"

"Mir was probably just surprised," I said. "I mean, you are wearing

Queen Rebecca's old necklace. Maybe he wanted a keepsake."

"I don't think so," she said. "You didn't hear him. He called it 'my necklace,' not 'my sister's necklace.' Plus, he just brushed past Hugo when he entered. It's like he doesn't even care that trolls killed his family. No offense, Hugo."

"None taken."

"Let's give him time," I said. "His whole world has been turned upside down. He needs a chance to breathe and consider his next move. In the meantime, what did you find out about the necklace, Mag? How did it stop you from going wild?"

"Hugo was starting to explain when Mir showed up," she said. "What were you saying, Hugo?"

"Oh, yes," he said. "Queen Rebecca's silver crescent. There have been numerous accounts of both its beauty and power. If you would kindly join me in the library, I have more information on the subject."

We stepped into the library. Hugo had done a lot of work already to fix it up, but it was still a mess. Most of the bookcases had toppled over and torn and battered books littered the floor, but right in the center of the library were a couple of upright bookcases, a table, and a few chairs. Books filled the shelves and, judging from their pristine covers, were well cared for.

"I love what you've done with the library, Hugo. Did you restore these yourself?"

"Yes. I've always had a unique affinity with books. It used to drive the other trolls mad."

"What do you mean?"

"Here, I'll show you." Hugo picked up a small, blue book. It was faded, the binding was peeling, and the pages were water damaged. Holding the book in one hand, he waved his other down the length of the spine. *"Beredan."* It glowed purple for a moment, before the binding snapped into place.

He flipped the book open. I could see the drooping, water logged pages, but I couldn't make out the writing before he waved his hand again. *"Tokelen."*

I watched, amazed, as water began to seep out of the paper. It was like something was drawing the water out, leaving the pages dry once more. Hugo tipped the book forward and the water pooled at his feet.

He wasn't done yet. Closing the book, he waved his hand for a third time, along the cover. *"Ernafen."* Purple light radiated out. I averted my eyes before it dazzled me. When it had faded and I was able to look again, I saw that the book had been restored. It looked as flawless as the day it was printed.

"That was amazing, Hugo," I said, awed. "Is this why the golden dragon is after you?"

Hugo slipped the book onto a shelf and nodded. "I believe so. I can do this with almost any ruined book. The golden dragon did his best to stamp out all knowledge during his first reign of terror. We can't let him try again."

"As fascinating as this is, could we please get back to the silver crescent?" Mag reminded us loudly. "You said you had a book that explained it."

"Forgive me, Mag, you're right." Hugo made his way to the table in the center of the library. "Step carefully now. The book we want is right this way."

"What kind of books have you restored?" Artie asked. "I'm guessing all historic tomes and illuminated manuscripts, right?"

"A few, yes, but I've also uncovered quite a few fiction novels. Did you know that Queen Winona had a fondness for romance books?"

"Really? Aren't those your favorite as well?" I asked, as I browsed through the titles.

"They are, but who doesn't love a good romance? Ah, here it is!" Hugo pulled a thick green book off the shelf.

"*A Dragon's War: Tales of the Past,*" I read. "By C.M. Aude. Cessala and Maude again."

"Yes," Hugo said as he flipped through the pages. Perched on his nose were his reading glasses. "After defeating the golden dragon, Maude and Cissy had quite the illustrious career as writers. Didn't they tell you?"

"No."

"You might want to ask them sometime. They're surprisingly astute scholars." While he talked, Hugo continued to search through the book. "Here it is." We crowded around him to look. The right-hand page contained text, while the left showed a portrait of the silver crescent necklace.

"It's beautiful," I said, running my hand down the page.

"Princess Marian drew it as a young woman," Hugo said.

Mag tilted her head. "Princess Marian?"

"Queen Rebecca's daughter," I explained. "And Queen Alana's mother."

Mag shrugged. "Never heard of her."

"She died soon after I was born," I said. "From what I understand, she was responsible for harsher laws on thieves."

Artie grimaced. "My dad hated her. According to him, Marian almost single-handedly destroyed the Quick organization." He paused and considered the picture. "She was a good artist, though."

"One of the best. Now, as for the necklace's history." Hugo buried his nose in the book. A few minutes of silence passed as we watched him read. He sighed and looked up. "It's a sad tale. I'll give you the abridged version.

"When the trolls attacked that fateful night, Rebecca was in the throne room with her parents, King Cecil and Queen Winona. A guard named Alexander was able to shepherd her to safety, while the king and queen held off the trolls. The only thing Rebecca was able to bring with her was the necklace, a gift from her mother.

"Once they were outside and far enough away from the trolls, Rebecca collapsed on the ground and started to weep. Alexander tried to comfort her, but her grief was too strong. She began to sing, lamenting all that was lost that day. A tear slid down her cheek and onto the crescent.

"Now, in those days, far more people had magic. The tear was imbued with Rebecca's own magic, infusing the necklace with her longing, regret, and sorrow."

"This is heartbreaking."

"It is," Hugo agreed. "The necklace can do amazing feats, like protect you from evil magic, increase your strength, and even negate other spells, but it will always take something from you in return."

"Such as?"

"Well, Rebecca lost her family, Marian lost the love of the people, and Alana, well, I don't know what, if anything, she's lost."

"What about me and Mag?" I asked nervously. "What will we lose?"

Hugo shook his head sadly. "I don't know. We'll have to wait and see."

"Is it possible to use the crescent's magic without losing anything?" Artie asked. "It gets its power from regret and sorrow. Could we somehow change that to love and hope?"

"Actually, there might be a way," Hugo said, turning back to the book. He read, frowning the entire time. This did not bode well. Finally, he said, "I'm sorry, Penelope. I don't know."

"It doesn't tell you?"

"No, it definitely describes the silver crescent's magic, but I can't translate it. This section is written in elvish. I knew I should have studied more elven texts."

"Hugo," Artie said. "Can you read any of it?"

"Enough to know that you're going to need help from the elves, both to translate the writing and to nullify the necklace's side effects."

"What do the elves have to do with this?" I asked. "Maude and Cissy wrote the book. Why is part of it in elvish?"

"The elves were the ones who made the necklace," Hugo explained.

"They probably asked Maude and Cessala to keep the information secret, so it wouldn't fall into the wrong hands. It might be a good idea to visit them and learn more."

"Where can we find the elves?"

"In Vanguard Forest. Luckily for us, Elton Castle was built right on the edge of Vanguard. You'll have to make your way to the elven capital of Ilyana Glen, which is in the heart of the forest. Simple."

"Oh yeah, really simple," Mag said, rolling her eyes. She stood and stretched. "Let's get this over with. The less time I have to spend with the elves, the better."

"What about Maude and Cessala? They're expecting to meet us here," I said.

"I'll tell them where you went," Hugo promised. "They know their way around Vanguard."

"Tomorrow morning, then," Artie said. "We'll get a good night's sleep and head for the forest at dawn."

"In that case," Hugo said, smiling warmly, "welcome to my home. Let me show you to your rooms."

Chapter Twenty-One

Fairy Hollow

Before following Hugo upstairs, Mag, Artie, and I headed outside to find Mir.

"He did say he was going out into the garden, right?" Artie said, as we stepped out into the gathering twilight.

"I think so. Remember we need to be gentle with him. Being displaced from your own time would overwhelm anyone."

Mag rolled her eyes, but didn't speak.

We rounded the corner of the castle and stopped dead in our tracks. I'd never been behind Elton Castle before. We were standing in an overgrown garden, the centerpiece being an enormous apple tree. Flowers grew everywhere. Borders meant nothing to the plants.

"This is a mess," Mag said. "How are we going to find anything in this jungle, let alone one arrogant prince?"

"Oh, come on, Mag," I said, smiling. "Look on the bright side. These flowers are beautiful. Who needs straight lines, when all you need is for things to grow?"

"Well, they're definitely growing," Artie said, "but where are the paths?"

"There." I pointed toward some cobblestones. "Those seem to be leading to the apple tree."

"Good luck following it, though," Mag said. "The plants are growing wild over the cobblestones, as well."

"If Mir is indeed in the garden, I don't see where else he could have gone," I said. "We might as well check out the tree."

Nobody had any better ideas. The garden was enclosed by Elton Castle on three sides. On the fourth, it was backed by a forest.

"Vanguard Forest," Artie said. "Home of the elves. Mir's not in there."

"How can you be so sure?"

"The elves are protective of their territory. Trust me. There's no way Mir could have entered."

As we talked, we picked our way carefully across the cobblestones, so as not to step on the plants. We reached the tree and looked around. There was no sign of Mir, only an old and broken bench.

"No entitled, whiny prince here. Where is he?" Mag said, swatting at a shining insect buzzing around her head.

The insect landed on my arm and said, "I could tell you, if your friend would stop trying to attack me."

"What would you know about it, bug?" Mag said dismissively.

"I'm not a bug." The light around it faded, revealing a six-inch tall woman. A pair of glowing wings were on her back. "I'm a fairy. Pleased to meet you. My name is Greta."

"Penelope Bogg, Magma Everett, and Arthur Quick," I said. "I don't mean to be rude, Greta, but where have the fairies been all this time? I thought you were…"

"A myth?" Greta finished. "Don't worry. I'm not offended. It's been many years since we fairies have ventured out of our hollow and into Alsmora proper."

"What are you doing in Elton Castle's gardens?"

"The fairies live here. We always have."

"In the castle?" Artie asked.

"No, the garden. We had a deal with King Bernard, Cecil's grandfather. We allowed him to build Elton Castle here and we even shared some of our magic. In return, he and his descendants would protect the garden. I haven't seen anyone around lately, though. You're the first humans I've met in a long time."

"I'm a dragon, thank you very much," Mag muttered.

"You haven't seen a black-haired boy around, have you?" I said, ignoring Mag. "He said we could find him here. His name is Mir."

"Mir? I think there used to be a Mir in the castle. I never liked him. He always stepped on the flowers."

"I'm sorry, Greta," I said sympathetically. "Maybe he just doesn't understand."

"His sister understood. Rebecca used to always come out into the garden and spend time with us. I really miss her." Greta sighed. "Our ruler, Lady Annabel would like a word. Neither humans nor dragons have been seen at Elton Castle for a century and she wants to know what brought you back."

"You live inside the flowers, right? Is Lady Annabel coming out to see us?"

"No, you're going in to see her."

"How?" Mag said, bending over the flowers. "Hello! Lady Annabel, we're here! Come on out!"

"Not like that," Greta said. She reached into a small pouch around her waist and pulled out a tiny, glowing wand.

"What are you doing?"

Greta smiled, flew over our heads, and tapped us each with her wand. Instantly, the world began to grow, or more accurately, we began to shrink. Within seconds, we were standing on the ground next to Greta, who was now taller than both Artie and me and eye-to-eye with Mag. A rose petal was drooping over our heads.

"You might want to move," Greta advised. "That petal is drenched in water droplets. You do not want to be standing there if it falls."

"Greta, where are we? Why did you shrink us?"

"We're on the border of Fairy Hollow. If you want to meet Lady Annabel, then please, follow me."

* * *

I couldn't believe that a fairy was leading us through the Elton Castle gardens, nor that I was five inches tall.

"How long will this last?" I asked. "We won't return to our normal sizes in the middle of Fairy Hollow, will we?"

"No, no," Greta said, laughing. "I'll have to use my wand when you leave. I can't change your sizes without it."

We were strolling along the cobblestones, with flowers gently waving in the breeze above our heads, when a faint light sailed past and crashed into the ground. The light died and a fairy stood, teetering slightly.

Greta hurried over and steadied the other fairy. "Lady Annabel! Are you all right?"

"Great, Greta!" Lady Annabel said brightly. "I've been flying around on my own for the last hour and Kirsten is none the wiser." The fairy leader turned toward us. She had an angular face, bright green eyes, and the same shade of red hair as Mag. She smiled when she saw us. "Welcome to Fairy Hollow. I'm Lady Annabel, Queen of the Flowers. You must be Penelope, Artie, and Mag?"

"Yes," I said, curtseying slightly. "It's a pleasure to meet you, Lady Annabel."

Annabel laughed in delight. It wasn't what I was expecting, but nothing about the fairy queen seemed normal. I had imagined her laugh to be like tinkling bells. Instead she guffawed, leaning on Greta for support.

"Lady Annabel," the other fairy said, sounding exasperated.

"Oh, come on, Greta," Annabel said. "Not all fairies can be as refined as you and Kirsten are. I have to get out and spend time with my subjects." She rolled her eyes and loudly whispered, "Greta and Kirsten are my advisors. Every now and then, I have to get away from them. They don't seem to like that, for some reason."

"We're just trying to ensure your safety, milady," Greta said. "You can't blame us for being concerned for our ruler, can you?"

"I suppose not, but it all becomes a bit tedious after a while." Annabel's eyes flashed and she suddenly became serious. "I'm sorry. I don't mean to bore you, but we have important matters to discuss. I have it on good authority that the golden dragon has returned."

"Who told you?" Mag said sharply.

Annabel waved her hand airily. "My friend Olivia."

"Who's Olivia?"

"Not important. Now, what do you know about the night Elton Castle was abandoned?"

"The trolls attacked, the king and queen died, and Rebecca escaped," Artie said.

"Also, yada, yada, silver crescent," Mag said, inspecting her claws, trying to act casual, but I could tell she was still rattled about turning wild.

"The golden dragon was first sighted a week later," Annabel said. "The timing is highly suspicious. Why did he only appear *after* Cecil and Winona died and Rebecca ran for her life? I think it was someone with a grudge, someone who wanted the royal family out of the way, to make it easier to take over."

I frowned. "What are you saying? That the golden dragon helped the trolls ransack Elton Castle and murder the king and queen?"

"That's exactly what I'm saying. What's not widely known is that the trolls had an accomplice."

"What?! Why did Hugo or Rebecca never tell us?"

"You've been in contact with Queen Rebecca?" Annabel said. "Interesting."

Greta cleared her throat. "Lady Annabel. The accomplice."

"Thank you, Greta. Simply put, I don't think Rebecca ever knew and it wouldn't have been in any of Hugo's history books. Nobody but the trolls, their confederate, and the fairies knew the truth and even then, we don't have the full story.

"You see, a hundred years ago, on that terrible night, one of my fairies reported seeing a hooded figure with Kelraz, the leader of the trolls. She couldn't hear what they said, but after the two talked for several minutes, they separated. Kelraz led the other trolls into Elton Castle, while the human disappeared without a trace."

"Do you know who he was?"

Annabel shook her head. "The human never reappeared, but we did hear a dragon roar about the same time."

"You're right. That has to be the golden dragon," Mag said, clenching her fists. She didn't seem to notice or care that her claws were still out. "How did nobody recognize him?"

"We never saw the human's face. We can't say for sure that the hooded figure was the golden dragon, though it seems likely."

"Where does that leave us?" Artie asked.

Annabel smiled sadly. "It looks as if the golden dragon either lived or worked at Elton Castle. I'm sorry, but it could've been anyone who wanted the royal family out of the way. Whoever it is, it's clear that he's ancient, powerful, and dangerous. You'll have to be extremely careful how you proceed. My suggestion is to head to the forest. Talk to Gideon. He was alive then. He should know the golden dragon's identity."

"You're the second person to tell us to visit Gideon," I said. "You and Hugo."

"There's good reason for that," Annabel began.

"Shh!" Mag said suddenly, her eyes wide. "I hear something!"

I could hear it too. *Crunch! Crunch!* Someone was walking over the gravel at the very edge of the garden. And not walking alone.

Chapter Twenty-Two

The Fairy and the Warrior

"Mir! Wait!" a deep, husky voice called. It sounded strangely familiar, but I couldn't quite place it.

"What do you want?" Mir demanded. I couldn't see him or the other man through the flowers, but their voices clearly carried to us. Annabel and Greta flew up to get a better look. Mag, Artie, and I waited below.

"Does Queen Alana know who you are or have you swindled her as well?"

"You have me mistaken for someone else," Mir said stiffly. "I've never met her before in my life. I only woke up today."

"Drop the act. That poor, scared prince routine isn't going to work on me. How would Hugo's guests react, knowing what you truly are?"

"You're crazy," Mir said. There was a crunch of gravel again, suggesting that he had turned away.

"Am I?" There was another crunch, as if the second man had stormed up to Mir. "Maybe I'll just have a little chat with Queen Alana, to satisfy my curiosity. Then, we'll see if you're lying, *Mir*."

"Be my guest, *Lupine*. But, I wonder, who will the queen and Hugo's guests believe? Wild, savage Lupine? Or innocent, confused Prince Mir?

You'll be laughed out of court or better yet, thrown into the dungeon, where mangy mutts like you belong."

"I am human, you conniving—"

"I may be conniving, but at least I'm fully human, unlike you. Oh, sure, you may look human now, but we both know the truth," Mir said. "You'll never be anything but a wolf."

"You're one to talk. You weren't exactly the ideal prince a hundred years ago."

"The Alsmora royal court is full of deceit and deception," Mir said dismissively. "Even my parents and perfect sister were guilty of that. My father promised to make me king and then he turned around and gave it to Rebecca. She was always good at getting our parents to do exactly what she wanted. So, go ahead and accuse me of anything you want. Think what you like, but I never lied to my sister."

"And what's that supposed to mean?"

Mir laughed, a cold, clear laugh that made the hairs on the back of my neck stand on end. "Does your *pack* even know where you are, Lupine? I don't think so. Maybe I should tell them myself. Then you might stop running."

"Don't you dare," Lupine growled. "If I hear you've been anywhere near my family, I will find you, Mir."

A cloak swished and I heard Lupine retreating through the garden and out of earshot.

"As if you could do anything to stop me, wolf," Mir said and then he too left.

Annabel and Greta flew back down to us. Their faces were deathly white.

"Did you see Lupine?" I asked. "Who is he? What does he look like?"

"He was wearing a hood," Greta said. "We didn't see him."

I sighed. I wasn't any closer to learning Lupine's identity. Who was his family? He didn't seem to like them very much if he was running. But, then again, he did seem protective of them. I shook my head. Lupine was a mass of contradictions.

"What I want to know," Artie said, "is what Lupine meant about Mir swindling Queen Alana. He's never even met his great-niece."

"You're right," I said. "It doesn't make sense."

We lapsed into thoughtful silence. The flowers swayed to the rhythm of the breeze, dowsing us with dewdrops, just as Greta warned.

"If Mir has been absent for a hundred years, how do he and Lupine know each other?" Mag asked.

Artie and I looked at each other, then back at Mag.

"I… don't know," I said. "By all accounts, they shouldn't. Annabel? Greta? Any ideas?"

"Sorry," Annabel said. "I've never seen this Lupine before. I know nothing about him. As for Mir, he stepped on a few flowers when he was a child, but he hasn't caused any problems for the last century."

"He claims to have been asleep," Artie said. "Is it even possible to sleep for a hundred years?"

"There are spells that can force you into an enchanted slumber," Annabel said, "but, I've never known it to last that long." She sighed, looking weary. "I must return to the other fairies. We have much to think about, especially if the golden dragon has returned. Greta, take our guests back to the garden's edge and restore their normal sizes. I'll be in the throne room with Kirsten."

She turned to go, but paused and flitted back to us. "Good luck, Penelope, Mag, and Artie. I hope we meet again."

"Thank you for everything, Lady Annabel," I said.

She smiled faintly, before flying off, further into the garden.

* * *

It didn't take long for Greta to lead us out of Fairy Hollow. Night had settled fast. A lit candle drew our eyes to the library, where we could see Hugo's massive silhouette framed in the window.

"Who would have thought it," Greta murmured softly.

"What?"

"That a troll would be living in Elton Castle, after what they did to King Cecil and Queen Winona. The fairies were ready to drive him out, until we got to know Hugo. He is the kindest, gentlest troll I've ever met. We're lucky that he found Elton Castle, instead of Laborc and the other trolls. Hugo is a gem."

"They almost took the castle this afternoon," I said.

"Yes, but thanks to Gideon, you were able to conjure a wind and send them down the river."

There was that name again.

"Hugo and Milo gave me the spell. Who is Gideon? Nobody will tell us."

Like everyone else, Greta didn't answer.

Mag sighed. "This is getting us nowhere. Would someone kindly explain, *who* is this Gideon? I feel as if I've heard his name before, but I can't quite place him."

"Talk to Olivia. She can tell you. Now," Greta said, taking out her wand, "I should return you to your proper sizes."

"Wait," Mag said. "Don't change the subject. We don't know who Olivia is either. Tarboone mentioned her, but all he said was that she's protective of Gideon. We need answers."

Greta opened her mouth to respond, when a familiar voice called, "Hey! What's going on here? Why are you so tiny?"

We all looked up to see Milo the crow flying toward us. I smiled, remembering how he had saved me from that troll. He landed beside us.

"Hello, Milo," I said. "What are you doing here?"

He clacked his beak, obviously pleased. "I was following the trolls. Ha! They were washed so far downriver that I doubt we'll being seeing them anytime soon."

"That's great, Milo," I said. "Really, it is, but we're a little busy. Can this wait?"

He didn't seem to be paying attention. He was staring at Greta.

"Easy, Milo," she said. "What are you—"

Before Greta could finish her sentence, he darted forward and seized her wand in his beak. Transferring it to his claws, he screamed, "Shiny!" and flew off toward the apple tree, alighting on a branch and startling a couple of chipmunks, who dashed down the trunk and out of sight.

The rest of us stood there, shocked and unmoving. We needed that wand and Milo snatched it because it was shiny!

"Greta, how are we going to get to Milo when we're five inches tall?"

"I'm six inches," Mag corrected me. "And we fly, of course."

"You can still transform into a dragon?" Artie said eagerly. "Will that break Greta's magic?"

"Well, actually," Greta began, when Mag interrupted.

"Naturally. We dragons are powerful. We can break some puny fairy magic. No offense, Greta."

"None taken," she said. "But, Mag…"

"Stand back," Mag said, "unless you want to be crushed!"

Artie and I retreated under the flowers. I readied myself to cast a protection spell. Greta, however, hadn't moved. She was hovering with her arms folded.

We waited and waited for Mag to transform. Nothing happened. After several minutes, Artie and I poked our heads out from behind the flowers. Mag was still in human form.

"Need some help, Mag?" Artie called.

"I'm fine," she snapped. "*Aargh!* Why isn't this working?"

"Maybe it's because of my magic," Greta said. "Are you finally ready to listen?"

Grumbling under her breath, Mag nodded.

"Good. Fairy magic blocks all other enchantments. Until it's reversed, you're all as mundane as the rest of your kind. Even you, Mag, are more human than dragon at the moment. Your powers will return the moment I get my wand back."

"Sounds like you need our help."

We turned to find two chipmunks and a squirrel standing beside us.

"Shell, Mel, Willow," I said. "What are you doing here?"

"We came to find you," Willow said.

Willow was a squirrel and the leader of the Woodland Warriors, a group of animals who patrolled woods and forests. She wore a green vest with a quiver of arrows on her back. In her paw was a squirrel-sized yew bow. Her bushy tail was standing up straight as she surveyed the area.

Shell and Mel were known as the Riddle Chipmunks. They were siblings who liked to give us riddles whenever we met. Unfortunately, they didn't seem to realize that their 'riddles' were more like questions spoken in rhyme. As far as I was aware, nobody had ever corrected them.

The warrior squirrel and riddle-challenged chipmunks towered over us.

"What happened to you?" Shell asked. "We've never seen humans so small."

Mel chuckled. "Hey, Shell, I have a riddle for you. What do you call…?"

Shell put a paw on her brother's shoulder. "Mel, now's not the time for riddles. Why don't you try and figure out how to take the wand from Milo?"

Mel glared at Shell, looking highly affronted, before leaping into the tree.

"Thanks," Artie said gratefully. "I don't know what we'd do without you, Shell."

"You'd have to deal with Mel on your own."

I laughed. "True. Now, Willow, Shell, any ideas on how to get the wand back?"

"Way ahead of you," Willow said, notching her bow.

Artie's eyes widened. "You're not going to shoot Milo, are you?"

"Of course not. But it does make a good distraction."

She spun around and fired the arrow. I watched breathlessly as it struck the trunk, a foot from Milo. He squawked in surprise and looked up. Mel took the opportunity to spring out of hiding and jump onto the crow's back.

"Mel!" Shell cried, as the chipmunk and crow rolled off the branch and crashed onto the ground, wrestling with each other. The wand was left behind, teetering on the edge.

Greta darted forward and grabbed her wand, holding it up triumphantly. "Got it!"

The rest of us were doing our best to separate Mel and Milo, but given our size, Mag, Artie, and I had to keep ducking their flailing paws and wings.

"That's wonderful, Greta!" I called, as I got a mouthful of Mel's fur, when he was knocked against me. I spat the fur out. "But we could use some help!"

I was straightening up, when I felt a sharp tap on the top of my head and everything began to change. One moment, I was watching two oversized animals scrabbling against each other, and the next, they had shrunk to a more reasonable size. No, they hadn't shrunk. I had grown.

I looked around and saw that Mag and Artie had returned to their normal sizes as well. I reached out and seized Mel, pulling him away. Artie did the same for Milo.

They panted, staring darkly at each other. In unison, they cried, "You attacked me! No, I didn't! You did!"

"Enough, both of you!" Mag snapped.

They both stopped at once.

"Now," Mag said. "You both attacked each other. I don't care who started it. Work it out between yourselves, but *we* have to get back inside and talk to Hugo." She turned on her heel and stalked back to the castle. "Nice seeing you again," she called over her shoulder to Willow and Shell. "Greta, thanks for the magic."

Artie and I let go of Milo and Mel. They didn't move, but looked at each other awkwardly. We turned toward Mag. She was already at the castle's door. She swept inside and out of sight.

"Thanks again, Greta," I said. "It was a pleasure to meet you."

"The pleasure was mine. Now, go. Follow Mag. The fairies can do no more to help you."

Greta gave us one last wave and flitted back into the flowers.

We started for the castle. Halfway there, I noticed that Shell, Mel, and Willow were scurrying beside us. Milo landed on my shoulder.

"You didn't think we would let you get away that easily, did you, Penelope?" Willow said. "After Laborc's attack, we're going to see if Hugo needs any help."

"All of you?" Artie said. "Shouldn't we wait for the Woodland

Warriors, Willow?"

"We are the Woodland Warriors," she said. "Even Milo."

Milo puffed out his chest. "I may be only an honorary member, but I'm ten times the Woodland Warrior that Mel is."

"Cool it, you two," I said, before they could start again.

They grumbled, but didn't say anything.

"Good. After you, Willow."

"Thank you," she said, heading for the door. She had barely crossed the threshold, when someone screamed inside Elton Castle.

Chapter Twenty-Three

Memories of a Queen

We charged into the entrance hall as someone screamed again.

"Where is that coming from?" The hall was big and empty and the cry echoed around the room.

"The library," Willow said, her ears twitching. "I think Mag's in danger!"

I sprinted for the library with Artie close behind. We burst into the room, where I stopped and stared. Mag was lying on the ground, gripping her arm in pain. Hugo knelt beside her, speaking softly.

"Mag! What happened?" I asked, rushing forward.

"Mir," she groaned. "He attacked me and fled out the side door!"

"He what?"

"Mir attacked me," Mag repeated. "Hugo and I walked into the library and Mir slashed at me with a knife, injuring my arm. I didn't like that, so I burned him. He escaped out the side door. If you hurry, you can probably still catch him."

Artie and I hurried to the door and stepped outside. All was quiet. Not even the leaves on the trees stirred. Mir was nowhere to be seen.

"Missed him," Artie said, shaking his head. "What do you want to do, Pen? Stumble through the forest's underbrush to find him or go back inside to Mag?"

"Go inside," I said. "The library may hold a clue to Mir's strange behavior. Willow, do you think the Woodland Warriors could search for him?"

"Leave it to us, Penelope," Willow said and the four animals raced into the forest.

Artie and I reentered the castle. Mag was sitting up now as Hugo tended to her wound.

"Just a scratch," she said. "But I can't wait to get my claws into Mir. Did you find him?"

"No," Artie said. "Nobody was out there, Mag."

She muttered angrily under her breath.

"We won't let Mir get away with this," I promised, "but we're not going anywhere until your arm is healed. The Woodland Warriors are looking for him now."

Mag stood. "I can't sit here doing nothing! I'm going to help them."

Hugo gently pushed her into a soft, comfortable reading chair. "You're not getting off that easily. That wound needs treatment. Stay here until I get back. I need to gather some herbs. They grow right at the forest's edge. I won't be long."

"Umm… Hugo. Why don't I just use this?" I said, holding up my amulet. "I do know a healing spell."

He shook his head. "You're my guests, Penelope. It's the least I can do after you saved not only me, but also Little Darling, from Laborc and his army. Besides, Mag's injuries aren't deep. I can easily heal her with a *gemser* plant. Save your magic. I've no doubt you'll need it."

Hesitantly, I nodded.

Mag yawned. "As long as someone heals me. Just hurry up, will you, Hugo?"

"Patience, Mag. Penelope, Artie, don't let her go outside."

"She won't leave. Right, Artie?"

He nodded. "You can count on us."

Mag rolled her eyes.

Hugo smiled, picked up a nearby basket, and headed out the side door.

Mag waited until he was gone, then jumped to her feet.

"Mag," I said warningly.

"What?" she said innocently. "I'm not going outside. I'm simply walking around the library."

I glanced at Artie. He shrugged. What could we do?

Mag strolled to a bookshelf. "Oh, look," she said smirking, pulling down a book with a green cover. "*The Cheese of Love*. The story of two mice, one from the walls of a country cottage and the other from the basement of a castle, who bond over a wedge of cheese." She chuckled. "Apparently, it's a romance."

She put it back and selected another book, this one smaller, with a blue cover. It was the same one Hugo had restored earlier. "No title, but it has to be more interesting than the cheese book." She opened it. "Hey! Isn't that Rebecca's name?"

I hurried over. Mag was right. There was Rebecca's name, written in small, neat handwriting. "I've seen this before."

"Where?" Artie said, stepping forward for a closer look.

"In Rebecca's memory. Her spirit, or whatever she was, offered me tea. This book was sitting next to her." I turned the page and skimmed the first entry. "It's her diary, all right."

Artie's eyes widened. "This must have been what Mir was after."

"And why he attacked me," Mag said ruefully. "Hugo and I interrupted his search."

I flipped to the last entry and paused. It was dated the day the trolls attacked Elton Castle. I started to read.

Monday, October 12th.

The morning has a crisp, new smell in the air. I believe winter is almost upon us. Mother said not to get my hopes up, that we probably won't see the first snow for another month, at least. I know she's probably right, but I do love the snow.

After lunch, I headed to the river to think. Mother and Father have been hinting that they're ready to name the heir to the throne. They said they wouldn't decide until Mir and I are old enough. They only want the best ruler for Alsmora. Is that me or Mir? I have no idea. I get along well with the people and Mir is, well, he certainly is passionate about ruling, I'll give him that.

We were just in to see our parents. Mir strutted around the room, a bit like a peacock, until Mother and Father delivered their news. They've chosen an heir. To both Mir's surprise and mine, they chose me! I can't believe it! Will I make a good queen? I don't know, but I'll try my best. Mir stormed from the room, calling as he went that he would be king one day. His words were rather chilling. C

I reached the end of the page and stared at the last letter. Was that a 'C'?

Artie peered over my shoulder at the page. "Find something interesting, Pen?"

Nodding, I gave him the diary, as Hugo returned.

"Mag, what are you doing?" he said.

"Relax, Hugo. I'm sitting," she said, plopping herself down in the chair again. "We were looking through your books. Is *The Cheese of Love* one of your favorites?"

Hugo blinked in surprise. "Why, yes. It is. I read it all the time. Now, hold still, Mag. This might sting a bit." He pulled a blue flower from his basket. A *gemser* plant. He began working on her arm.

While Mag and Hugo were busy, Artie handed the diary back to me. "Pen," he said, worried. "What was that last word Rebecca was trying to write?"

"Maybe she was trying to repeat the word 'chilling'?" I suggested. I had no other idea what it could be. It certainly wasn't her initial.

"What do you have there?" Hugo said, as he finished bandaging Mag's arm. She hopped off the chair and both dragon and troll walked over to us. I held out the book. Hugo's eyes widened and I knew he recognized it.

"I need to talk to Rebecca," I said. "This has to be the reason why Mir attacked Mag. Rebecca is the only one who can tell us more about her brother."

"What kind of secret is worth injuring someone for?" Artie asked.

"I don't know, but I intend to find out. Mag, could I borrow the silver crescent necklace?"

* * *

A few minutes later, I was sitting in a chair, the silver crescent around my neck.

"Are you sure this is going to work?" Hugo asked, looking up from the diary. The way he peered at me through his reading glasses reminded me of an owl. I tried not to giggle at the thought.

Everyone was staring. Clearing my throat, I said, "It'll work. Rebecca told me it would."

"All right," Hugo said. "Go ahead, Mag."

Mag started to sing a slow, lilting song. As my eyes started to close, Artie reached out and gently squeezed my hand. "See you when you get back, Pen."

I smiled as I drifted off to sleep, wishing I could take Artie into the dream with me.

* * *

When I opened my eyes, I was alone on the grassy hill outside Elton Castle, overlooking the river. Pushing aside my disappointment that Artie couldn't come with me, I looked around. At first, I didn't see anything, not even birds in the trees. Then, I spotted a blonde girl watching me from the edge of the river.

"Rebecca!" I called, running up to her.

"Greetings, Penelope. What brings you here?" Unlike my mad dash,

Rebecca strolled toward me at a more sedate pace.

I stopped in front of her and tried to catch my breath. Once I could speak, I said, "Rebecca! I have to ask you about Mir!"

"Slow down, Penelope. What does my brother have to do with anything?"

"I've met him, Rebecca. I found him in front of Elton Castle, in the present."

Rebecca froze, her expression was of shocked disbelief. After a moment, she covered her eyes. She began to shake and through her hands, I could see silent tears sliding down her face.

Sniffling, Rebecca looked up. Even through the tears, she was smiling. "Thank you, Penelope. After all these years, it's nice to know that Mir lived a long and happy life."

"Well, actually," I said and told her the story of Mir sleeping through the last century, yet not aging a day. "And he attacked Mag," I finished. "We think he was after your old diary. The last entry was the day Elton Castle was attacked. You ended with the letter 'C.'"

"Oh, dear," Rebecca said quietly. "I had hoped that Mir wasn't up to his old tricks."

"What tricks? Rebecca, you're not making any sense."

She sighed. "I haven't been entirely honest with you, Penelope. Mir is not my brot…"

"He's an imposter?"

"Brother's name. Mir is not my brother's name."

"Oh," I said, blushing. "'Mir' is a nickname, isn't it?"

"It is," she said. "You know his real name, Penelope. I know you do."

"Mir. Casimir," I whispered. "Your brother is Casimir."

"Correct," she said. "The last sentence I meant to write in my diary was: *Casimir can be intense, but he is my brother and I love him.*"

"He certainly is intense," I agreed. "I've known him since I was fourteen."

* * *

Casimir was Queen Alana's magical advisor. He had shown up one day about two years ago and offered his services to the queen and her husband, King Marcus. Marcus was delighted by Casimir's 'bag of tricks' and accepted immediately. Sadly, the king died in battle soon afterward.

"Rebecca," I said, "are we sure we're talking about the same person? I know both Casimir and Mir. Casimir is in his thirties. Mir is only a teenager."

"Come now, Penelope," Rebecca scolded. "I thought you would know better than that."

"He used magic to change his appearance," I said. "He only looks fifteen."

"You're catching on fast," Rebecca said. "Casimir is really one hundred fifteen. He clearly hasn't been asleep for that century if you already know him. Who knows how he survived so long. Magic can extend your life only so far."

I nodded distractedly, my mind on something even more troubling. "Rebecca, why did Casimir lie about his name and attack Mag? What was the point? He could have told Alana that they were related when they met two years ago."

Rebecca sighed. "I don't know, Penelope. Why did Casimir stay away from me, his own sister? I would've welcomed him with open arms if he had let me. No, Casimir is up to something."

"But what? I don't understand. Yes, he's a bit creepy, but it's not like he's…" I trailed off as it suddenly dawned on me. "Rebecca, when did the golden dragon first appear? Before or after your parents died?"

Rebecca bowed her head, deep in thought. "After," she finally said. "I didn't see the golden dragon until after Alexander and I reached Kelton Castle. It was considered the family's vacation castle. Why?"

"Would you show me your first memory of the golden dragon? I have to be sure."

"Of course, Penelope." Rebecca closed her eyes and the scene around us changed. We were no longer standing in front of Elton Castle in the middle of the day. It was now twilight and we were in an upper tower of Kelton Castle.

Someone knocked softly on the door and Rebecca called, "Enter."

A young woman carrying an armload of books, scrolls, and papers walked into the room. I couldn't see her face, because her pile was so huge. As I watched, the topmost scroll fell to the ground.

"Oops!" the girl said, wobbling a bit from her uneven load. "I'm sorry, milady. It's a bit heavier than I thought."

"No matter, Victoria. Just set them down on the table," Rebecca said, taking some books from the stack. "And be aware of the fallen scroll."

Too late. Victoria had stepped on the scroll, which caused her to fall face first on the floor. As everything tumbled to the ground, I reached out to help her, but Victoria ignored my hand and scrambled to her feet. I stared at the back of her head, confused, until I remembered that she couldn't see or hear me.

"Are you all right, Victoria?"

"Yes, milady. Thank you for your concern."

That's when she turned and I got a good look at her face. I gasped. She had brown hair and green eyes and when she smiled at Rebecca, her eyes lit up. It was the same smile I had seen hundreds of times before.

Victoria looked like my mother, Alice.

"Mom?"

Neither Rebecca nor Victoria responded.

Victoria began gathering the dropped papers and arranging them on the desk. "Milady Rebecca, may I ask why you need all this information on trolls? Our informant was very wary about approaching them."

"Let's just say I'm interested in learning all I can about their leader, Kelraz."

"The troll who killed your parents?!" Victoria seemed to realize what she said, because she coughed and continued, "My apologies, Queen Rebecca. I misspoke."

"Nonsense," Rebecca said. "Victoria, I wish you would remember that you're not only a trusted advisor. We're friends. You can tell me anything."

Victoria smiled as a young man burst into the room. He had brown hair, blue eyes, and wore a guard's uniform. A medal pinned to his shirt front denoted him as a captain. His hair was disheveled and his eyes were wide with worry.

"Alexander!" Rebecca exclaimed. "What's wrong?"

"Look outside," he panted. "You won't believe this."

Together, Rebecca, Victoria, and I rushed to the window. The other two looked stunned, but I watched grimly.

The rogue golden dragon was flying across the valley, straight at us. Even from a distance, I could see the smoke curling from his nostrils and his toxic green eyes glittering with malice. Now, they were mud brown. No, one was brown, while the other was green. I grimaced. His eyes changing color was all the proof I needed.

"Call in Maude," Rebecca ordered. "I don't think we can take on that monster with our non-magical weapons. Ah, the joys of being *mundane.*"

Victoria dashed from the room, leaving Rebecca and Alexander. As she left, I decided to follow her. Why was she an exact copy of my mom? But when I got to the door, all I found was a white void where the hallway should have been. I remembered that this was a memory. I could only see and hear what Rebecca experienced at the time.

Turning back, I saw the ruler of Alsmora and her guard captain standing side by side at the window, holding hands. Rebecca even put her head on his shoulder. After several seconds, she sighed and took a step away from Alexander.

"I'd love to stay like this forever, Alex, but I need you to alert the guards."

"Of course, Bec. I'll head there now."

But they didn't move. They continued to stand there, staring at each other, while the golden dragon flew ever closer.

The moment was broken when Victoria rushed back into the room, with Maude in tow. Rebecca and Alexander jumped apart.

Alexander was the first to recover himself. He cleared his throat and said, "Right away, milady. I'll assemble the guards, just as you ordered." He brushed past Victoria and Maude and hurried out of sight.

"Mistress Maude, as you requested, Queen Rebecca."

"Yes, thank you, Victoria. You may go."

As she turned toward the door and Maude approached Rebecca, the whole scene suddenly stopped. Victoria and Maude seemed to be frozen in place. Only Rebecca and I were still moving.

"Is that enough, Penelope, or do you want to see more of the memory?"

"No, that was perfect. Thank you." I glanced outside at the immobile golden bane of Alsmora, with his two differently colored eyes. "I now know the identity of the rogue dragon."

Chapter Twenty-Four

Golden Identities

I awoke to find Artie still holding my hand. Groaning, I sat up, wondering why I felt so lightheaded.

"Mag! Hugo!" Artie called. "Penelope's awake!"

"Not so loud," I said, clutching my head.

"You okay, Pen? You've been asleep for a long time."

I looked out the window and saw that the black sky had light streaks of gray. Dawn was approaching.

"I'm all right," I said. "But my head…"

"Here," Hugo said gently, handing me a plate piled with sandwiches. "I think what you're suffering from is referred to as hunger. I made enough for everyone."

As Mag, Artie, and I all reached for the platter, I saw that Mag's arm was already fully healed from Mir's attack.

"I see you're feeling better, Mag."

She glanced down at her arm and shrugged. "Those *gemser* plants can heal anything."

"I can see that," I said. "Oh, Hugo! I love what you've done with the books!"

Artie stared at me closely. "Anything wrong, Pen? What did you learn from Rebecca?"

I sighed. I had hoped to avoid this talk until later, but Mag and Artie deserved the truth. "I found out the golden dragon's identity." I closed my eyes, waiting for the onslaught of questions.

"You *what?*"

"How did you find out?"

"Where is he?"

"Is it someone we know?"

Mag clenched her fists. "The golden dragon will rue the day he tried to turn me into a wildling."

"And he will, one day," I said, "but for now, we need to focus. He doesn't know that I know."

Mag rolled her eyes, but nodded for me to continue.

"Thank you. The golden dragon…"

Knock. Knock.

Someone was at the front door.

Before anyone could react, Willow leapt through an open window and headed straight for Hugo.

"Willow? What's going on out there?"

She ignored me and whispered in Hugo's ear. He frowned, nodding as she talked. When she was finished, she took off through the window again.

Hugo stood and started toward the entrance hall. "Excuse me, I have a guest to greet."

"Who is it, Hugo?" I asked nervously, reaching for my amulet.

He glanced back at us and said, "Penelope, whatever you have to tell your friends, tell them now. I'll keep our guest occupied. I don't know how long I can keep her out of the library. With Olivia, you never know where you stand. Go outside. I'll send word when it's all clear."

"Annabel's friend? Who is she, Hugo?"

Without another word, Hugo headed out of the library to welcome our visitor.

* * *

Hugo's voice floated back to us as we stepped out of the side door into the garden. "Olivia, it's been too long." His voice was deep and guarded.

"Yes, it has," a woman answered. "May I come in, Hugo?"

"It would be an honor."

The front door closed and I glanced at Mag and Artie. They looked as mystified as I felt.

"Why is everyone so secretive about Olivia and Gideon?" Mag said. "What makes them so special?"

Artie and I shook our heads. We were in the dark as much as Mag.

We stood by the side door, listening for Hugo and Olivia, but they didn't enter the library.

Once we were sure they weren't coming outside, Mag led us deeper into the garden. "Enough stalling, Penelope. Who is the golden dragon?"

I unclasped the silver crescent necklace and dropped it in Mag's hand. "Put that on first. I don't want you to go on a rampage after I tell you."

"Ha, ha," Mag said, as she put it around her neck.

Satisfied that she wouldn't turn into a wildling, I said, "What do either of you know about Mir?"

"Not much," Artie said. "He's Queen Rebecca's younger brother, he attempted to steal his sister's diary, and he attacked Mag. What else is there to know?"

"I'm getting to that. Now, what do you know about Casimir?"

"Who?"

Artie frowned. "Queen Alana's magical advisor?" He shrugged. "I know less about him than I do Mir. I barely glimpsed him at the gala last week."

I sighed. Why were they not getting it?

"The eyes. Describe Casimir's eyes."

"How should we know?" Mag said. "Neither of us ever truly saw him."

"What about the golden dragon?"

"Brown," Artie said.

"Green," Mag countered.

They looked at each other, confused.

"You're both right," I said. "The golden dragon has one brown eye and one green. He cast a spell on himself that confuses people into seeing only one color at a time. Either brown or green, never both."

"But why would he do that?" Artie asked.

"Because Casimir has one brown and one green eye. Don't you see? *Casimir* is the golden dragon. His spell prevents anyone from making the connection."

Silence. Neither Mag nor Artie moved. Then, the explosion of rage happened.

"Casimir! That stooge of an advisor! He attacked Alsmora a hundred years ago! He changed the dragons into… into this!" Mag gestured at her human form.

"I thought you liked being human," Artie said.

"I do, it makes it easier to walk through towns, but it's the principle of the matter!"

She paused, breathing heavily and I cut in before she could continue. "That's not the worst of it."

Mag's amber eyes were glowing. I would have to tread carefully. One wrong word could set her off again. I decided to get it over with and said, "Casimir and Mir are the same person."

The silence didn't last as long this time. Just long enough for Mag to close her eyes, take a deep breath, and scream, "We had the golden dragon within claw reach this entire time!"

"Mag, calm down," Artie said. "Hugo and Olivia will hear you."

"I don't care who hears me! I just…"

"Want your revenge," I finished. "Mag, you'll get us caught. Stop yelling."

"But—"

I placed my hand on her arm and tried to send calmness through our dragon guardian bond. It seemed to work to a degree. Mag's eyes stopped glowing.

"Good," I said. "Now, this is what we're going to do. After we talk to Hugo, we're going into Vanguard Forest. We have to find the elves. We still need their help with the silver crescent and its side effects. We'll have to be careful, though. If Casimir escaped into the forest, he might be heading for the elves as we speak. We need to warn them."

"Consider us warned," a voice said from behind us. "We don't like Casimir any more than you do."

We turned and saw a raven-haired girl staring at us. She was about my height, with a narrow, angular face and bright green eyes that seemed to gleam with a shrewd intelligence. Her arms were crossed and she was leaning casually against the wall. She was wearing an emerald green dress and brown cloak. She looked like she was one with the forest. Hugo was nowhere to be seen.

"Who are you?" Mag demanded. "Where's Hugo?"

"He's off getting some tea," she said easily. "Would you care to join us? I'm sure Hugo would love the company and I've never had tea with humans or a dragon before. I'm Olivia. You must be Magma Everett, Arthur Quick, and…" She broke off when she saw me. "Penelope Bogg," she finished.

"Did Hugo tell you about us?"

"I know enough," she said. "I've heard nothing except your name, Penelope Bogg, for the last few days. I'm here to escort you to Gideon."

* * *

We followed Olivia back into the library. Hugo was there, pouring tea into two cups. He looked up, startled, when we entered.

"We appear to have guests, Hugo," Olivia said. "More tea, I think."

"Of course," he said, as he set out more cups. "I didn't realize you all knew each other."

"We just met," I said. "Olivia was saying that she's going to take us to see Gideon."

I walked up to Hugo, who leaned closer, so I could whisper in his ear. "Hugo, what's going on? You said you would keep Olivia away. She found us almost immediately."

"Sorry," he said. "She made a beeline for the library the moment she entered. I couldn't stop her. Then, she asked for tea. What else could I do? I had to be a good host."

I sighed. "I understand, Hugo. Who is Olivia? What does she want?"

"If you two would stop whispering, I could tell you."

Hugo and I turned and found Olivia standing beside us. She was holding *A Dragon's War* by C.M. Aude. Mag and Artie were watching, their tea forgotten on the table.

Olivia smiled. "I love this book, especially the parts written in elvish. My father taught me to read the old script. I can translate it for you, if you like. That is, unless you wish to finish your tea first."

"Why should we trust you?"

"Good question, Penelope." Olivia reached up and pulled her hair away from one of her ears. It was pointed. "I'm an elf. If you want to meet Gideon without stumbling around Vanguard Forest, I suggest we leave now, before it's too late."

"Isn't Casimir hiding in the forest?"

"Thankfully, no, but the situation is still dire. Our scouts saw him skirting the tree line, until he was out of sight of Elton Castle. He transformed into the golden dragon and flew off in the direction of Kelton."

"And you did nothing?" Mag demanded incredulously. "You couldn't have at least tried to fight back?"

"Mag," Artie whispered reproachfully. "Show some respect."

"You'd be wise to listen to your friend," Olivia said coolly. "That attitude won't get you far with Gideon."

"Could you tell us more about him?" I said. "Who is he? Is he an elf too?"

Olivia sighed. She seemed to deflate slightly. "Yes, he's an elf, but his identity is complicated. Please, I can explain everything, but not until we're under the protective cover of the trees."

I glanced at Mag and Artie. "What do you think?"

"I say we go after Casimir now," Mag said. "We should strike when he's least expecting it, not stroll through a forest looking for some elf."

"You need our help, dragon," Olivia warned.

"After you let him slip away, I don't think so, elf," Mag said. "Where were you a hundred years ago when the golden dragon was first gathering power? We can do this on our own."

"What do you have against the elves?" Artie asked.

"They never do anything to help when Alsmora truly needs them," Mag said, glaring at Olivia. "They leave it to the dragons to do their dirty work."

"Is that why dragons are considered a myth among humans?" Olivia said. Her tone had bypassed cold. It was downright frigid. "At least humans know that elves are real."

"Don't make me laugh," Mag said. "Elves are as much myths as dragons are, at least as far as humans are aware."

"Plenty of humans know," Olivia countered. "My grandmother, for instance."

Mag rolled her eyes. "Of course. Just because your grandmother said so, it must be true."

"Hey! My grandmother happens to be—"

Aaroo!

We all rushed to the window and looked outside. Lupine was standing in wolf form at the edge of the forest. He nodded to the right. I looked over and gasped. Coming over the hill was a writhing, scuttling mass of black.

The scorpions, the *yikties,* were on the way.

Chapter Twenty-Five

Wolfish Pride

"I don't believe this! I thought we were finished with those scorpions," I said. "Wansetop was trapped in that cave in!"

"Just because we defeated their leader doesn't mean that the other *yikties* wouldn't attack," Artie pointed out. "They must be working for Casimir."

"Fine by me," Mag said, smoke curling from her nostrils. "I could do with setting those scorpions on fire."

"NO!" Olivia tucked the elvish book into her cloak pocket and pulled on Mag's arm. She began dragging her to the side door. "It'll cause more problems. We have to retreat to Vanguard Forest. They can't get us there. Hurry!"

"And leave Hugo to fend for himself? Not likely. We barely saved him from the other trolls," Mag said, yanking her arm free. "Who knows what the *yikties* will do to him."

"*Bechulen,*" Olivia said, flicking her hand carelessly toward Hugo. "There, only Hugo and his friends can enter Elton Castle or its grounds. Now, let's move!"

I turned toward the lovable troll. During Mag and Olivia's argument, he had been quietly arranging the tea table. "Will you be okay?" I asked.

"Of course," he said, smiling slightly. "Don't worry about me. You can trust Olivia and her magic." He placed Rebecca's diary in my hands. "Keep this with you. I'll see you soon, Penelope."

"Stay safe." I hugged Hugo and turned to leave.

Olivia led us to the side door and out onto the grounds. As we passed by Fairy Hollow, I waved to Greta, who was watching us intently. She nodded and flew back into the flowers.

We got to the border between the garden and forest before Olivia stopped. I wasn't sure why, since the *yikties* were fast approaching.

"Olivia."

"Shh! I'm concentrating."

"On what?" Mag groused. "You're just standing there."

"Do you want to be left behind?" Olivia said. "We are about to cross into Vanguard Forest. Dragons are not permitted to enter, with one notable exception. *You,* Magma Everett, are not that exception, so if you want to join your friends and meet Gideon, keep quiet."

Mag grumbled, but didn't say anything.

Olivia, smiling smugly, turned back to the magical barrier.

Artie leaned in and whispered, "I'm getting really tired of these two snapping at each other."

"Me too. Is it my imagination, Artie, or are those *yikties* getting closer?"

"Yes, they seem to be coming toward us rather quickly," he said. "Um, Olivia?"

"Would you all be quiet?" she said. "I'm taking down the Vanguard shield. It's a very delicate process. Our tress are alive. More so than your puny saplings."

"I understand," Artie said. "But if you would just…"

Olivia huffed angrily and glared at us. "Just? Just what? Let me just stop my extremely important spell because you humans want to talk. What is it?"

"Look," I said.

She turned and her eyes widened in shock when she saw the scorpions. "We can't let them reach the trees or all is lost." She gave a short whistle and Lupine appeared at her side.

"What's going on?" he asked.

"*Yikties.* A whole hoard of them. Faster than we anticipated. Lupine, could you take Mag and Artie and slow them down? Penelope and I will work on the barrier."

"What can I do?"

"You have magic, don't you? I need you to cast another temporary shield around all of Vanguard Forest, while I work to alter this one. As a human, it won't hold long over elf territory, but it only needs to last a few minutes."

Taking a deep breath, I said, "All right. I'm ready."

"Thank you, Penelope," Olivia said, sounding relieved. "My dad and grandfather are in there. I couldn't bear it if anything happened to them."

She returned her attention back to the shield and started muttering a spell.

"Will you be okay, Pen?" Artie asked.

"I think so. You'll know if I need help."

Mag, Artie, and Lupine hurried off to intercept the *yikties*. I closed my eyes, placed my hand on the nearest tree, and listened. I listened to the dew dripping from the leaves. I listened to the wind whistling past, making the branches scrape against each other. I listened to the birds chirping their songs to the air. I listened and imagined the trees extending far out over the land.

This would be one of my biggest spells yet. Holding my amulet with my other hand, I said, *"Bechulen."*

As I stood there, the birds and wind grew louder. It sounded as if the entirety of Vanguard Forest was ringing with their voices. I clapped a hand to my ear. Then, I started to shake.

My energy was fading. It was being absorbed into the tree. I tried to pull my hand back, but it was merging with the trunk!

I swayed on my feet, about to faint, when someone took my hand and yanked me back. I was free! I fell into my rescuer's arms and sobbed with relief when I saw Artie.

"I thought you might need some help."

I laughed, not caring that I sounded slightly hysterical. Artie held me gently as my energy started to return and I got my laughter under control. When I was reasonably calm, I gave Artie a hug and looked around.

Olivia's eyes were closed as she concentrated on the barrier. Mag and Lupine, meanwhile, were fighting off dozens of *yikties*. Mag was in dragon form, breathing fire at the scorpions, while Lupine was swiping at them with his claws and snapping with his teeth. As I watched, he deftly dodged a fireball that flew over his head. I glanced at the trees, worried that they might be set ablaze, but my spell was holding. The flames were bouncing harmlessly off the newly erected shield.

But Mag and Lupine were still outnumbered. There were quite a few dead scorpions scattered around them, but they just kept coming.

"Artie, we have to help them."

"Are you sure you're up to it?"

"Yes. I can do this."

We jumped into the fray. I wasn't confident enough to use my magic yet, so I drew my sword. Artie unsheathed his knife. I slashed at a *yikty* creeping up behind Mag.

The scorpion let out a hideous scream that made the hairs on the back of my neck stand on end. Mag glanced around, grinning. I shuddered. Her fangs were stained with blood.

"Pen! To your right!"

Artie's voice brought me back to reality. I ducked as another *yikty* tried to strike me with his poisoned tail. If I had been hit, the poison would have worked its way into my bloodstream, paralyzing me. As I moved, the momentum tore me away from Artie. I grasped desperately for his hand, but I lost my balance and had to somersault to safety, which took me even further away from my friend.

I stood, trying to recover, when a scorpion, larger than the rest, slammed into me, driving me facedown to the ground. I grunted in surprise and pain as my attacker rolled me onto my back, pinning me in place. The sword dropped from my hand and my assailant kicked it away. Looking up, I recognized the *yikty* at once. "Wansetop?"

He laughed cruelly. "Very good, Bogg. I was hoping we would meet again. You'll pay for trying to trap me in that cave. Luckily, my master saved me. Now, good-bye."

I was short on magic, had no sword, and couldn't even reach the silver rose tucked in my sheath. I did the only thing I could and braced for his attack.

Instead, a massive ball of fur launched itself at Wansetop, knocking him off my chest. Gasping, I sat up and saw Lupine, snarling and wrestling with the *yikty* leader. The two broke apart, panting, and started circling each other. I jumped to my feet, seized my sword, and looked for an opening to help.

"Why do you fight us, werewolf?" Wansetop spat. "My master would welcome you with open arms. Join us. Turn on the witch."

"I don't think so, scorpion," Lupine said. Dawn was fast approaching, but he didn't seem to notice. "I would never betray my fa— friends."

"Friends?" Wansetop laughed. "Don't you mean another 'f' word?" He glanced at me and called out, "Hey, Bogg! I think the word this mangy mutt is looking for is 'fa—'"

Lupine growled, so low and menacing that I scrambled back. He turned at my movement. That's when I saw the pain in his eyes. Before I had time to wonder at its meaning, however, Wansetop scuttled forward, his barbed, poisonous tail at the ready.

"Watch out!"

Too late. Lupine tried to leap out of the way, but he was too slow. The stinger got the wolf in his left front paw.

"NO!" I cried, my exhaustion forgotten. I fumbled for my amulet. *"Beredan!"*

Ropes sprang out of the ruby and wrapped themselves around Wansetop, sending him crashing to the ground. Without bothering to check on the hated scorpion, I dashed forward to help Lupine. He was hobbling toward the trees, seemingly desperate to reach the shade, but whimpering all the way.

"Lupine! Wait!" I called, catching up easily. I put my hand on his bristled back and he gasped. "It's okay. It's just me."

He didn't look too relieved, however, and redoubled his efforts to pull away.

"Lupine. Stop. You can't walk on that leg. Please. I don't want anything bad to happen to you."

He ceased trying to escape and looked up at me. "I know, Penelope. I know you want to help, but you have to let me go. I can't stay here. You wouldn't understand."

"I know you can transform into a human, Lupine. I don't care. You're still my friend. We're like family. Family? Is that what Wansetop was trying to say?"

Artie and Mag walked up beside me, the rest of the scorpions defeated, but I only had eyes for Lupine.

The wolf glanced between me and the forest, before looking up at the sky. Sunrise was upon us.

"I'm sorry, Penny. I should have told you sooner."

Lupine stepped into the light of dawn, wincing on his injured foot. He started to change.

His spine straightened and his height increased as he stood on his hind legs, which were now human. His front legs were now arms. The gray fur was dropping away, leaving only brown hair on the top of his head. He was wearing a rumpled and stained dark blue uniform dress shirt and black pants. The muzzle shrank, revealing a human face.

I stared, gaping at the man, not believing my eyes. After all this time, I finally found him. He teetered forward, but Mag caught him before he fell. She lowered him gently to the ground. His left hand was turning purple from the paralyzing *yikty* poison.

"Penny," Malcolm murmured, slipping into unconsciousness.

Chapter Twenty-Six

The Cottage in the Forest

My whole world was turning upside down. I tried to make sense of what I was seeing. All the *yikties* were either dead, gone, or in Wansetop's case, tied up. Mag was back in human form and, to my relief, her teeth were no longer stained with blood. Meanwhile, my captain of the guard, fugitive brother was a wolf. It was all too much.

Artie and Mag were staring at me and I knew we would have to move soon. Malcolm needed treatment for that wound.

"Abselen," I said.

His hand became a lighter shade of purple with the healing spell, but otherwise didn't change.

"You won't be able to do it on your own."

Olivia was striding toward us. Her expression was grim.

"What do you suggest then? Do you have a spell I can use? Should we go to Hugo for help?" My voice rose a full octave by the last word. I took a great, shuddering breath, trying to calm down. "Please," I said desperately. "He's my brother."

Olivia gazed off into the distance. "I met Lupine recently. He came to my aid when I needed it most." She gave me a small, sad smile. "We need to go through Vanguard Forest and find Gideon. Only the elves and those trained by them have the skills to heal this type of injury."

"The dragons can heal him too," Mag said. "We should go to Aldrich."

"Gideon is closer," Olivia argued. "I know where he is at the moment. It's your choice."

"Can Gideon really help?"

"He can."

I glanced at Malcolm. His eyes were closed and he was shivering. "We'll follow you to Gideon."

Olivia nodded. "Wise decision. Come."

She started walking into Vanguard Forest, when she paused and spoke to a nearby bluebird. "Would you kindly tell Hugo that Wansetop is tied up by the Vanguard shield? We don't want to leave pests like him littering the forest."

The bird nodded and flew off toward Elton Castle.

"Like that pathetic troll can hold me," Wansetop spat, straining against his bonds. "Beware, elf. You have made a powerful enemy. My master, the golden dragon, will take great pleasure in burning down Vanguard Forest." He laughed cruelly.

Without looking back, Olivia strode into the forest. "Are you three coming or not?"

Being the strongest, Mag scooped Malcolm into her arms. "Four, Olivia. There are four of us," she said.

"Of course," Olivia said, her voice wavering only slightly.

With one last glance at the bound Wansetop, we followed her into the forest.

* * *

Barely ten feet into Vanguard Forest, a cloaked and hooded figure stopped us.

"Olivia," he said. "Well done. I see you found Penelope Bogg." His voice broke when he said my name. The man cleared his throat.

"Who are you?" I said, standing protectively in front of Malcolm. I gazed suspiciously at Olivia. Had she lured us into a trap?

"Where are my manners?" the man said, throwing back his hood. He had a narrow face, with angular features. His black hair and green eyes looked exactly like Olivia's. "I'm Xavier," he continued. "Olivia's father."

"Pleasure. Now, would you kindly move?" Mag said. She gestured toward the shaking, unconscious Malcolm. "We're in a hurry."

"Mag," Artie hissed. "Be quiet! You don't know who these two are."

"Should I care?"

"You should," Artie said. "I may not know who Gideon is, but I know one thing. Xavier is Gideon's son."

* * *

Mag and I both started talking at the same time.

"Gideon has a son?"

"How do you know this, Artie?"

"Maybe I can answer," Xavier said. "Do not worry, Miss Bogg. I will be brief. Then, we can get your brother the best medical attention available. I promise to take you there myself."

I motioned for him to continue. We started walking as Xavier began his tale.

"Several months ago, I was inspecting the perimeter of Vanguard Forest, when I came across a young man, apparently lost and alone. I was about to reveal myself and escort him out of the forest, when he tensed, staring at something in the distance. As I watched, one of my few human friends, Abigail, came strolling into view. I was worried that the boy would try to rob her, when another man came striding up. The boy ducked out of sight, peering through the trees.

"The newcomer introduced himself as McGraw and asked Abby several questions, but she simply shook her head. That's when McGraw became aggressive. Before I could even move, the young man bolted out of the trees and defended my friend. Both men pulled knives, glaring at each other. The younger man muttered something to Abby. She took off running for her house at the bottom of the hill.

"I stepped in and the two backed off immediately. McGraw made some snide comment and departed. The young man thanked me profusely. After a short conversation, I sent the boy on his way. Isn't that the way it happened, Artie?"

"Sounds right to me," Artie said. "Tristan McGraw is a bully. Every thief knows it. I'm just glad I was able to help your friend, Xavier. I never caught her name. She was a sweet, old lady. She invited me into her house before I left and offered me some apple pie. The only things I learned from her were that her son and husband were dead and that I should call her Mrs. B."

"I think you were very brave, Artie, but what does that have to do with healing Malcolm?" I asked.

"Abigail is the best healer for miles around," Xavier said. He stopped walking on the top of a high hill and pointed down. A neat little cottage was nestled against the trees. "If anyone can heal your brother, it'll be her. Dad's visiting her now. They would like to meet you, Penelope."

* * *

When I saw the house, I froze in my tracks. I had a feeling I had seen it before, but I'd never been here. Had I? Everything seemed so familiar. Xavier started the descent down the hill, with Olivia and Mag carrying Malcolm close behind.

Artie paused and looked back. "You okay, Pen?"

"Yeah, fine." I took his hand and we followed the others to the house.

It was a pretty, one-story cottage, with a sea of golden marigolds in the front yard. The two window boxes were filled with delicate pink peonies and red tulips. The front door was open and I could see a man and a woman sitting at a table.

"Dad and Abigail," Xavier said. "We shouldn't keep them waiting."

As we stepped into the front garden, there was a clatter from inside and the woman cried, "They're here!" She scrambled to her feet and stood framed in the door.

Abigail looked to be in her late sixties. She had curly white hair, brown eyes, and wore a blue dress and a white apron smudged with flour. She smiled when she saw us, but faltered when she spotted Malcolm.

"Oh, dear," Abigail murmured. She rushed to Mag and checked

Malcolm's forehead. "Please, bring him inside. Penelope, Xavier, could I have a word?"

Mag, Artie, and Olivia stepped over the threshold, leaving me, Xavier, and Abigail gazing anxiously into the house.

The man, Gideon, stood and spoke to Olivia as she approached. Gideon was a tall, regal-looking elf. Like his son and granddaughter, he had black hair, green eyes, and a narrow, angular face. He wore a beautifully tailored brown dress shirt, brown pants, and a green cloak with embroidery on the back. I couldn't quite make out the design. Olivia said something in response, her expression dark. I was sure she was telling him about Wansetop.

"Your brother will be fine with Gideon for a few minutes," Abigail said. "He's a skilled healer, as am I." She put her hands on my shoulders and studied me. "You look so much like her. Like both of them."

"I'm sorry. I… I don't…" I stammered, when I saw the tears in Abigail's eyes. I looked at Xavier, pleading silently for help.

He cleared his throat. "Abigail, maybe we should explain before we scare Penelope. She has a right to know."

"Yes, yes, of course," she said, letting go of my shoulders and taking my hands. "Penelope, my name is Abigail Bogg. I'm your grandmother."

* * *

I didn't have many memories of my father, Edric. He died when I was eight years old, but I could still remember the hug and the proud smile he gave me when I saved that pack of wolves. Looking at Abigail now, I could see the hurt losing her son had caused.

I stared into her eyes. *They're the same brown as Dad's,* I thought. *And her smile. It's the same as his.*

"Grandma?" I said tentatively. The word sounded foreign to my ears from lack of use. "I never had a grandma before."

"I'm sorry, Penelope," she said softly. "I should have been there for you more." She paused and her voice became hoarse. "Your grandfather, Lucas, was very ill these last few years. It was all I could do to care for him. I couldn't take Alice and you kids in when Tealeaf was destroyed. When Lucas died last year, I didn't know where to find you."

"Grandma," I said. It still sounded odd. "There's nothing to forgive. You did the best you could. Grandpa needed you." I squeezed her hands. They were cold. "Malcolm, Lydia, and I were well taken care of. I would like to make up for lost time, though."

Abigail laughed happily and pulled me into a hug. "You are truly your parents' daughter, Penelope. Remember that."

When we broke apart, Xavier was wiping his eyes.

"Why, Xavier, you sentimental elf, are you crying?" Abigail said, a teasing note to her voice.

"I'm just happy for you two." He sniffled. "That's all."

"Well, come on," Abigail said. "My grandson isn't going to heal himself. Gideon, skilled as he is, can only do so much. Penelope, if you would grab that basket, please."

I glanced down and saw a basket overflowing with flowers and herbs. Picking it up, I followed Abigail and Xavier into the house, feeling dazed.

"Pen, what happened?" Artie asked as I rejoined him and Mag.

Malcolm was lying on a couch with Gideon and Olivia standing over him.

"Tell you later."

"Right, Gideon," Abigail said, waving her hands at him, shooing him away. "Away from my grandson. I'll see to him now."

"That's not fair, Abby, and you know it," Gideon said in a deep, sad voice.

"Grandson?" Mag muttered. "Penelope?"

I sighed and whispered, "Abigail just told me she's my grandmother."

Artie's eyes widened. "Of course! Mrs. B! Mrs. Bogg!"

"That's right," I said, but I was distracted by Gideon. He kept glancing at me, like he wanted to talk.

"Penelope, could I have the basket?" Abigail asked.

I stepped forward, brushing past Gideon, and handed it to her.

"Penelope…" he began, before trailing off.

"It's a pleasure to meet you," I said, holding out my hand to shake his. "I've been looking forward to this, ever since I read your name on that piece of paper."

Gideon looked taken aback. "Piece of paper?"

I pulled the crumpled scrap from my bag. "Lupine, I mean Malcolm, helped me retrieve it from Maude's house."

He barely looked at it, instead gazing straight into my eyes. "Penelope, I… I don't know how to say this, but I'm… I'm…"

"Oh, Dad, tell her." Xavier sighed. "Penelope, Alice is my sister and Gideon is your grandfather."

Chapter Twenty-Seven

Ravenwood

When I was little, my mom told me stories about the elves. The stories were always the same. The brave elves would go up against some horrible threat, like scorpions, bloodthirsty trolls, and even a horse-lizard-crab creature I had made up when I was five. I always wondered why the elves were never the villains. Now I understood. If Xavier and Gideon were to be believed, my mom was an elf and that would make me…

"I'm half-elf?" I croaked. I felt as if my whole life was a lie. Suddenly, the strange magical signature on Maude's bookcase made sense. If I wasn't human, what was I?

"Quarter-elf, actually," Xavier said. "Alice and I are the half-elves."

"Don't worry, Penelope," Gideon said, smiling. "If we head farther into the forest, I can teach you everything you need to know about being an elf."

I took a step back. "Elf training? You can't be serious. I'm *not* giving up my humanity for anything. I won't leave my friends and family and seclude myself in Vanguard Forest for all time. I'm not abandoning Lydia!"

"No, Penelope, you misunderstand me," Gideon said. His smile faded.

"I think she made it quite clear," Mag said coldly. "She doesn't want to go with you. And why would she? You've never been in her life until now."

Gideon opened his mouth to respond, when Artie called from the window, "Somebody's coming!"

Eyes wide, I rushed to join Artie. I looked outside. About twenty elves were making their way to the cottage.

"Unbelievable!" I said, turning angrily toward Gideon. He looked taken aback by my animosity. "You're going to *kidnap* me and *force* me to behave like an elf? I am not an elf! I'm human!"

Gideon said soothingly, "I'm not forcing you into anything, Penelope. Please, listen. I just want to teach you about your heritage."

But I didn't trust him. Mag was right. What kind of man was this to ignore me my whole life and then try to change me?

I backed up toward the front door, whispering to Artie as I went, "Don't let him take Malcolm. I'll be back as soon as I can."

Without another word, I bolted out the door and ran blindly, deeper into the forest.

* * *

In hindsight, running into the elves' forest probably wasn't the smartest idea, but I didn't know where else to go. And I always felt comfortable around trees.

I hurried as fast as I could, dodging low-hanging branches and ignoring the startled cries of birds, heedless in my mad dash away from my grandfather.

Grandfather, I thought scathingly. *How do I know he's telling the truth? I've never met him before today. Why should I believe him?*

Ah, a stray thought chimed in, *but how is he any different from Abigail? You never met her before today and yet you were overjoyed.*

That's different. But even to me that sounded like a weak excuse. *She was busy taking care of my other grandpa.*

You didn't even give Gideon a chance to defend himself, the Stray Thought argued. *What's the harm in hearing him out?*

I stopped running as I reached a small glade and took in my surroundings. I had no idea where I was. All I could see were trees, trees, and more trees. The only thing to break up the monotony of trees was a tiny spring off to my right. Feeling thirsty, I knelt and dipped my hands in for a drink and caught my reflection.

The change that had started when I took up the silver rose was nearly complete. I hadn't looked recently, but my brown hair had almost finished reverting to gleaming silver, my natural color. I looked older, more tired, and, I supposed, wiser. My travels had taught me that it was all right for me to leave my comfortable job at Kelton Castle, that I could look after myself, that I was a witch.

You've grown so much, the Stray Thought said. *So, you're part elf? Big deal. That doesn't alter who you truly are. Your mother raised you to be the young woman you are. No amount of elf blood in you is going to change that.*

But what if going with Gideon means he tries to turn me into something I'm not? What if I want to stay human?

You are human, Penelope. Three-fourths of you is human. It doesn't matter if you're fully human, fully elf, or something in between. You can make your own choices. Your mom did.

True, I thought. *I should at least give Gideon a chance. I had the feeling he misses my mom just as much as I do.* I stood up and squared my shoulders. *Thanks, random thoughts in my head.*

Whoever said I was some random thoughts. Look behind you, Penelope.

I spun around and found Mag and Artie standing at the edge of the clearing.

"That dragon guardian bond really works," Mag said. "Happy we had that talk."

* * *

"How did you do that, Mag?" I asked. "I didn't know we could use the dragon guardian bond to speak telepathically."

"I didn't either," she said. "Artie suggested it, I tried it, and it worked."

He shrugged. "All I did was ask Mag if she could track you through the forest with the bond. If anything, Gideon's the one who told us it would work."

I sighed. "I need to go back. That little talk we had set me straight. I should apologize to my grandfather."

"Apology accepted."

We turned and found Gideon, Xavier, and the twenty elven guards striding into the glade. Gideon and Xavier were in the lead.

"Y- you heard me?" I stammered.

Gideon walked right up to me, stopping several feet away. Like me, he looked extremely awkward.

"Every word," he said. "One of my elves saw you running through the forest, with Mag and Artie close behind. We are the stewards of Vanguard. It wasn't hard to find this meadow." In almost a whisper, he added, "This was your mother's favorite place in the whole forest. It's fitting that you should find it too."

I nodded, unable to speak. I felt as if I were intruding on Mom's secret hiding spot, but at the same time, I thought she would be pleased that I had found it.

"Thank you," I rasped, my throat tight with emotion.

He smiled and I knew, without a doubt, that Gideon would always love me. I suddenly felt proud to be his granddaughter.

The moment was broken by another elf, who cleared his throat and tentatively said, "My liege?"

It took me a moment to realize that he was talking to Gideon.

"Yes?"

"We just received word from Abigail and Olivia. They need help."

My blood ran cold. "Malcolm's in danger?"

The messenger nodded. "It seems that they can't heal him of the *yikty* poison, because he's, well, a werewolf. His inner wolf is fighting them, making it difficult for them to proceed. He's also muttering in his sleep, saying that Lydia is in trouble."

I glanced anxiously at Mag and Artie and motioned them to the side. Once we were out of earshot of Gideon and his guards, I said, "What do we do? Do we stay and help Malcolm or return to Kelton Castle and find Lydia?"

"Lydia is safe for the moment," Artie reasoned. "She's protected by the barrier. Malcolm is the one who needs us."

"Agreed," I said. "How do we help him?"

"We need the *Lenahen Plum Flower,*" Mag said. "It healed my friend Venn when he was attacked by a *yikty.* I don't know how Malcolm became a werewolf or why that would stop the cure from working, though."

"Why don't we ask someone who knows?" I said, walking back up to Gideon.

"Grandfather?" He turned to look at me and I was struck by how tall and impressive he really was. "What are you to the other elves?"

"I'm King Gideon Ravenwood, ruler of the elves."

"Is it true that Malcolm is a werewolf?"

"Yes. I'm sorry."

"How do we save him from the *yikty* poison?"

Gideon tilted his head as he considered me. "Abigail has the *Lenahen Plum Flower.* What you need now can only be found in the elf capital of Ilyana Glen. Alice's room in Hightower Hall hasn't been touched since she left twenty-five years ago. She has exactly what you need."

Chapter Twenty-Eight

Hightower Hall

"Was Grandma a human?"

Gideon looked surprised by my question. "Yes, she was. Why do you ask?"

The others had gone ahead as we made our way through the forest toward Ilyana Glen.

"Xavier said he and Mom are half-elves. If Grandma was an elf too, they would be full elves."

Gideon chuckled. "You're exactly like your mom, Penelope. The moment she was old enough, she immediately started asking questions. She wanted to know why she and Xavier were not like the other elves. When she found out the truth about her mom, Alice became interested in the humans of Alsmora. It was all I could do to stop her from running off with Edric Bogg the moment they met. Then again, they were always perfect for each other."

"Who was my grandmother?" I asked eagerly, as we stepped into the bustling elven village of Ilyana Glen. "What was she like? What kind of human marries the king of the elves?"

"More questions," Gideon said, smiling. "Okay, Penelope, I'll tell you. Your grandmother's name was Vi—"

A horse whinnied and we looked up. A woman was riding straight toward us. For a moment, I wondered if it was my grandmother, but then I spotted the purple lizard sitting on her shoulder.

Grinning, I ran up, calling out, "Maude! Cissy! When did you get here?"

Maude cackled. "We arrived early yesterday morning. A storm blew us off course. We couldn't make it to Elton Castle. What took you three so long?"

"Got held up at Elton," Mag explained. "Nothing we couldn't handle."

"I can see that," Maude said, looking straight at the silver crescent necklace around Mag's neck.

She shifted awkwardly under Maude's gaze. "Necessary precaution," Mag muttered.

"Uh huh."

"Have you met Gideon, Maude?" Artie asked. I smiled at him, grateful that he had changed the subject for Mag's sake.

Maude turned, beaming, toward Gideon. "I thought that was you, Gid! How's my favorite elf?"

He smiled. "Hello, Maude, Cissy. What brings you here?"

"We're here for your granddaughter, naturally. We have to get her trained if she wants to take on the golden dragon.

"We know the golden dragon is Casimir."

"Oh, good! That simplifies matters! We can get on with the training."

"We can't, Maude, not now," I said. "Malcolm is hurt."

Cissy chirped, shaking her head.

"What's she saying?"

"She says that we need to start your training, before it's too late."

"I'm not abandoning my brother!" I cried. "And I won't leave my little sister to fend for herself either!"

"Not even to save all of Alsmora?" Maude asked, her eyebrows raised.

I took a deep breath. "I will do everything I can to save Alsmora from the golden dragon, but I need a few days to help my siblings. I promise you, Maude, and you too Cissy, that once I heal Malcolm and check on Lydia, I will return for training."

Maude and Cissy glanced at each other, before turning back to me. "Go. Be with your family," Maude said. "We should be able to hold off Casimir for a few days."

"Thank you," I said, hugging Maude. Cissy chittered softly next to my ear.

"Very well," Gideon said. "Penelope, Mag, Artie, if you'll follow me, I'll show you to Alice's room. Xavier, stay here with Maude and Cissy. I'll be back soon."

He started for Hightower Hall, a magnificent castle at the other end of the elven village. With a brief backwards glance at Maude, I hurried after him, Mag and Artie close behind.

"What were you and your grandfather talking about, Pen?" Artie whispered as we jogged in the wake of Gideon's much longer strides.

"That I'm a lot like my mom and that she was interested in the humans of Alsmora. He also started telling me about my grandmother."

"Abigail?" Mag asked.

"No. My other grandmother. Her name was Vi, I think. It might be short for something. Maude interrupted before Gideon could tell me anything about her."

"Might have been Violet," Artie suggested. "Or even Viola."

"I know a Viola," I said, smiling. "I don't think it's the same person, though."

Mag gave a short bark of laughter. "Doubtful," she said. "Common enough name."

"If I could interject…"

We all looked up in surprise to find that Gideon had slowed down to talk.

"Your grandmother wasn't named Violet or Viola," he continued. "She was Victoria."

* * *

"Victoria! I saw a Victoria in Queen Rebecca's memory! She was working as a handmaiden, just like I did at Kelton Castle."

"She's one and the same," Gideon said. "I first met her a hundred years ago, when she stumbled upon the edge of Vanguard Forest. She was badly injured and almost unconscious. I brought her back here to heal. Once she was well enough, I got the full story. The golden dragon had attacked her and her friends, separating them, forcing her to take shelter by the forest. Victoria kept saying she would return to them, but…"

Gideon paused, emotion constricting his throat.

"She never did, did she?" I said quietly. "Victoria stayed here in Vanguard, with you."

Gideon nodded. "She did. We fell in love. Eventually, we had Alice and Xavier. You know the rest."

I nodded. Mom had met Dad and Malcolm, Lydia, and I had been born.

We reached Hightower Hall. Gideon let us in through a back door and up some stairs to what looked like a set of bedrooms.

"Alice's room," Gideon said, pointing to the third door on the right. "I'll be downstairs in the throne room. Unlock the door with *Anoffen*. I must leave you. I haven't entered since Victoria died. I can't bear to go in now."

"Grandpa."

"I'll be all right. I hope you find what you're looking for, Penelope."

He walked away, shoulders back and head high, leaving Mag, Artie, and me alone in the hallway.

I approached the door, but stopped short.

"What's wrong?" Artie said.

"This is my mom's old room, Artie. I'm not sure I can go in there. It feels like I'm invading her privacy."

"We can't stand here forever," Mag said and put her hand on the doorknob. It wouldn't open. "Penelope, I'm going to need you to say the spell. I can't get in on my own. What was it again?"

"*Anoffen*," Artie said, "but Mag, maybe Penelope's right. Maybe we are invading…"

There was a click and Mag turned the doorknob. It opened easily.

"Well, that's convenient," she said, strolling inside. "Come on, you two."

"I'm sorry, Pen," Artie whispered.

"It's okay," I said. "Really. I'm just scared of what I might find, but I need to do this to help Malcolm."

I stepped inside the room.

Chapter Twenty-Nine

A Search Through the Past

My mom's old room was smaller than I had imagined. Since this was the elves' capital, I had expected it to be gigantic, but this was a modest space, about the same size as my own at Kelton Castle.

A bed sat at the far side, opposite the door. A wooden desk was between the bed and an open, sunlit window. A bookcase and the closet were near the door. A braided rug lay on the floor. The only thing out of place was a chair, which lay toppled on its side.

Everything was coated in dust.

Mag was examining the bookcase, a book in her hand. She blew dust from the otherwise pristine cover. "What are we looking for exactly, Penelope?"

"Wherever it is that can help Malcolm."

"This is going to take forever."

"Maybe not," Artie said thoughtfully. "The room isn't too big. If we split up, we'll find it in no time."

"Fine," Mag said, handing me the book. "I'll take the bed. You can have the desk, Artie, and Penelope can search the bookcase."

"Mag, you're not sleeping on my mom's bed."

"Oh, come on, Penelope! She might have hidden a clue there!"

"No, Mag," I said sternly. "You take the closet. Come on, let's get started."

"I wasn't going to sleep," Mag muttered as she made her way to the closet. "Much."

Trying not to laugh, I smiled at Artie. He smiled back.

As I turned to the bookcase, I glanced down at the book I was holding: *A Brief History of Alsmora* by Victoria Caulfield. I opened it and saw a message written on the cover page.

To my beautiful daughter, Alice.
May you grow into a strong, intelligent woman.

Love,
Mom

Artie looked up from where he was searching the desk. "Find something, Pen?"

Wordlessly, I passed him the book. He read my grandmother's message and handed it back. "Think this is what we're after?"

"I doubt it. I mean, there might be something in the book, but I don't think it's the message itself."

He nodded and we kept searching.

Turning back to the book, I flipped to the first chapter and began to read.

Alsmora has always had a unique and varied history. Home to many different magical and mundane races, it is believed that everyone, no matter who they are, has at least a degree of magic.

Some races have more magic than others, including elves and dragons. Humans are different in that they are both magical and mundane at the same time. Witches and wizards are born with magic, but some mundane humans can gain magic later in life, most notably if they are bitten by a vampire or werewolf.

My eyes widened when I saw the word *werewolf.* I started skimming further ahead, but there was nothing else of interest. I was about to give up and close the book, when I remembered the table of contents.

Running my finger down the page, I spotted 'Chapter Nine: A New Moon.' Figuring that it might have something to do with werewolves, I turned to Chapter Nine.

Werewolves are one of the most interesting groups in all of Alsmora. They start off as humans, but are turned if they are scratched or bitten around the full moon. They can only transform in the dark of night and must return to human form at dawn.

The next few paragraphs detailed werewolves and their attributes. I didn't find anything useful, until the next page.

Werewolves are not inherently vicious, unless they are so as humans. For the most part, though, they will never willingly attack humans, except on the full moon. That is the one night of the month where they have no control over their actions.

Herbs and plants have strange effects on werewolves. The gemser plant, for example, is the necessary ingredient to treat yikty poison. It is completely harmless to humans, but deadly for werewolves.

The only way to combat this is with the water from Ilyana Glen, the mysterious elven waterfall, for which the nearby village is named. The werewolf must drink it at the same time the gemser plant is being administered. This will cure them of the yikty poison, but there is no known cure for being a werewolf.

No known cure for being a werewolf.

I stared at those seven words, my heart sinking each time I reread them. "Malcolm," I whispered.

"Mag?" Artie said, jolting me to my senses. "What have you done?"

I tried not to groan. Mag had taken all the clothes in the closet and tossed them out, littering the floor.

"Nothing in the closet," she said. "Now what?"

"Mag," I said, exasperated. "Why?"

She shrugged. "You said to check the closet. Well, I checked the closet. The only problem was, there were too many clothes in the way."

I decided not to point out that she had just made a bigger mess and instead said, "Did you find anything?"

"Nothing. It was a complete waste of time."

"I hate to say it, Pen, but Mag is right," Artie said. "I didn't find anything either."

"I did," I said, holding up the book. "We need to talk to Gideon. The only thing that will help Malcolm now is the water from Ilyana Glen."

* * *

We got lost on the way to the throne room. Gideon had forgotten to give us directions, so we were left to wander the halls.

"This way," Mag said. "I'm sure it's this way."

"Mag, you said that five minutes ago," Artie said. He stopped and leaned against the wall, his arms crossed. "Face it, we're lost."

"We're not lost," she snapped. "I'm just not sure where we are at the moment."

"That's the definition of lost, Mag." I glanced out the window and saw a waterfall in the distance. If I had to guess, that was probably Ilyana Glen. I'd have to visit it before leaving Vanguard Forest. I scanned the courtyard below, but didn't see anyone. There went my hope that somebody would come up and guide us back down.

"What if we jump out a window?" Mag suggested.

Artie and I both stared at her.

"What? I'll fly us down," she muttered defensively. "It's not that far."

"We'll leave that as a backup plan," I said. "I'd rather not risk the elves panicking if they see you with your dragon wings."

"Oh, come on! There's nobody down there who would see!"

"No, Mag. Not in the elf capital. You'll just have to wa—"

Crash!

"What was that?" I gasped. "An earthquake."

"The ground didn't shake."

"I'll tell you what that was," Artie said grimly. "Glass breaking. Come on. The sound came from Alice's room. There's a thief in the castle."

* * *

We peeked around the door into my mom's room, which Mag had left ajar. Two shadowy figures were moving about. As we watched, one of the thieves tripped over the pile of clothes Mag had left in the center of the room and landed facedown on the floor.

"Gary, what are you doing?" the other thief hissed. "Get up and start looking before Bogg and her friends find us."

"Tristan," Artie whispered.

Tristan McGraw had once worked for Artie's father, Leopold. They had had a falling out when the rogue thief sided with the golden dragon. I balled my fists as I remembered Xavier's story of Tristan threatening Abigail.

"What are we doing here again?" Gary asked, scrambling to his feet.

"I told you, you idiot," Tristan snarled. "Master Casimir said that if we find some old book in Alice Bogg's old room, we can prevent her from ever returning. Now, start looking!"

"Seems like someone beat us to it," Gary muttered, kicking some clothes out of the way.

"Just look."

I pulled Mag and Artie further down the hall, away from the door. I needed to vent, but didn't want Tristan or Gary to hear me.

"We have to get them out of that room! I can't let them hurt my mom!"

"Pen, they're probably searching for Victoria's book," Artie said. "We have the book. They won't find it."

I sighed. "I know, but I can't let them get away with this."

"Great," Mag said, rubbing her hands together in glee. "I can't wait to use my claws on those two fools."

"Not you, Mag," I said, pushing Victoria's book toward her. "Get Gideon. Tell him what's happening. Hurry. Artie and I won't be able to keep them busy for long."

"Why do I have to go?" Mag asked sullenly. "And why are you giving me the book?"

"You wanted to jump out the window," Artie said. "You can land safely. Pen and I can't. And the less chance Tristan has of getting that book, the happier I'll be."

"I don't like it," Mag said. "But I see your point. I'll return as fast as I can with Gideon and his elves." Her wings sprouted out of her back. "Good luck, you two."

She hurried over to the windows, threw them open, and leapt out, leaving me and Artie with two thieves rummaging around my mom's old room.

"Come on," I said, taking Artie's hand. "Your friends are waiting."

Chapter Thirty

Ghosts and Guards

Artie's father Leopold was the leader of a highly successful gang of thieves. Everyone lived in fear of them, but in the short time I had come to know Artie, I had learned that he was nothing like his family. The Quicks and their allies were ruthlessly efficient. It was unwise to even blink around them, lest you lose your valuables.

Artie, however, was different. He was a thief, but he only stole to help those in need.

Unlike the two searching my mom's room. When I first met Tristan, he tried to burn all the *gemser* plants in the Quick Hideout in an attempt to hurt Mag. I didn't know anything about Gary.

I gritted my teeth as Artie and I watched Tristan make an even bigger mess than Mag. He was ripping clothes apart and tossing them aside. Gary was flipping through books and setting them carefully on the floor.

I leaned in and whispered, "Why is Tristan searching the clothes? He said they were looking for a book."

"No idea," Artie said, not taking his eyes off Tristan. "I think he just likes being a jerk. How do you want to do this, Pen?"

I glanced between Artie the two rogue thieves. "What do you think of becoming invisible?"

* * *

The plan was simple. Turn Artie and myself invisible and scare Tristan and Gary out of Hightower Hall.

Artie had some doubts, however.

"I don't know, Pen. Tristan doesn't scare easily."

"What about Gary?"

Artie tilted his head thoughtfully. "I've never known Garrett Hopkirk to be what you would call brave. Greedy, yes. Courageous, no."

"Greedy?"

"Yeah. Do you see the way he's stacking the books?"

"I do."

"Knowing Gary, he's going to try and sell all those books to the highest bidder. Who wouldn't want rare, priceless books from Hightower Hall? If Tristan doesn't watch him carefully, Gary'll make off with the entire room."

I clenched my fists. "So, Tristan is in league with Casimir to take over all of Alsmora and Gary will plunder everything. Just great!"

"That's about the size of it," Artie said. "We'd better get going, before it's all gone."

I nodded and took Artie's hand, while keeping my other hand on my amulet. "*Aun evas comren.*"

A moment later, we were invisible.

"Your magic seems to work faster each time you use it," Artie said.

"I think it has something to do with Gideon. Ever since I read that spell from Maude's house, I've felt more in control of my magic. I feel as if he's been helping us on our journey."

"Maybe it's all part of being quarter-elf," Artie suggested. "I wonder if your mom or Xavier ever had problems with their magic."

I shrugged. "We can ask Xavier later. Let's hurry, Artie. I don't know how much longer Malcolm can hold out. We still need that water, after all."

He nodded and we made our way to the door. Carefully, we eased inside. Luckily, neither Tristan nor Gary seemed to notice.

Letting go of Artie's hand, I picked my way to the open window, while he stayed by the door. Once we were in position, I slammed the window shut, causing both Tristan and Gary to jump.

"Who's there?" Tristan demanded, drawing his knife.

In a low and haunting voice, Artie responded, "Fools! Did you think you would be able to steal from me? I am the guardian of Hightower Hall. I see everything!"

The moment he finished speaking, we were both on the move again. I retreated to the bed, while Artie slipped past Tristan's outstretched arm to the closet.

"Tristan?" Gary gulped. "What was that?"

"It's just some stupid trick," he snapped. "Keep looking!"

Gary nodded, though he still looked frightened.

"*Brinze*," I whispered and an eerie wind began wafting in the room.

Artie laughed humorlessly. "Wrong choice, thieves! Prepare yourselves for my wrath!"

"Tristan!" Gary yelped, sprinting for the door. I stuck out my leg, causing him to trip, while at the same time pouring more magic into my spell. The wind's power increased.

"Get up, you idiot!" Tristan yelled, yanking Gary to his feet. "We're not leaving, not until we've found *A Brief History of Alsmora*!" His voice rose to be heard over the wind.

Gary gestured toward the books on the floor. "Can't find it! I'm getting out of here, Tristan! No money is worth this! I'm not dealing with ghosts!"

"There are no ghosts!"

Artie snuck up behind Tristan and shoved him, causing the rogue thief to go sprawling on the floor.

"Who did that?"

"Ghosts!" Gary cried and he ran out the door into the hallway.

Artie and I hurried after him, but not before I aimed my amulet at Tristan and said, "*Beredan!*"

Ropes sprang out of the amulet's center and wrapped around Tristan.

Ending the invisibility spell, we left my mom's old room. Gary was on the ground, unconscious. We hadn't done that.

"Gary!" Artie exclaimed. He bent over the fallen thief. "What happened?"

Groaning, Gary opened his eyes. They were wide and scared as he stared at a point above our heads.

"Artie!" Gary rasped. "Behind you!"

We turned.

A figure stepped out of the shadows. She had gray eyes and stringy brown hair. Her dark blue uniform dress shirt was stained and rumpled, while her silver breastplate was tarnished in places. A cruel smile twisted her lips into a sneer, as she slammed and locked the hallway door.

"Hello, Quick," Rowena said. "There's no escaping me this time."

*　*　*

"What are you doing here?" I said, taking a step forward.

"Stay where you are, Bogg," Rowena ordered. She was breathing heavily, her eyes alight with manic glee. "I'll get to *you* later. Right now, I want to savor my victory."

She walked up to Artie, only stopping when her face was an inch from his. He stared back coolly.

"How I've waited for this moment, Quick," she said, panting with excitement. "I've dreamt of capturing you for years."

I couldn't take it anymore. "Rowena, you've got the wrong idea."

"Shut it, Bogg! You're not off the hook either. I want a word with you about your dear brother."

"My brother is none of your business," I said coldly.

"Really? I have evidence that you've not only spoken to him, but also know where he is. Tell me now and I might forgive you for harboring a fugitive."

"Last I checked, I didn't need your forgiveness."

Rowena snarled and leapt at me, drawing her dagger as she went, resting the cold steel against my neck.

"What are you going to do?" I said. "Kill me? You'll never find Malcolm then." *Where are Mag and the elves?*

Rowena smirked, running her finger down the chain of my amulet, before yanking it off. I watched in dismay as she tossed it to the floor, the chain broken.

"There's still Arthur," she said. "I could force the information from him, in exchange for his freedom."

"Not on your life, Rowena," Artie said, drawing his knife. "If you want Malcolm, you'll have to go through both of us."

Even with a dagger at my throat, I smiled gratefully at Artie.

"So sentimental," Rowena said, suddenly releasing the pressure on my neck.

Maybe she's letting us go, I thought, but my hope was short-lived when she spun around and held the dagger against Artie instead.

"Drop it," she ordered and, reluctantly, he dropped his knife.

"Didn't you do this at the Storm Knights' base, Ro?" Artie said. "I think you might need to come up with some new tricks."

"Who asked you?" Rowena snapped.

Someone started pounding on a nearby hallway door. "Penelope! Artie! You in there?" Mag called. "I think the door's locked!"

"I'm feeling generous, Bogg," Rowena said. "Since I'm in Gideon's house, it would be impolite to kill his granddaughter. You stay there and don't move, while Arthur and I start our trip back to Kelton Castle. I'm not completely heartless. I still want to see our little thief here brought to justice."

"You can't take Artie!" I said, raising my voice slightly, so Mag and any reinforcements she brought could hear me.

"Watch me." She moved her dagger to his back and marched him to a door at the opposite end of the hall, away from Mag. "Nobody there," Rowena said, placing her ear to the door. "Open it for me, Bogg."

I didn't move.

"Unless you want me to put Arthur out of his misery," she said, nodding toward the blade at his back. "Now."

"Just do it, Pen," Artie said. "I promise I'll be all right."

Slowly, I picked up my amulet, walked past Rowena and Artie, and placed my hand on the doorknob.

"Well?" Rowena said impatiently. "Unlock it."

I glanced behind me, desperate for Mag's help. How could I unbolt the other door when I was all the way over here?

Then, it hit me.

"Whoops," I said, dropping my amulet. I stooped quickly to retrieve it, but batted it with the back of my hand. It rolled away from me.

"Be more careful," Rowena growled. "And make it quick."

I nodded, but I wasn't really listening. As I fumbled for the amulet, I quickly thought, *Mag? Can you hear me?*

Penelope? What's going on in there?

Rowena's holding us hostage. She's making me open the south door. Hurry! She's taking Artie!

The connection ended, I picked up my amulet and smiled innocently at Rowena. "Sorry about that."

She glared at me suspiciously. "Unlock the door and no funny business."

Turning back to the doorknob, I muttered, "*Anoffen*." There was a click and the door sprang open.

"Finally," Rowena said and pushed Artie over the threshold. "Don't move a muscle until we're gone, Bogg. I'll know if you do."

I nodded obediently and waited for them to disappear. Once their footsteps had faded, I ran back down the hallway, grabbing Artie's knife as I went. I reached the north door and gasped, "*Anoffen*."

Mag and Gideon stepped through immediately.

"Penelope," he said. "Mag said Rowena took Artie."

"Yes! Rowena ambushed us! We have to save him!"

Gideon smiled. "Thanks to your warning, it's already being done. Look."

We all gathered around the window to watch. I almost burst out laughing in relief.

Rowena had exited Hightower Hall, her dagger still at Artie's back. Maude, Xavier, and twenty elves leapt out of hiding and surrounded her. Rowena raised her knife threateningly, when she suddenly dropped it. She began to hop on the spot, her arms flailing wildly. Artie stumbled away from her, into Maude's embrace.

"What happened?" I said and then I saw the tiny, purple lizard scurrying away from Rowena. I started to laugh. Cissy must have jumped on Rowena, surprising her so much that she forgot all about Artie.

I whispered, "Thanks, Cissy."

"We should return to the throne room," Gideon said. "I have some guests to welcome and then we need to discuss a certain book written by my wife."

CHAPTER THIRTY-ONE

WATER, WATER, EVERYWHERE

We finally made it to the throne room, with help from Gideon. He led Mag and me inside as Artie entered with Xavier. Rowena and Tristan, both bound with rope, were pushed in a moment later.

I rushed to Artie and gave him a hug. "Don't ever sacrifice yourself like that again, do you hear me, Artie?"

"She was threatening you, Pen."

"That's sweet," I said, pulling away enough to look him in the eye, "but she's after you, not me."

"Ahem!" Gideon cleared his throat behind us.

We quickly straightened and went to stand in the corner next to Mag, out of the way. I handed Artie his knife back. Gideon turned to face the prisoners.

"Tristan McGraw," he said, "it's been a while. I haven't seen you since you accosted Abigail all those months ago. Thieves like you aren't allowed in Vanguard Forest."

Artie shifted awkwardly.

Gideon glanced at us and smiled. "You are the exception, Arthur Quick. I know you are a thief of honor."

Artie bowed low. "Thank you, King Gideon. I appreciate your faith in me."

"You earned it, Arthur. You not only saved Abigail, but you've been a good friend to my granddaughter." Gideon turned back to Tristan. "You, however, are not honorable, McGraw. From what Penelope has told me, you were actively trying to prevent my daughter Alice's return. Do you have anything to say in your defense?"

Tristan spat on the ground. "The golden dragon will take over this whole pathetic forest. I'm not scared of you, *King* Gideon."

"So be it. You are to be thrown into the dungeon. Take him away." He nodded toward the guards.

As they dragged him away, Tristan called out, "Your days are numbered, Ravenwood! You'll be sorry you ever angered my master."

The door closed on his threats and we all breathed a sigh of relief.

"One down, one to go," Artie whispered, as Rowena stepped forward.

"Good riddance," Mag said, glaring at the twisted royal guard.

I couldn't agree more.

"Rowena Hartford," Gideon said, his tone icy. "You are one of Queen Alana's guards. Why would you willingly come into elven territory and try to kidnap one of my guests?"

Rowena snorted. "Guest? I'm sorry to inform you, *Your Highness*, but said guest is a wanted thief. It is a crime for him to even be here. If you don't want a war with the humans of Alsmora, I would suggest you free me and arrest Quick. I'll escort him back to Kelton Castle, where he'll answer for his thieving ways."

Gideon did not look amused. "The elves' treaty with the humans states that people seeking refuge in my domain will be given protection, as long as they are not criminals. What you are forgetting, Rowena, is that Arthur is not a criminal. He has shown no aggression toward anyone, nor tried to steal anything. *You*, on the other hand, invaded my castle and tried to not only kidnap him, but threatened both Penelope and Malcolm, my grandchildren.

"Therefore, we will honor our treaty with the humans and lock up a dangerous criminal. Guards, take Rowena down to the dungeon as well. I'm sure she and Tristan would love a chance to become better acquainted."

Rowena departed quietly with the guards. I could see the malice in her eyes, however. I shivered slightly as she passed.

Once we were alone again, Gideon sighed and turned toward us. "What have you three learned about Malcolm's condition? Was Victoria's book helpful?"

"It was. We need water from Ilyana Glen," I said. "A flask should do, Grandpa."

"Say no more," he said. "Head to the waterfall and find Maude and Cissy. They can help you from there."

* * *

We caught up to Maude and Cessala outside of town, by the waterfall. Maude was at the edge of the water, staring into the distance, toward a bright light on the opposite shore. Cessala was stretched out in the sun, apparently asleep. It looked like the elves had no problem with her dragon form in their territory. Mag transformed as we walked up to them.

"Ah, there you three are," Maude said. The light across the water dimmed and blinked out. Cessala turned sleepily at our approach.

"Thanks for saving me from Rowena, Cessala," Artie said, grinning.

The mighty purple dragon yawned and stood. "My pleasure," she said. "I didn't like that Rowena. No respect for anyone."

"None," Artie agreed.

"Now that we've established that Rowena is awful," Mag said, "we are in a hurry."

"That's right," I said. "We need some water to take back to Malcolm."

"Of course," Maude said, stepping aside. "Dip your bottle or flask or whatever you have into the water and you're all set."

I reached into my bag and rummaged through it. Almost immediately, I found a bottle, but as I pulled it out, I froze. I couldn't use this one. The Ruby Ship was in it.

The Ruby Ship was a mystical vessel that shrank to the size of a toy when it was on dry land and expanded in water.

Maude saw my dilemma and laughed. "Is that the Ruby Ship? Can't use that bottle then, can you?"

"Why not?" Mag said. "It's a bottle, isn't it?"

Cessala shook her head. "If you put water in that bottle, then the ship will grow to its proper size. Either you release the Ruby Ship and leave it behind or the bottle will break. I don't think you want that."

"No," I said. "What do we do?"

"Easy," Artie said, pulling something out of his own bag. "We use a different container."

I stared at him. "Where did you get that?"

"Abigail," Artie said. "Before Mag and I chased after you, Abigail gave me this. She hinted that it might be useful."

I smiled. "Thanks, Artie and thank you, Abigail." I stowed the Ruby Ship safely back in my bag and took Artie's bottle, dipping it in the water.

Once it was full, I leapt to my feet and ran to Mag, grabbing Artie's hand as I went. We climbed onto her back, as she stood and spread her wings.

"We'll be back soon," I called down to Maude and Cessala.

"Good luck!"

Mag flapped her wings, lifting us into the air, and headed for Abigail's house.

"Hold on, Malcolm," I whispered. "We're on our way."

CHAPTER THIRTY-TWO

BROTHER CARE, SISTER LOVE

It didn't take long to get from Ilyana Glen to Abigail's cottage. Mag landed in front of the house and I scrambled from her back. Olivia was sitting in the garden, reading. She looked up as I approached.

"Did you find the cure?"

I held up the flask of water. "Got it. Is that…?"

Olivia held up the book. *A Dragon's War* by C.M. Aude. "Yes. Nothing yet. I'm still working on translating the Elvish to English. It could take longer than I anticipated."

She stood and, turning away from me, called, "Abigail, Penelope's back!"

Olivia returned her attention to the book.

A moment later, Abigail came bustling out of the house.

"Grandma," I said, my voice hoarse. "Am I too late?"

"Malcolm's fine," she reassured me. "At least for now."

"I want to see him."

"No," Abigail said firmly, plucking the bottle from my grasp. "You've been through enough for one day. I want you all to relax. Malcolm is in good hands." She turned and hurried back inside.

I yawned, suddenly exhausted.

"Are you okay, Pen?" Artie asked quietly.

"I'm fine." I looked up at Mag. "Thanks for getting us here."

She smiled. "Of course, Penelope. Anything for a friend."

I grinned back, swaying slightly on my feet.

Artie took my arm and lowered me gently to the ground. "Sleep, Penelope," he said. "You need it after everything you've been through."

I nodded, too tired to argue.

* * *

My dream started like the others. I found myself in a completely different location from where I started, but that's where the similarities ended. I was not on a peaceful hillside, but instead, I was standing in the Kelton Castle gardens.

As I tried to get my bearings, I heard a terrified voice yell, "They're almost through!"

Turning, I saw my little sister, Lydia, run toward the castle. I tried to follow, but I was stopped when a large, black lion leapt in front of me, blocking my path.

"Cadmus?"

"You need to return to Kelton," he said. "Your sister needs you."

"I know, but Malcolm is injured."

Lydia suddenly reappeared at my side. "I need your help, Penelope. Casimir and his forces are at our front doors!"

I looked between the two. "How bad is it?"

"See for yourself," Lydia said, motioning out toward the valley.

I peered around them and gasped. Lydia had conjured a purple protection bubble around the entirety of Kelton Castle and the nearby village. The golden dragon was on the other side of the bubble, breathing fire at its glittering surface.

"We don't have long," Lydia said. "Another day, at most." She winced. "It's taking all my magic to keep Casimir out. I need you here, now. Please."

Lydia or Malcolm? I thought. *Which one needs my help more?*

The answer was obvious.

"I'll be there as soon as I can," I promised. "Hold on, Lydia."

"Easier said, than done." She grimaced. "I'll try, Penelope. Hurry."

"I promise to come, Lydia," I said as the dream started to fade. "I promise. I promise. I promi…."

* * *

"I promise!" I shouted, as I jerked awake. Artie and Mag crowded around me immediately.

"Pen!"

"What happened?"

"Lydia's in trouble," I said. "We need to get to Kelton Castle, before it's too late."

* * *

I checked in with Abigail before we left.

"Grandma," I said, pulling her aside. "We're leaving for Kelton."

"Don't be silly, dear," Abigail said. "You've only just arrived. Stay and rest, at least until Malcolm has recovered."

"I'd love to, Grandma, but Lydia needs me. I'm sure Malcolm will understand."

Abigail reached out and gave me a hug. "We'll be fine here. Go do what you need to do. Promise me that you'll bring Lydia with you when you return."

I hugged her back. "I promise, Grandma."

Chapter Thirty-Three

Battle of the Air

The ride back to Kelton Castle was nerve-racking. I kept going over all the horrible things I might find when I got there. Lydia could be injured, or Casimir could break through the barrier, or we could be intercepted on our way there, or…

"Pen?" Artie said. "You're tensing."

Startled, I looked over my shoulder at him. Artie was sitting right behind me, with his arms wrapped around my waist, so he wouldn't fall off.

"I am not tense," I snapped, then realized how I sounded. My shoulders slumped as I took a deep breath, trying to calm down.

"Better?"

"Yes. Sorry, Artie. I'm worried about Lydia and Malcolm and what's happening at Kelton Castle."

"Pen, you're doing it again," Artie said. "Breathe."

I stared at him in surprise, before taking his advice.

"Let's talk about something else," he suggested. "Tell me about the first time you listened to the plants."

I laughed. Artie was referring to the ability I had to put my ear near plants and instantly know what was going on in their world.

"Ten years ago, when I was six," I began, "I was in my backyard in Tealeaf. My parents were busy with Lydia, who was two, and Malcolm was at an age where he didn't want to be seen with his little sister. I had no other friends to play with, so I started observing the garden. It didn't take long before I heard the leaves rustling, water trickling over the roots, and even the plants growing. Soon, I noticed the sounds of the birds and the bees and the animals going about their day. I spent hours listening to the plants after that." I smiled at the memory.

Artie grinned back. "There you go," he said. "That's the Penelope I remember."

Mag cleared her throat. "If I could interrupt your touching story of vegetation for a moment, we're here."

Artie and I looked up in surprise. At first, I couldn't see anything but trees, but then Mag banked to the left and Kelton Castle came into view.

It was protected by a glittering, purple bubble, like I'd seen in my dream. An army of humans and scorpions was gathered at the base, while Casimir, in dragon form, battered at the shield with his wings and fire.

"How are we going to get through?" Artie asked.

"Go in through the back," I said. "I know how to break through the barrier." *I hope,* I added silently.

Mag flew low toward the barrier, so as not to be seen. We were halfway to the ground, when Casimir started to turn in our direction. A jet of purple light shot from the ground, narrowly missing him. Casimir dodged the spell by ascending higher into the sky, leaving the barrier unattended.

We made it to the back and approached the barrier.

"*Anoffen*," I said, once we were close enough. The barrier flickered out of existence long enough for Mag to fly through, before it reappeared as a glittering blue bubble behind us.

"Did he get in?" Artie asked.

"I don't think so," Mag said. "Where are we going, Penelope?"

"Over there," I said, pointing. "I think the spell came from the garden." I could see two figures, one human and one feline, waiting for us.

Mag landed and I ran to greet my baby sister, at last.

"Lydia!" I cried, pulling her into a hug.

"Penelope! I've been waiting forever for you to return!"

"We got here as fast as we could." I smiled at my favorite lion. "Hi, Cadmus."

"Good to see you, Penelope. You came in the nick of time. It's hard to talk to Lydia."

"Penny, why is this lion here?" Lydia whispered to me.

I stared at the two of them, confused, until I remembered that Lydia couldn't speak to animals like I could. I would have to translate.

"His name's Cadmus," I said. "I'll explain later. First, I'd like to introduce you to my friends, Mag and Artie. Mag, Artie, this is Lydia."

Thankfully, Mag was back in human form. She gave a slight, curt nod to Lydia. Artie, meanwhile, smiled and said, "Nice to meet you, Lydia."

"Nice to meet you, too," she said. "Penelope, we have a dragon outside the barrier!"

"I know. Casimir. Lydia, who is in the castle?"

"Queen Alana, Viola, Hazel, and a couple of others," Lydia rattled off. "Everyone else got out before I created the barrier."

"Right, keep everyone inside," I said. "Mag, Artie, and I will go take care of him. Try to keep the barrier up as long as you can. Cadmus, stay with her."

Lydia nodded and she and Cadmus headed back inside Kelton Castle.

"What's the plan, Pen?"

"Defeat the golden dragon, naturally," Mag said.

"And reinforce the barrier," I added. "What else can we do? I'm not strong enough to defeat him. Not yet."

Mag returned to dragon form and Artie and I climbed on. She leapt back into the sky and flew toward Casimir.

He watched us silently as we approached. In a way, it was more unnerving than if he had roared. There was nothing but cold calculation in his menacing, two-toned eyes.

Mag stopped twenty feet from him. The only thing between us and him was the barrier. The only sounds were Mag and Casimir beating their wings to stay airborne. Casimir's army of scorpions and humans seemed strangely muted on the ground.

Casimir finally broke the silence. "Penelope Bogg, have you come to surrender?"

Before I could respond, Mag snarled, "Like we'd ever surrender to an imposter like you!"

Casimir clicked his tongue in disapproval. "Temper, temper, Magma. What would dear Storm say?"

Smoke curled from Mag's nostrils. I could feel her rumbling beneath me. If Casimir wasn't careful, she would be breathing fire any moment.

"Don't you *dare* talk about my father," Mag growled.

"Easy, Mag," Artie said soothingly. "Don't let him get to you."

"Ah, Arthur Quick," Casimir said, turning his attention to Artie. "The noble thief who won't steal. I always wondered what was the purpose of a thief who went against his very nature. I'm sure your family is so proud."

Artie did not look impressed. "Nice try, Casimir, but I came to terms with my decision years ago. I may be a talented thief, but I refuse to use my gift to hurt others."

"Pity." Casimir's gaze shifted to me. I stared coolly back. Gone was my sympathy for the prince lost in time. Now I saw him for the monster he truly was.

"Penelope Bogg," he whispered. He sneered, his fangs glistening. A shiver ran down my spine. "Such a pretty barrier, Bogg. I'm impressed. Not many people can create anything capable of stopping me. But wait, is it yours or your sister's? Dear Lydia conjured it to keep me out initially, but you removed it so you could slip through. So, who's in charge of the barrier now: you or Lydia? Shall we test it?"

"What are you talk—" I began, when I heard a screech and a scream from the ground. Alarmed, I looked down and saw that Casimir's army of humans and *yikties* was pounding on the barrier, with Lydia and

Cadmus standing on the other side. They had come out of the castle to help! Cracks were appearing in the glittering blue surface!

"No!" I cried.

"How is that possible?" Artie said. He was squinting at the army. "You'd need something strong enough to break a magical barrier." His eyes widened. "It can't be."

"Can't be what?" I tore my gaze away from my sister and looked instead at the army. There was something off about the humans. There were bright lights surrounding all of them. I blinked, trying to understand what I was seeing. I stared in horror.

Fire! And coming from their mouths!

"That's right, Bogg," Casimir said smugly. "Those aren't normal humans. Wildings, transform!"

At Casimir's command, every wilding shimmered and grew into their true dragon form. I counted a dozen in all, all in a variety of colors, but all with blank, white eyes.

"No," Mag whispered. She turned furiously toward Casimir and shouted, "NO! What did you do to these dragons?!"

Casimir laughed cruelly. "Like what I did, Magma? I helped to unlock their true selves. Now, they do *my* bidding. Wildlings, more fire!"

The wildlings opened their mouths wider and more fire streamed out, bathing the barrier in a sickly orange light. The cracks crisscrossing the surface deepened.

Lydia and Cadmus still stood on the ground. Cadmus was in lion form and Lydia had her face buried in his fur. She wasn't focused on the barrier.

Then, how was it still up?

"Ah, I see you realize the truth," Casimir said. "Yes, Bogg, Lydia isn't controlling the barrier. *You* are. Why else would it change from purple to blue? *You* are the only thing standing between me and taking my rightful place as king of Alsmora."

I was shaking. The effort to hold the barrier against twelve wildlings and a horde of scorpions was immense. I was sealing the cracks as fast as the wildlings were making them. It didn't help that the *yikties* were still pounding on the weakened, vulnerable spots.

I gasped as the mental strain of the magic reached a fevered pitch. I fought to ignore it. My force of will was the only thing preventing the barrier from collapsing. Bright spots appeared in my vision. If the wildlings didn't stop soon, I would pass out. I closed my eyes.

Dimly, I heard Artie yell, "Cadmus! Get Lydia to safety!"

A moment later, a door slammed and I breathed a sigh of relief. Lydia was safe.

She wouldn't be for long, though, if the barrier fell. I poured my magic into it, but it made me feel dizzy and lightheaded. I wouldn't be able to hold out much longer.

"Give up, Bogg," Casimir said quietly through the haze. "Give up and release the barrier. You can't win. My forces are almost through. Nobody can help you now."

"That's what you think," Artie said. It sounded like he was talking from a distance. I felt him take my hand. New power surged through me and I was able to open my eyes. My breathing came easier. "Penelope has us."

"Artie's right," Mag said. "Penelope doesn't fight alone." More magic flowed into me.

The bright spots had disappeared from my vision. I didn't feel dizzy anymore. The cracks in the barrier were closing, as if they'd never existed at all.

"Thank you."

Casimir laughed derisively, but I could see the fear in his eyes. "You think this changes anything? Wildlings—"

But before he could issue an order, Mag flew at him, faster than I thought possible. She went through the barrier like it was nothing and rammed Casimir in the stomach with her head.

He let out a great whoosh of air in surprise.

"I thought nobody could go through that magic," I muttered.

Mag flashed me a grin. "We control the barrier. It *listens* to us, if you know what I mean." She gave me a meaningful look, before glancing pointedly at the wildlings. They were still breathing fire, but nothing was happening to the glittering, blue surface.

My eyes widened in realization. "Keep him distracted."

Mag nodded and swiped at Casimir with her claws. Casimir, who had just recovered from her last attack, raised his wings to block her. Mag countered by flying around him and breathing fire at his exposed back. Twisting away, he dodged her deftly by climbing higher into the sky. He started to circle above us.

"Hurry, Penelope. I don't know how much longer I can keep this up." Mag breathed more fire, but Casimir evaded it easily.

"What are you going to do, Pen?" Artie asked. He was still holding my hand.

With my free hand, I placed my palm on my amulet and turned to face the wildlings.

"Do you trust me, Artie?"

"Of course."

We ducked as Casimir tried to dive at us, but Mag kept him away with another burst of fire.

Acting like nothing had happened, I said, "I need you to focus all your might on the silver crescent necklace, the barrier, and the wildlings. Imagine the magic flowing from the necklace through the barrier and into the wildlings. And say *Abselen*."

"But I'm a mundane," Artie protested.

"No, Artie," I said firmly. "You're more than a mundane. Now, please, help me."

Casimir was still high above us, watching us warily. We would only have one chance at this.

Taking a deep breath, I imagined a pulse of magic beating in the necklace Mag wore, even in dragon form. I imagined this pulse traveling from the necklace to Mag, followed by Artie, and then me, connecting all three of us. I imagined the pulse working its way into the barrier, infusing the surface with the bond I shared with my friends. Finally, I imagined the pulse of magic jumping from the barrier and into each and every wildling below.

"One, two, three."

"Abselen," Artie and I said together.

A minute passed. One horrible minute in which I thought nothing had happened. Then, slowly, the fires stopped as each wildling dragon blinked, shook their heads, and closed their mouths.

They were free!

There was a hideous scream of rage from above. We looked up in time to see Casimir diving straight toward us. Before we could react, he had slammed so hard into Mag that she went tumbling head over tail in midair. Artie and I were barely hanging on. As she righted herself, I felt something cold, hard, and sharp wrap around my middle, yanking me upward, tearing me away from Mag and Artie. Casimir had grabbed me in his claws! He dove for the ground, before pulling up sharply and hovering in midair.

"Pen!"

I kicked and struggled against Casimir's iron grip, but he was too strong. Panting, I stopped and looked at my captor. He had raised me up, so I was face-to-face with his cruel, hate-filled eyes.

"You cost me my army, Bogg! Now, you will pay!"

He opened his jaws. I could see the fire building in his maw. I was nearly out of magic from my little stunt with the barrier and I couldn't reach my sword. I braced for impact.

A flash of red caught my attention. Mag was circling above. Artie was on her back, poised to jump.

Several things happened at once. I twisted violently enough in Casimir's claws for him to loosen his grip slightly. With that bit of leeway,

I plunged my hand into the side pocket of my sheath. At the same time, Artie jumped and fire began streaming from Casimir's mouth.

My hand closed on the silver rose. This was an emergency worthy of its powerful, but limited magic. I felt new energy flood my body. *"Bechulen!"* The protection bubble appeared moments before the fire engulfed me. The flames bounced harmlessly off my shield.

Casimir looked furious, but before he could ready himself for another attack, Artie landed on his back. He pulled out his knife. Casimir twisted his neck to look at him, sneering.

"Trying to play hero, Quick?"

"I'm not playing hero," Artie said quietly. "I am one." He lunged forward and slashed at Casimir's arm, the one holding me. Casimir howled, Artie must have found a chink in his scales, and he opened his clawed hand, dropping me.

I was falling. I couldn't tell which way was up and which down. Artie called, "Pen!" from somewhere, but I was so disoriented, I couldn't find him. I was still clutching the silver rose, but the wind rushing by at breakneck speed made it impossible to speak.

"Ohen!"

I hadn't said that, but my descent slowed. I was still falling, but now it felt more like I was floating. I righted myself, so my feet were pointed toward the ground.

"Pen!"

I looked up and saw Artie floating down toward me. Sweat beaded his forehead from the effort. He caught up and took my hand.

"Ohen," I said, adding my magic to the spell. Artie sagged against me in relief, his face pale.

"Whew," he said. "That was close. Are you all right, Pen?"

"A little shaken, but I've survived worse. Thank you."

Artie wrapped me in a hug. "I couldn't let him hurt you. Although, it looked as if you were doing fine on your own."

"I may have blocked Casimir's fire, but he looked ready to crush the life out of me. You stopped him." I pulled away slightly from the hug and smiled at my rescuer. "And don't forget the spell."

Artie looked confused. "What spell?"

"The spell that's keeping us in the air," I said, gesturing around us.

His eyes widened in alarm. "But I didn't... did I?"

Before I could answer, there was a roar from above. We looked up and saw Mag grappling with Casimir.

"We should help her," I said.

"I think you two have done enough."

Artie and I looked down in surprise, for the voice had come from below us. We were sitting on the back of a red dragon, this one male. Without noticing, we had gently landed on his back.

"Who are you?"

"My name is Volcano, Cano for short. I'm one of the wildlings you saved. Thank you."

"You're welcome," I said, "but Mag..."

Cano gave a short, but loud growl. The eleven former wildlings abandoned the smoldering remains of the *yikty* army and took to the air.

Cano calmly flew through the barrier, returning Artie and me to the ground. The other dragons joined Mag, surrounding Casimir.

As one, the twelve dragons breathed fire at Casimir, battering him from all sides. The silver crescent glittered brightly against Mag's throat.

With a defiant roar, Casimir dived away from the fire circle. For a moment, he hung motionless in midair, his body coated in flames. Then, he spun in a tight roll, extinguishing the fire. I stared in shock. He was completely fine. There wasn't even a trace of scorch marks or injuries.

He shot his own fire at the dragons. Mag managed to dodge at the last moment, but the former wildlings began to shriek in pain as the flames lapped over their scales. They all hastened to the ground, spinning like he had done to put out the fires. Unlike Casimir, they all looked burned.

Laughing maniacally, Casimir leered at me through the barrier and called, "Don't get too comfortable, Bogg! Your shield may be keeping me out for now, but I will find a way to break it. Keep those poor excuses for dragons. There are others I can tempt to my side. This is only the beginning!"

He wheeled around and flew away, golden scales glittering harshly in the sunrise.

CHAPTER THIRTY-FOUR

REUNION

We found ourselves in the throne room, in front of Queen Alana, Lydia, and Cadmus. He was the size of a house cat, sitting with his back to us on a nearby windowsill, tail twitching. I was sure he was keeping a lookout for Casimir.

Queen Alana didn't seem to notice our furry guard. She smiled at Mag, Artie, and me in turn.

"Welcome back, Penelope," she said. "And welcome to you as well, Arthur and Magma."

Casimir's threat was still ringing in my ears. I tried to ignore it as I said, "It's good to be back."

"Thank you for the warm welcome, Queen Alana," Artie said politely.

Mag glanced around the room. "Nice castle you have here," she said, before joining Cadmus at the window.

Queen Alana raised an eyebrow, but didn't say anything. Instead, she gestured at our guest. "And who is this?"

Cano, in human form, had been standing behind us. He had the same red hair and amber eyes as Mag, but he was bigger and buffer, his skin tanned from the sun.

"Volcano, Your Majesty, but please call me Cano. I was one of the wildling dragons under Casimir's control."

"Are you and the other former wildlings a threat to me and my people?"

"No more so than any other dragon, thanks to Penelope, Mag, and Artie."

Looking over, Mag frowned. "How do you know our names?"

Cano stared pensively out the window, as if he hadn't heard her. The injured dragons were huddled together on the grounds.

"They're confused and disoriented," he murmured to nobody in particular. "Lost in more ways than one."

I reached out and touched his shoulder. He turned to me, his eyes widening in surprise.

"I hope the other dragons feel better soon."

Cano seemed taken aback. "So do I." He laughed awkwardly. "Forgive me. Sympathy is a luxury we haven't experienced for a long time. I sometimes forget how easily it comes to you humans."

Queen Alana cleared her throat, turning back to us. "Will the barrier hold?"

"I believe so," I said, as Cano returned his gaze to the window. "I don't know for how long, but at least for now, it should block Casimir."

Queen Alana nodded. "Thank you. All of you."

"Our pleasure, Queen Alana," Artie said.

"Glad we could help," Mag said. She was still staring curiously at Cano.

"Milady," I said, "could I borrow Lydia for a bit? We need to go to Vanguard Forest."

Queen Alana smiled. "Of course. Say hello to Gideon for me."

* * *

"Where are we going?" Lydia asked, as Mag flew us toward Vanguard Forest.

"To see someone special."

Lydia turned to Artie. "Has Penny gotten more cryptic since you've known her or is it just me?"

Artie laughed. "I think it's just you, Lydia."

She leaned toward Artie and whispered loud enough for me to hear, "Do you like my sister?"

"Lydia!" I spluttered.

"What? It's a simple question," she said innocently.

I smiled and shook my head. I couldn't stay mad at her, not after finding her again. I ruffled her hair affectionately and turned back around to watch for Abigail's house.

* * *

Abigail was waiting for us. She stood outside her cottage, her eyes shaded against the sun, watching our arrival. The moment we were on the ground, she hurried up to us and gave me a hug.

"Penelope! I'm so glad you're back!" She turned to my sister. "And this must be Lydia. So good to finally meet you!"

"Hello," Lydia said shyly. She gave me a confused look.

I took her hand and gently tugged her forward. "This is Abigail Bogg, Lydia. She's our grandmother."

Lydia's eyes widened and she said, "Are you really? You have to tell me everything there is to know about our father!"

"Of course, my dear. Where to start?"

"Grandma, before you begin, is Malcolm…?" I left the question hanging, too scared to finish.

"Go inside," Abigail said. "Lydia and I will be along in a minute."

Together, Mag, Artie, and I stepped into the house. Artie took my hand.

"It'll be all right, Pen," he said.

I squeezed his hand, grateful.

There was nobody in the living room. "Malcolm?" I called. "Are you in here?"

A young man stepped out of the kitchen, full guard uniform and all. "Hi, Penny," Malcolm said. "What kept you?"

CHARACTER LIST

- Penelope: Witch-in-training, also known as the Silver Rose, Mag and Artie's friend.

- Mag: Dragon, dragon guardian to Penelope, Penelope and Artie's friend.

- Artie: Thief, quick to help others, Penelope and Mag's friend.

- Malcolm: Captain of the royal guards, though currently a fugitive on the run, Penelope's brother.

- Lydia: Witch-in-training, created a magical shield to protect Kelton Castle, Penelope's sister.

- Maude: Witch, Cessala's friend, Penelope's eccentric magic teacher.

- Cessala (Cissy): Dragon/lizard, Maude's friend, Mag's long lost aunt.

- Queen Alana: Present Queen of Alsmora.

- Casimir: Queen Alana's magical advisor.

- Rowena: Royal guard, obsessed with chasing Artie, Fiona's twin sister.

- Fiona: The Storm Knights' second-in-comand, Rowena's twin sister.

- Commander Ashcroft: Leader of the Storm Knights.

- Tristan: Thief, works for the golden dragon.

- Wansetop: Scorpion, works for the golden dragon.

- Hugo: Troll, scholar and caretaker of Elton Castle.

- Milo: Annoying crow.

- Cadmus: Cat, part of the Gilded Lions pride.

- Lupine: Wolf, asks for Penelope's help in Tealeaf.

- Tarboone: Goblin, Little Darling's friend.

- Little Darling: Crocodile, Tarboone's friend.

- Ash: Dragon, former wildling.

- Volcano: Dragon, former wildling, also known as Cano.

- Greta: Fairy, Lady Annabel's advisor.

- Lady Annabel: Fairy, leader of Fairy Hollow

- Queen Rebecca: Former Queen of Alsmora, Queen Alana's grandmother, only seen in Penelope's dreams.

- Victoria: Advisor to Queen Rebecca, Gideon's wife, only seen in the past.

- Alexander: Royal guard to Queen Rebecca, only seen in the past.

- Gideon: King of the elves, Victoria's husband, father of Alice and Xavier.

- Xavier: Gideon and Victoria's son, Alice's brother, Olivia's father.

- Olivia: Xavier's daughter, Gideon's granddaughter.

- Abigail: Penelope's grandmother, Edric's mother.

- Alice: Penelope's mother, Gideon and Victoria's daughter, Xavier's sister, hasn't been seen for two years.

- Edric: Penelope's father, Abigail's son, died when Penelope was eight.

- David: Storm Knights guard, young wizard.

- Patrick: Storm Knights guard, was once Malcolm's partner in the royal guards.

- Willow: Warrior squirrel, leader of the Woodland Warriors.

- Shell: Riddle Chipmunk, Mel's sister.

- Mel: Riddle Chipmunk, Shell's brother.

- Gary: Bumbling thief, helps Tristan in Ilyana Glen.

- The Golden Dragon: Villain, destroyed Tealeaf and ruined Elton Castle a hundred years ago, wants to take over Alsmora.

Glossary

Abselen: Heal

Anoffen: Open

Aun evas comren: Invisibility

Bechulen: Protect

Beredan: Bind

Brinze: Wind

Ernafen: Renew

Endoraken: Reveal

Entalen: Awake

Funner: Fire

Lanasan: Slow

Ohen: Up

Tokelen: Dry

Yikty: Scorpion

If you enjoyed both Silver Rose and Silver Crescent, please consider leaving me a review. Thank you for reading. The story will conclude in:

Silver Storm

www.ingramcontent.com/pod-product-compliance
Lightning Source LLC
Chambersburg PA
CBHW021037310726
48969CB00006B/1696